SUSAN SWAN

The Dead Celebrities Club

SUSAN SWAN

The Dead Celebrities Club

A Novel

Cormorant Books

The publisher gratefully acknowledges the support of the Canada Council for the Arts and the Ontario Arts Council for its publishing program. We acknowledge the financial support of the Government of Canada through the Canada Book Fund (CBF) for our publishing activities, and the Government of Ontario through Ontario Creates, an agency of the Ontario Ministry of Culture, and the Ontario Book Publishing Tax Credit Program.

LIBRARY AND ARCHIVES CANADA CATALOGUING IN PUBLICATION

Swan, Susan, 1945–, author
The dead celebrities club / Susan Swan.

Issued in print and electronic formats.
ISBN 978-1-77086-544-0 (Softcover). — ISBN 978-1-77086-545-7 (HTML)

I. Title.

PS8587.W345D43 2019   C813'.54   C2018-906274-6
C2018-906275-4

Cover design: angeljohnguerra.com
Interior text design: tannicegdesigns.ca
Printer: Houghton Boston

Printed and bound in Canada.

CORMORANT BOOKS INC.
260 SPADINA AVENUE, SUITE 502, TORONTO, ON M5T 2E4
WWW.CORMORANTBOOKS.COM

For M.

PROLOGUE

A TALL MAN with a head like an emperor on a Roman coin is lashed to a swim chair. His mouth, his hands and ankles, his arms and chest are bound with duct tape. How absurd. He's as good as glued to the plastic while an oaf with a pea-sized brain is getting the best of him, an ill-bred ruffian who isn't fit to kiss his big toe. A friend's warning rushes back: *You should get the hell out of the country.*

But he didn't leave when the going was good. And now it's humiliating to be tied up and gagged like a victim, to understand that no matter how hard he struggles, he's helpless. What are the odds he won't get out of this one? Best last guess: one hundred to one. If he could talk, the odds would be even money.

Ready for a little joyride? His assailant presses a button, and the fancy-schmancy chair swings out over the pool, its seat rocking. The man experiences a rush of light-headedness as the chair inches downward. Soon he feels the oddly intimate sensation of water touching the soles of his feet. Now his calves. His knees. The water of the pool laps against his waist. The chair keeps moving down, carrying the man to his unhappy fate, like a witch on her ducking stool.

PART ONE

HOOSEGOW

MY NAME IS Dale Paul. Not Dale. Not Paul. But two names together like the Pope. I was born in an age of swindlers. A time when fraud was as natural to the human race as breathing.

1

Dale Paul

MOTHER HAS FALLEN asleep in her chair, her dinner tray on her lap, her snores rising and falling with the soft, pestering sound of the rain on the windows. Outside, thunderheads lie across the Adirondacks. Twilight has brought a late spring storm. I spot one or two misty lights across Strawberry Lake. Well, maybe three. It doesn't matter. The reporters are still out there in the darkness.

Perhaps you think I deserve their contempt. Or perhaps you, too, believe in getting what is owed you, but aren't brave enough to admit it. If that is the case, then you should keep reading.

Unlike Mother, who remains stuck in the rut of binary oppositions, assuming things are either this way or that, I know there is always a third alternative, the somewhat murky nether region — the creative in-between, in other words, where I often find myself living, a zone that lends itself to playful experiments.

But tonight, I'm at a loss. How did I get myself into this position? Before you can murmur the phrase *wire fraud*, I have been convicted and sentenced to twelve years in a low-security prison.

If Earl were here, he would know what to do.

2

WHEN I LEFT the land of the pessimists for the land of the optimists to make my fortune, it was Earl who encouraged me to improve my prospects. He picked me up at LaGuardia in his limo and said he wanted to sell me a house he'd bought for his mistress, Kimberly Roderick. She sat between us in Earl's limousine, a tired-looking blond woman who worked in Manhattan real estate, although she didn't have much to say about buying houses that day. She knew Earl was going to give her the money from the sale because he was planning to marry his newest conquest, a former Miss Universe who disliked Earl's habit of acquiring women like racehorses and then dumping them when they demanded too much of his time.

Kimberly's thirteen-bedroom mansion was pleasingly located on the North Shore of Long Island, and as soon as Earl's limo passed the village of Flower Hill, I knew I'd be happy just to be in the environs, smelling the ocean air with the other money men such as myself, the financiers and investment bankers, the lawyers, and the scions of wealthy families whose riches go back through the generations.

I was struck by the river birches and butternut hickories shading the blacktop roads; the surfeit of trees evoked a primeval age, when the Montauks had the run of the place, centuries before the money barons built louche monstrosities along the old Aboriginal paths.

We drove through Sands Point and then turned down Half Moon Lane, where a For Sale sign was visible in front of Kimberly's house. Modelled after a Hôtel de Ville in Normandy, the mansion's gables and its singular eyelet window in the third-storey roof were new versions of the old style. As the ad in the real estate magazine said, there were too many features to list: fireplaces of imported Italian marble, heated floors, classic chef's kitchen: two refrigerators, two freezers, two dishwashers, and two hemlock wood islands adjacent to the butler's pantry. There were also a sauna with a massage room, a wine cellar, and heated paths to the Rockefeller rose garden, along with the four-car garage with double mahogany doors.

Admiring the wisteria vine climbing up the pillars of the veranda, I imagined my own name set off by a garland of gold rosettes on the tall stone columns that supported the wrought iron gates.

Already I was known for betting large amounts of money on small, over-looked companies with growth potential. I had founded Quaestus Capital, doubling the pension money I'd borrowed from the family firm by buying and selling undervalued corporations that were broken up and sold off in parts, far exceeding the purchase price paid for the whole.

Here in Sands Point I would be free, far from the jowly faces around the tables in northern boardrooms, the host of sleepy pooh-bahs who stared blankly at me when I explained derivatives such as interest rate swaps.

Across Long Island Sound sparkled the world's greatest metropolis, with its thundering horde of schoolteachers and politicians and television producers and bank managers and receptionists and waitresses and bellhops and taxi drivers and out-of-work pizza delivery boys, an army of willing bodies and minds who believed the world was still a decent place. They were waiting for me, and I was ready for them.

3

TWENTY YEARS LATER, it was Earl who told me the fraud charges were going down. From the sound of his voice that day, I knew my fortunes were about to change.

Earl was well into his fourth marriage by then, and photographs of his latest beauty queen wife appeared regularly in the media. My own marriage had collapsed. Esther and I were divorced, and she was living in Port Washington with my son, Davie. I stayed on at our home at Half Moon Lane. (It was my house, after all.)

I welcomed Earl warmly. He had come a long way from our days at

Munson Hall, where he had been a round-faced boy with large eye sockets and odd ears that lay flat against the side of his head. Before I met him, he had been expelled from a private school in upstate New York for some unspecified crime, and his parents had sent him to the civil-tongued northlands to learn manners. "A common American," Pater remarked contemptuously after meeting him for the first time. Earl seemed oblivious to my father's jokes about my friend's Brooklyn accent, although Earl never said anything as primitive as "toity-tree and a turd," which was how gangsters talked in the movies we saw as boys.

I saw myself as a pale reflection of Earl and his success, a moon to his sun. His financial empire covered half of the western world and included television stations and newspapers in most English-speaking nations. His holding company on the New York Stock Exchange was valued at over twenty billion dollars, and he held court at his press conferences as if he were one of the robber barons whose summer homes had made my neighbourhood in Long Island famous.

I gamely accepted Earl's fist bump, although such macho genuflections embarrass me. Earl was wearing one of his cut-rate suits and a garish Van Heusen shirt tightly buttoned to his chin, as is his habit.

Making friendly small talk, he followed me into my den, where we seated ourselves on a Montauk sofa that I had carefully positioned to set off the Sir Alfred Munnings engraving of fox hunters chasing the hunt master. Something was on Earl's mind. I sipped my espresso, waiting for him to come out with it, but he kept turning our conversation back to his wife's spending habits.

I asked him if he wished he hadn't dropped Kimberly Roderick so many years before, and he looked at me warily as if he thought I was being critical.

On the road, there was the noise of a vehicle, and I glanced out the window and saw a police car, black with the telltale white doors, an unmistakable replica of the cruisers in *Highway Patrol*, the old TV show with Broderick Crawford. Noisy gas-guzzlers, every one.

The police car parked on Half Moon Lane, and two burly men, cartoon caricatures of officers of the law, got out and began walking up the drive.

WIDA, my boyhood motto. *When in doubt, avoid.*

Speaking into the intercom, I directed my butler, Dieter, to lock all the doors so the police would think there was nobody home.

Let me handle this, okay? Earl hitched up his belt and headed for the door, moving in his odd shuffling gait.

Moments later I heard him talking jovially to the officers, who sounded astonished to find him in my home.

Earl, we got a ticket for the owner of that car, one of the policemen said, likely pointing at my Mercedes sedan.

Silence. Then came the noise of backslapping and Earl guffawing, followed by the sound of the door closing and his steps returning to the den.

Earl stood in the doorframe, grinning. You don't need to worry about this, okay? He handed me an unpaid parking ticket for three thousand and five dollars. A harmless tchotchke, considering what was about to unfold.

I've got something to say, he blurted.

I waited a few seconds before I replied. You're going to get another divorce.

Yeah, well, maybe not. I'm going to run for president.

You, our commander-in-chief, I exclaimed, chuckling.

His face turned a candy apple red. I was all too aware of the warning signs, so I exclaimed: Good sir, that takes courage. Running for president. You've talked about it before, haven't you?

This country is totally fucked up. I'm going to fix it, okay? He assessed me with his peculiar eyes. You don't think I can?

If you can't, nobody can, I replied. My answer seemed to satisfy him. He nodded as he headed toward the door. Then he paused. I hear something's going down with the Department of Justice.

What did you hear? I asked coldly.

Earl dropped his gaze. Nothing good. You should get the hell out of the country.

Nobody's going to kick me off my front porch.

I think that's how I'd feel too. If I was you, he said, and left.

4

IT IS RAINING harder now, and through my hotel window, the mountains of the Adirondacks are dissolving into the evening mist. Sipping a bottle of hoppy local ale, I consider my options. Should I call Earl? I am a sixty-three-year-old man with a bad heart, and my lawyer, Malcolm de Vries, says my time in prison will go more easily for me if the warden knows about my social connections. Malcolm has seen Earl's photograph in my office, Earl's hand on the president's shoulder. Behind the two men, in sagging, matronly folds, rise the tasteless velvet drapes that some addle-pated decorator chose for the White House.

Malcolm doesn't know I've called Earl countless times without getting anywhere. When I ring, an assistant says Earl's busy schedule is the reason he isn't returning my calls, but the other day I found an old phone number I had misplaced. I take it out of my pocket now. I don't want to wake Mother, so I make the call in her washroom, and Earl's voice rumbles hello.

Oh, it's you, he snarls. You fucking woke me, Dale Paul, he says before the line goes dead.

What's the matter with my old pal? Has something gone amiss between us?

I emerge from the washroom, feeling troubled. To settle my nerves, I pick up a hotel notepad and begin to doodle. Like Pater, I am an inveterate doodler, although my crude designs aren't as fine as the dense, imaginative art of serious doodlers. Wielding my black Sharpie, I sketch a stooped woman whose figure radiates frustration. Underneath her I write GOOGIE in big block letters, and then I add a stick woman with only one eye and write KISTER.

Next, I draw a stick man with ten darts sprouting from his head, the darts representing the ten charges of fraud against me.

As I yoke together the figures like apples hanging from a bough, Caroline and Meredith burst through the door.

How can you joke at a time like this? Meredith cries, staring at my doodle. You're going to be locked up for twelve years. You could die in there!

My cousin has forgotten to speak in a lowered voice, and Mother's eyelids flutter open, her head still slumped at an odd angle, as if someone has cleaved her in two and pasted her back together.

Dale Paul, don't tell me you and Meredith are arguing again, she exclaims.

Dale Paul is joking about going to prison, Meredith says, her good eye blazing. She lost her right eye in a childhood accident and wears a pair of hideous glasses to disguise the fact that it's false. Like Pater's side of the family, she is tall and big-boned, although her bulk is offset by her dainty, feminine head and the two grey braids hanging down her broad-shouldered back.

Darling boy! You mustn't joke, Mother exclaims. You could be raped!

I'm going to a federal prison, Mother. Most of the men are doing time for non-violent crimes. It's only the state prisons that house rapists and murderers.

You'll see, Googie. He'll talk his way out of trouble. My girlfriend, Caroline, bless her, gives Mother a reassuring smile.

I hope you're right, dear, Mother replies. There's nobody better than my son at convincing other people what to do.

I'm not sure whether Mother is trying to insult or praise me. Things have come to a pretty pass when you don't know if your own mother has stopped believing in you.

Meredith, can you do something with my tray? Mother asks. And when are you going to fix yourself up? Older women shouldn't wear their hair long.

It hurts to see Meredith's pained expression. Alas, Mother has trouble accepting anyone outside the core family, and her blood racism gets worse if you draw attention to it. I pretend not to notice and stick my sketch inside my briefcase, the usual receptacle for my doodles. I am a flâneur of the line — a fan of the hard-edged images we see around us, the flattened, cleaned-up look of comic books. All I need is smooth paper and a felt-tipped pen, although a ballpoint also works. It makes a bold line naturally, and it can make a very light line too.

5

THE NEXT MORNING, I file thoughts of Earl away in The Vault of Unpleasant Things and prepare myself for the act of self-surrender. After our breakfast of scrambled egg whites and Canadian bacon, I say goodbye to Mother, who clings like a child to the tail of my suit jacket until Meredith gently pries me loose.

My cousin settles, grim-faced, behind the wheel of my Mercedes sedan while I slide into the front passenger seat and unfold the map the hotel clerk made to guide us. The map shows a back road to the prison, a route the journalists are unlikely to know.

I've never had a driver's licence, so the sight of Meredith sitting behind the wheel doesn't bother me the way it might other men who aren't going to drive for a while. Caroline, tall and lithe, jumps into the back seat, clutching her untidy bag of manuscripts. She is an editor at a London publishing house, where she tends her authors like a junkyard dog, and she has brought along some work in case there is a long wait at the prison.

I know what you're thinking — nobody in her right mind would do such work when escorting her lover to prison. You don't know Caroline. The more stress she feels, the harder she goes at it. If I ask her to put down her piles of typed papyrus, she smiles absent-mindedly and stares right through me.

Onward we drive, away from the ersatz inn with its air of faded luxury, its baronial fireplaces built from ledge rock chipped out of the hills. Off and away we sail down potholed roads lined with rundown clapboard bungalows and ugly shingled houses.

In the back seat, Caroline stops making notes. We're being followed, she whispers, widening her lovely eyes.

Meredith looks up at the rear-view mirror and sees a van with a satellite dish. I point at a side road. Go down there, Kis.

My cousin drives slowly at the best of times, but today she makes the tires squeal as she turns off the main road and speeds down a driveway winding through a birch forest. At a fork in the road, she turns again and continues to drive at high speed until we find ourselves on an overgrown laneway. She switches off the motor. There isn't a sound in the entombed hush of the woods, so I light up the joint I've brought for the occasion. Meredith quickly pushes the button to lower the car windows, and the two women exchange eye-rolls as they wave the smoke from their faces.

A few yards down the road, a derelict mansion stands in a shady grove of aspens, its outside beams covered in shaggy slabs of bark. I know enough from visits upstate to recognize the Great Camp style of the region. An image of Teddy Roosevelt's old house in the Adirondacks springs to mind: the handmade twig chairs, the garland of yellow birch bark scrolls over the fireplace, and the same design repeated above the wooden doors of the house — everything homey and yet costing the earth.

It's all coming back: Mother's stories about Teddy's quaint home away from home, and Melvil Dewey ordering the Lake Placid Club to use his idiotic spelling reforms on the club menus. Dewey's motto had been "Simpler spelin," and club menus regularly featured dishes of Hadok, Poted beef, Parsli, Letis, and Ys cream.

Always alert to the need for apology, Meredith decants her broad shape from the driver's seat and strides over to the mansion. Nobody here, she calls after peering into one of its broken windows. From the woods comes a faint melancholy trill. *The lament of birdsong.*

Back on the main road, the van with a satellite dish has disappeared. We drive until we see a small wooden sign that says FCI, which stands for Federal Correctional Institute. Meredith makes an abrupt right turn. Immediately we come to one of the wild blue-black rivers you see upstate. We don't know our car has already passed under a hidden surveillance camera, and we drive in full innocence into a long meadow surrounded by pinewoods.

A tall hill, a small mountain really, rises up behind a low ridge that accommodates two immense fenced-in compounds. The prison's maximum- and low-security buildings are separated from each other by a few miles of service road. The larger compound sprouts guard towers that evoke the medieval campaniles you might see on a rinky-dink castle.

On the ridge, a white pickup truck with police lights on its roof drives along the service road that joins the two compounds, dipping in and out of view as it winds through the trees.

Do you remember Mr. Eric driving you to boarding school? Meredith asks.

Only too well. I shake some Tums into my palm and chew them distractedly.

Meredith winks at Caroline. Dale Paul used to sing *clang-clang* whenever we drove through the school gates. It used to make Mr. Eric laugh.

Don't be absurd, I retort. Mr. Eric never liked anything that made me unhappy.

Or so you thought, darling. Thrusting her tongue against her white, even front teeth, Caroline thinks for a moment before she points at the maximum-security prison and exclaims: Oh my god, those guard towers.

Look. I'm not staying there. At least, as far as I know.

I'm glad you find it funny. Caroline rolls her eyes, and Meredith makes a prissy *tock-tock* sound against the roof of her mouth with her tongue.

6

THE ROAD AHEAD is blocked with cars and satellite trucks. When the journalists spot us, some of the reporters climb out of their cars and run over, their cameras flashing like meteor bursts. I get out of my sedan, followed by Caroline and Meredith.

How does it feel to be a felon? a man shouts. Did this feckless scribe really think I would answer such a question? Several reporters yell more egregious remarks: Traitor! Scum! You ripped off our vets!

It's shocking to experience head-on the vector of human anger; the effect is so extreme it feels impersonal, as if a tornado of hatred has been directed your way by malevolent natural forces.

Caroline places her hand on my arm. Don't talk to the journos.

But I'm already clearing my throat. Smoothing down my dark hair. Why bother hiding what I do well? Modesty is just a convention, and I know how to tap dance for the newshounds, how to digress into tangents that none of their pack has the wit to grasp.

As I turn to address them, the white truck I saw on the mountain road roars up, and a prison guard wearing a white peaked cap leans out his window and speaks to the newsmen. Most of the reporters jump back into their vehicles and drive away. Only one man stays behind to talk to the prison guard. It takes me a moment to recognize Tim Nugent. How typical of my dogged school chum.

I am too far away to hear what he is saying. Looking disappointed, he leaps back into his car and waves frantically at me through the open window. Then he, too, is gone, and we get back into my sedan.

Nice wheels, the guard calls as he waves us in. He has on navy pants and a sky-blue shirt. He says he is a correctional officer. A C.O., he adds proudly. A plastic pen set has been hinged onto his shirt pocket, while from his belt dangles a baton ring, a radio holder, and one too many metal keys. Craning his neck, he leers at me. How's the weather up there, big guy?

I shrug. Strangers always ask me about the weather, assuming, wrongly, that they're the first person to joke about my height.

By the way, a writer named Nugent says he knows you, the guard says.

True enough, I answer.

I told him to get the warden's permission if he wants to speak to you. She your wife? He points at Caroline.

My girlfriend. And the other woman is my kister. I smile crookedly.

Well, whoever they are, they can't accompany you past this point.

I kiss the women, tell Meredith to keep a close eye on Davie, and climb into the prison truck. The guard floors the accelerator, and we drive rattling and bumping all the way up the ridge to the low-security prison. In the rear-view mirror, I watch my po-faced girls grow smaller and smaller.

7

Tim Nugent

The stillness of these pines lining this damp yellow road along which they
were traveling; the cool and the silence, the dark shadows and purple and
gray depths and nooks in them, even at high noon. If one were slipping
away at night or by day, who would encounter one here?

— THEODORE DREISER, *AN AMERICAN TRAGEDY*, 1925

DEAR ALEXIS, TIM writes in an email to his editor. Dale Paul has no interest in rehashing his trial and conviction, and a ghostwriter can't do much if his subject won't answer pertinent questions.

But we've agreed on our process. Dale Paul will draft a version of what he wants in the book and I will rework it or tell Dale Paul if it is unusable.

By the way, I have no real answer to your question about why he picked me to ghost except that we roomed together at an exclusive boarding school for boys in Toronto. Was it about choosing the devil he knows?

Tim sends off the email and opens a new file. He needs to fill in some of Dale Paul's background, and he isn't sure where to start. Maybe he'll write his own journal about the project and call it "Not in the Book." Well, why not? He needs to let off steam somewhere. It's not as if he hasn't ghostwritten memoirs before, but this assignment could prove difficult. For one thing, Dale Paul is an old friend. For another, Dale Paul is what his father used to call "a handful." Aaron Nugent was referring to the way Dale Paul's confidence creates a force field that sucks people in. Unfortunately, Tim is almost half Dale Paul's size: five foot nine to his friend's six foot six. The height difference bugs the hell out of Tim, along with the fact that Dale Paul sometimes calls him by his boarding school nickname, a moniker for the parasite fish that attach themselves to sharks.

One of these days Tim intends to make a public declaration to his former pals: I'm a different person than the kid you knew at boarding school, although Tim doubts they would pay attention.

How tough can it be for an old pro like him to ghost a new book? He's heard Dale Paul talk for hours on end, decades of it, and his friend's voice has found its way inside Tim's head. Besides, he has monthly alimony to pay, and freelance work is getting scarce. Too many amateurs are willing to write online for free.

Meanwhile, the prison hasn't answered his calls even though he's sent several letters outlining his project to the Bureau of Prisons.

The prison is a fortress and he can't get in, so he's distracting himself with the musty copy of a Theodore Dreiser novel he picked up at the library in the village of Strawberry Lake. Maybe Dale Paul has read it. Or maybe he has seen A Place in the Sun, the movie adaptation with Elizabeth Taylor. Dreiser based his eerie tale on a real murder in the Adirondacks. It's the sort of bookish lore he wouldn't expect his old school friend to know, although Dale Paul can still surprise Tim. He seems to remember Dale Paul studying English literature at college.

He picks up the Dreiser and starts to read. Through the window, the aluminum roofs of the boat sheds glint in the sun. Occasionally, there's the noise of an outboard and the sound of its wash hitting the dock. Beyond lie the gentle hills of the Adirondacks. It's late May and the trees have just come out in leaf and Dale Paul's prison is somewhere in that mass of spring green, which isn't a solid colour as might be expected but a collage of shades — from light mint and dark jade to a green so yellow it glows like gold.

He's been in the village for three days, visiting the library and reading up on when the region was filled with TB sanitariums and most of the homes with glassed-in verandas were cure cottages. A sanitarium close to his motel is now a seniors' home; it's a natural segue, from invalids to old people.

At the library, Tim discovered that the prison had also been a sanitarium before it was turned into a camp for recovering addicts. They constructed snowmobile trails and logged the wilderness. Later, some of the buildings were used to host staff for the 1980 Winter Olympics in Lake Placid. It became a prison in 1983. The maximum-security down the road holds two thousand inmates, while Dale Paul's compound houses nine hundred and twenty men.

There are literary connections too. Sylvia Plath's boyfriend, known as Buddy in her novel *The Bell Jar*, had been sent there for TB in the 1950s and the famous poet had broken her leg skiing on a nearby mountain. When he's not at the library, Tim is prowling around the town's cobbled streets, eating tasteless resort food while young, dark-haired waitresses rush up and down wearing apologetic smiles.

He's made friends with the motel owners, two brothers — big, cheerful, outdoor types. According to the brothers, most of the people in the area work at the prison, and many of their guests are visiting incarcerated relatives. While Tim waits for a call from the prison, he drinks coffee in their homey office with its moose head on the wall and framed black and white photographs of winter sports at Lake Placid.

The brothers asked Tim how he knows Dale Paul, so Tim explained that they had met at Munson Hall, a boarding school in a wealthy Toronto enclave. Their fathers had run into each other on the first day. The men had been friends at university, although they seemed vastly different to Tim.

Aaron Nugent had become a dentist in North Bay, Ontario; he was a short, sandy-haired man with a diastema, as the gap between his two front teeth was known. It was an odd trait for a dentist to have, but Aaron claimed it would be too much hassle to fix it.

In those years, Aaron Nugent looked much as Tim does now. But unlike Tim, Aaron was overly fond of off-colour stories, and Tim had felt slightly ashamed of his father that first morning at Munson Hall. Dale Paul's father was tall and commanding, and he headed up the Fairfield

Furniture chain, although Mr. Paul didn't strike Tim as a business type.

After their fathers left, Dale Paul told Tim that he lived only a few blocks from the school, but his father had put him in boarding so he could pull up his marks. Tim appreciated Dale Paul's friendliness that day, and he was relieved when a wizened master said the boys would be rooming together in the red brick building behind the school's clock tower. The dormitory was faux Georgian in style, with high ceilings and tall doors that displayed gold lettering on the heavily varnished wood. Each of its five floors had been ranked according to the ages of the students, and Dale Paul and Tim slept on the top floor with ten other thirteen-year-old boys. During the first week, Tim and Dale Paul joined the United Nations Club. They spent most of their free time together, until Earl Lindquist arrived and changed everything.

For years after they had graduated, Dale Paul and his then-wife, Esther, sent Tim a Christmas card. It wasn't entirely a surprise when, a few months before the charges were laid, Dale Paul asked Tim to write Dale Paul's memoir. No doubt his old friend imagines Tim is still the impressionable boy he had been at school, a kid from the sticks that Dale Paul thinks he can boss around.

8

Dale Paul

CLIMBING OUT OF the truck, I hear the racket of lawn mowers and outboard motors coming from Lake Placid. Already the free world is beckoning, a haven of pleasure. Along the ridge sprawls the gulag.

The guard (I am having trouble calling him a C.O.) points at a hodge-podge of brick buildings surrounded by a razor-wire fence; behind the buildings are a scattering of wooden dwellings attached to one another by covered walkways. In the centre of the lawn, a shoddy fountain gurgles and sings next to a plot of dead daffodils as brown and wrinkled as burnt paper.

That's us, the guard mutters.

That open-air den of mole tunnels is my new home? I stand hypno-tized, and in my mind's eye I see the moth-coloured face of my old school's clock tower, its football fields, and the stone residences that housed boys like Earl and Tim and myself along with the ancient, yellow-teethed masters who taught us Latin and Greek.

What is waiting for me inside Essex prison? Will I be met by a congre-gation of bums and losers eager to crow about the fall of someone like me? The old saying that the market can be wrong a lot longer than you can stay solvent didn't apply to me; lo and behold, I have been sentenced to the hoosegow for exercising my talents.

Up ahead, the C.O. grumbles something I don't catch. Leading me around a stand of scrubby poplars, he points at the gully behind the prison. A *tranche* of blue fills my eyes. There's a small lake in the gully between the ridge and the mountain. By the north shore of the lake is a park that resem-bles the rundown recreation areas often found in small towns. There is no bandstand, but there are a few unpainted picnic tables and two dilapidated tennis courts without nets.

Should I have brought my tennis whites?

The C.O. shrugs. That's where our Michael Jackson dancers practise.

Before I can ask about the dancers, the C.O. points down the road at the compound with the watchtowers that had frightened Caroline. They put the real bad boys in there. The C.O. smirks. Deep in the forest, where they can't get out.

And that? I nod at a tall Alpine house on a graded slope outside the prison. By the house, rough-looking men are planting sapling trees.

The warden's place.

His own Great Camp? I ask.

Ha ha.

The C.O. doesn't grin. Clearly, he is a man who prefers laughing at his own wisecracks. As we stroll through an anodyne concrete archway, my heart begins beating wildly and I curse myself for leaving my pills in the car. Caroline usually makes sure I have them on my person, but she was too distracted this morning to remind me. I take Rhythmol for tachycardia — the affliction that taxes my old, fast-beating heart.

Anxiously, I follow the C.O. into a room in the Receiving and Discharging Building. It's the size of my walk-in closet on Half Moon Lane. I have purposefully worn an old, double-breasted suit, and when the C.O. asks if he should mail my clothes home, I suggest he burn them. The man doesn't crack a smile. He asks me to undress and then he searches my orifices; his latex-sheathed finger inside my rectum feels thick and unpleasantly warm.

I receive the standard prison issue: two large-sized khaki uniforms called "browns," two blankets, two sheets, and a pillow. I am also given undershirts, socks, and undergarments. I can buy sweatpants at the commissary. Then the guard marches me out into the yard and leaves me standing dizzy and frightened like a prison mole blinking up at the light.

Unfortunately, the dope has left me feeling light-headed. If you aren't subject to spells of dizziness, it's hard to fathom a sensation akin to a space opening behind your eyes, a portal that lets in air where coil upon coil of your brain matter should be. As soon as my dizziness kicks in, my heart begins beating too quickly. The sinus node, the body's natural pacemaker, is sending the wrong electrical impulses through the right atrium, increasing my heart rate. Because I make a crash when I fall, because a large falling man changes the environment no matter how much I might wish otherwise, because I will end up a creature of ridicule, I have no interest in fainting on my first day in my new home.

The tang of male sweat drifts my way. I force myself to turn around. Nothing has prepared me for the sight in front of me in the prison yard. I may as well have stepped into a scene from the television show *Oz*. Most of the ne'er-do-wells are black or Latino, while the beefy guards are white-skinned, and they all stand waiting for me to play my role in the tawdry prison melodrama to which I've been consigned against my will.

Over by the gate, an imposing black man wearing a Vandyke is heading my way, followed by three guards who are each restraining a German shepherd. The man's closely shaved head rests like a black bowling ball on his shoulders. As he comes closer, I see he is wearing rimless glasses and a dark business suit. His stiff military bearing and the way the other men look at him suggest I am about to meet the warden.

Nathan Rickard, the warden says, extending his hand. The tremor in his voice suggests my presence is having an impact. Celebrity has a habit of doing that, although you could chop up my Midas-like traits, along with the traits of other celebrities, and feed the parts into a blender and out would come some variation of a well-known financier and nobody would notice the difference. I was once mistaken for Wolf Kruger, the head of the securities commission. Wolf and I don't even look alike. Yet there is something there — a grave facial expression, a knowing gleam in the eye. The gold dust of celebrity does the rest.

Behind the warden, some of the prisoners are clapping and calling my name while others are yelling the same insults the journalists had used earlier: Fraudster! Crook! You get the gist. The warden ignores the men and steers me forward, his large dark eyes behind the lenses of his glasses

darting warily around the yard. We have almost reached the prison buildings when three men step into our path. Is one of the miscreants about
to stick me with a knife? They could be bubble-wrapped for all the good
my ability to read my fellow humans does me this morning. While I try to
quiet the arterial flutters of my heart, one of the scofflaws shouts, Make
us rich, Dale Paul!

With your money and my ideas, we'll go far! I execute a mock bow.

The scofflaws call out enthusiastic hurrahs. The German shepherds begin
to bark, standing on their hind legs, straining against their leashes; the
guards appear to be marshalling all their strength to keep the dogs under
control. A whistle shrills; the dogs drop to all fours, stop barking, and the
cries die away. By the time the warden and I reach my dormitory, the place
has assumed a churchy quiet.

If you figure out how to make money in here, let me know. The
warden smiles an odd, secretive smile.

You have my word, good sir, I reply.

Heck, you sound just like you do on television. He chuckles.

He doesn't realize I am serious. In the parking lot this morning, while
Nugent stood chatting with the guard, the idea of betting on the death of
aging celebrities popped into my befuddled brain like the ping of an email
dropping into my inbox. To qualify, you must be in the news and about to die.

Can you see where I'm going with this? *Well, all in good time.*

9

Each inmate is responsible for making his bed in accordance with regulations by 7:30 a.m. weekdays and by 10:00 a.m. on weekends and holidays. Workdays off during the week are considered to be the inmate's Saturday and Sunday. Each inmate is also responsible for sweeping and mopping his personal living area to ensure it is clean and sanitary. Lockers must be neatly arranged inside and out and all shelving must be neat and clean.

— FEDERAL BUREAU OF PRISONS, *INMATE*

ADMISSION AND ORIENTATION HANDBOOK

MY SLEEPING QUARTERS at Essex are in one of the two-storey wooden buildings attached to others by a covered walkway. From my research, I know that some of the original prison buildings were part of the athletes' village for the 1980 Winter Olympics. I'm not surprised to see five interlocking circles carved in the wood above the door.

The warden waves his hand at two men standing near the front of the building. I look them over carefully, feeling the curious sensation I often experience with my fellow humans — that they are not entirely real, or at least not as real as I am, although they keep making signals at me through a wall of Plexiglas. Perhaps everyone experiences a similar metaphorical wall, although I have always been shy about exploring that possibility. One of the men is a tattooed thug who wears his golden hair long and tousled like a Viking. The other one is a young ghetto tough, with dreadlocks and a facial scar. Something about the bashful way the dreadlocked prisoner holds himself reminds me of Arnie, Esther's golf caddy, except the scofflaw's front teeth have been filed into points. Arnie would never do anything to spoil his smile.

This is your bunkmate, Derek Williams. The warden smiles, and the Viking smiles back. Derek runs the Michael Jackson dancers program, the warden says.

The Viking shoves his face close. Nothin' else to do in here, mate! His facial tattoos make it impossible to read the man's expression.

Your other bunkmate is Marvin Bailey Jr., the warden adds.

Yo, the ghetto tough mutters.

I'm trembling. Thankfully, the men don't remark on my nervous state, and a moment later, a C.O. named Martino appears. He's an affable fellow with a beaky nose and a pair of round and slightly vacant eyes. After promising to get my meds, he leads me through the long rows of cubicles to my new bunk, where I am to stow my prison things. He says I will work at a prison job from 7:45 a.m. to 2:30 p.m., with a forty-five-minute lunch break, followed by a few hours of leisure time before supper at 5:00 p.m. For seven dollars a month I will tutor men who wish to get their high school certificate. Imagine. I used to earn more than seven dollars a second just a few short months ago.

After Martino leaves, my bunkmates show me how to scan my ID in the Chow Hall, grab a tray, and walk the food line. The vast room rings with coarse-sounding male voices. When I walk in, one or two white prisoners hurl the same ill-informed invective about letting down our vets. These men are clearly fools who believe the lies the media has been spreading.

Hey, mate, over here! Derek gestures to a seat next to Bailey. I take a few steps and hesitate. The rest of the room is banging tables and clapping. At what? At me? Yes, at me. It seems the vote is heavily in my favour: two-thirds for and one-third against. The nay faction is mostly white, I can't help noticing. Things could be a lot worse.

I was given a fork and a spoon and an ugly rectangular tray with depressions in the plastic for plates and cups. Neither the tray nor the cutlery looks particularly clean, so I pull out my white linen handkerchief, a keepsake from Caroline, with my initials embroidered in its corners. On the way in, I insisted the guard take my last twenty-dollar bill and he allowed me to keep the hanky along with a package of Tums.

My spoon is encrusted with half a spaghetti noodle, so I move my hands under the table and go to work.

A precautionary measure, I explain. Bailey looks incredulous, and Derek tips his chin at something across the room. The warden is making his way to us through the tables of men. I promptly rise; slowly, hesitantly, Bailey and Derek stand up too. The warden sometimes eats with his boys, and it turns out this is one of those days. A man in a chef's hat follows along behind, holding out a plate of the same steaming mush served in the chow line.

Gimme some milk, the warden tells the cook, and we all sit down. Derek and Bailey begin gobbling the disgusting gruel, and I avert my gaze as Bailey starts pushing the hamburger meat onto his spoon with his index finger.

May I please have a knife? I ask the cook, who has reappeared with the milk jug. The cook shoots me a wide-eyed look and hurries back to the kitchen.

Knives are dangerous in here, mate. Derek shrugs.

You bes' eat up, bro, Bailey adds. Ain't goin' be nuthin' left.

There won't be anything left, you mean. But I'm waiting for the warden to start, and you should too.

Bailey appears momentarily startled, and so does Derek, while the warden pours himself a huge glass of milk. Then, to my amazement, he, too, begins to gobble his food, shoving the goulash onto his spoon with his fingers.

Would any of you like some ketchup? I ask. The bottle is a tawdry brand called Catsup.

The warden grunts and shakes his head, so I turn my eyes to my bunk-mates. How about the two of you? I ask, waiting for them to offer it to me.

Instead Bailey grabs the ketchup bottle and squeezes what is left onto his plate, jabbing his fingers into the red goop in a repeat performance of his grotesque shovelling procedure. To my disgust, he licks his fingers clean.

Use this, good sir, I say, handing him my hanky. When I nod reassuringly, he solemnly takes the handkerchief and wipes off his fingers.

10

THE FIRST NIGHT, as I lie in my cot, I happen to look up at the planks supporting Bailey's bunk and notice the words *Northern Particle* stamped on the wood. Our beds have been made from particleboard, which is cheaper and denser than regular plywood, and the particleboard was manufactured by a company I used to own in British Columbia before a fire destroyed its warehouse. The fire dispensed toxic fumes into the forest like a sprinkling of lurid holy water and I lost a great deal of money.

I wanted to view the damage, so I took a floatplane up to the small coastal city where the factory was located. Pater came along in the hopes that he could talk me into going back to university. That day in Prince Rupert, he realized I was never going to become a professor who teaches the philosophy of history, which had been his ambition before Mother's father forced him to join the family furniture firm.

He was something of a business failure, my dear old Pater, a man who couldn't succeed even in a nepotistic job — a scholar manqué whose single hope had been to teach at some small, inconsequential college. As a boy, I imitated his manners and formal way of speaking, although the two of us rarely saw eye to eye.

For instance, Pater taught me it was wrong to reach out for what you want, so I ended up with the usual WASP inhibitions about declaring one's right to self-interest. I swore I would rid myself of my chains.

Humming to myself, I bring out the portable reading lamp that Derek has loaned me until I save up enough money from my prison job to buy one at the commissary. These lamps are made of cheap metal and don't open until you press down hard on the spring.

I clip the lamp onto my notepad, and, with the stub of a lead pencil I found under my bunk, I begin to sketch my father. What a good thing Pater is no longer with us — he would have shuddered at the idea of me bedding down with thugs.

Fortunately, he died before I moved to Long Island with Esther, my hard-drinking, golf-addled ex-wife; my son, Davie; and my mother, Gloria Paul (alias Googie), daughter of the Fairfield Furniture chain. Mother was born in the United States, and if I'm making it sound like my grandparents were a cross between a Montauk sofa and a Louis XIV chair, in many ways that is the case. Mother was distantly related to the Roosevelts of Oyster Bay. Her grandparents were good friends of Melvil Dewey, the education reformer, and the names of my maternal great-grandparents are in the old records at New York's Social Register.

Pater's social pedigree is not worth mentioning, but his father had been a lowly Presbyterian minister, and I've always thought this self-righteous forebear was the reason for Pater's antipathy to business. Lying on my cot, I doodle his angry face the day I told him I was going into hedge funds — his long, saturnine face used to cloud over during our talks, and that afternoon his expression had turned murderous — so I add a few boughs of pine, as if his shouts have singed the virgin timber.

I do my best to fringe their tips in a refined, Asian sort of way, but a cook is only as good as his utensils. That is to say, there is only so much you can do with cheap graphite, even if the 4B pencil comes in handy for shading outlines. How I wish I could put my hands on the brush pens I left at home. A brush pen would be just the thing for darkening in the branches of the pine tree.

Pleased with my sketch, I stick it in the drawer under my bunk and let my mind drift into the sort of meandering thoughts I indulged in at college, where I was attempting to live out Pater's plan for my life. In those years, my father tried to direct me away from airy flights of visionary thinking toward steadfast analysis of historical battles, as if the boundary between rational thought and daydreaming is ironclad instead of the mysterious palimpsest I know it to be.

I think again of my light bulb moment, my idea about a dead pool where the prisoners will be invited to bet on the death of aging celebrities. Nugent's appearance in the parking lot reminded me of our boarding school bet that let the overworked and underappreciated boys gamble on which of our teachers would be the first to push up daisies. (More on About to Die later.)

Outside, darkness is falling, and although I'm as circumscribed as an astronaut in his capsule, things seem less dire than they did this morning. At least tonight I'm free to doodle, and doodling is a form of thinking; it's less purpose-driven than the paintings an artist does in the heroic solitude of his studio, and doodling is more self-serving too, even if I am doing it in a room of fifty or more slumbering scofflaws. Like me, a few of them are still awake, and small halos of light spill from their reading lamps, each man a lighthouse in the gloom of the dormitory, where the overhead LED ceiling panels glow spookily, neither too dim nor too bright, illuminating the darkness.

11

Tim Nugent

A GOOGLE SEARCH for "North Bay, Ontario" turns up images of sandy beaches and broad-leaved trees, along with aerial shots of the town sitting like a footnote on a wide harbour that opens onto a large, light-filled lake. Tim finds these scenes reassuring because water and trees are what he remembers about his hometown, a forest outpost in which human buildings looked out of place. He was ashamed of the town's dusty red brick stores, nostalgic souvenirs of a more prosperous age when the town's logging and mining industries were going strong in what he and his friends jokingly called The Armpit of the North.

He hardly ever thinks of North Bay now; it has been thirty-five years since he moved to the States where people used to go to live out their best hope, and, just like Dale Paul, he wanted to be American. (Okay, so the United States used to be a nicer place, but he still likes it, even with the nasty political partisanship and the winner-and-loser mentality that explains why so many won't get help if they fall between the cracks.) He decided to immigrate to the U.S. the day he saw Robert Kennedy on television advising his kids to drink their milk so they could grow up and be president.

When he left North Bay to board at Munson Hall, the Pauls took him under their wing. Mrs. Paul talked the school into letting him go there for Sunday dinners on the "out" weekends, those twice-monthly occasions when the boarders could visit the homes of friends. Meredith had been kind to him too. Very kind. He blushes at the memory. And now here she sits at a table by the window overlooking Strawberry Lake. How long has it been since he saw her last? Twenty-five years? Thirty? She seems to be watching the play of light on the water, oblivious, if that is possible, to the chatter in the pub. Its decor reminds him of the après-ski lounges of their youth: barnboard walls, faux Tiffany lamps, and thick wooden beams on the ceiling.

Meredith has on a tie-dyed blouse and a long skirt. She has worn hippie clothes since he first knew her. What's more, she still wears her strange glasses — the result of a freak accident — and she's kept her hair is in braids. To his surprise, she's aged better than he has. Of course, she has lived a quieter life. She stands up and waves when she sees him, and he waves back. He always liked her husky voice and the way her face dimples up when she smiles. Googie Paul used to say Meredith was too "approachable" for a young woman, not to mention a young woman with one eye.

Meredith, you haven't changed much, he says, smiling.

Neither have you. She smiles back.

Liar. It's my years at the *Post*. And … He lets her fill in the blank. I'm freelancing now.

You should try teaching at a girls' college.

Hard job?

She hesitates. Well, not really. It suits me. Googie is sick, so we're staying up here for a few more days.

It's hard to believe she's eighty-six. She used to be beautiful.

In certain lights she still is. Meredith sighs and looks down at her lovely, long-fingered hands. Do you think Dale Paul is being persecuted for his attitudes?

Among other things. It's good to see you, Kis. We're old pals, aren't we?

The phrase *old pals* hovers in the air.

I suppose. Dale Paul tells me you're writing his memoir.

He's good copy, isn't he? And I know where he comes from. But I still need to research his early influences. You can help me fill in what I can't remember.

You want my help?

Of course I do. He pats her hand, and she jerks it away. Your recall was always better than mine, Tim adds, turning red. I'll be speaking to all his friends, along with business associates like Conrad Black and Warren Buffett.

I'm not going to betray him.

No one wants you to do that. But you know him as your kid brother. Who else can say that? Readers will soften toward him when they discover he has a vulnerable side.

She looks at him fearfully as if the word vulnerable makes her uneasy. I guess you'll want to know everything, then? Well, time to powder my face, she says. Her bad eye seems to shine as fierce and wild as her good one. Is she thinking about the messy business with Earl? Or what happened the last time they were all together? He's pissed with himself for not putting that together sooner.

12

Dale Paul

An inmate will be limited in the number of letters, books, photographs, magazines, and newspapers that can be stored in their
designated storage space. Nothing is to be tacked, stapled, or
scotch-taped to any surface except to bulletin boards. Ordinarily,
photographs, particularly those of family and friends, are approved,
since they represent meaningful ties to the community.... Nude or
sexually suggestive photos (individual prints or copies as opposed
to those from publications) present special concerns about personal
safety, security, and good order, particularly when the subject is an
inmate's relative, friend, or acquaintance....

— FEDERAL BUREAU OF PRISONS, *INMATE
ADMISSION AND ORIENTATION HANDBOOK*

THE NEXT DAY a note arrives from my mother in her shaky hand. She
and Meredith are still at the inn on Strawberry Lake because Googie
hasn't been well enough to travel. Unfortunately, the Bureau of Prisons
won't allow me visits for a month so I have time to settle in. (Settle in! As
if I am at some folksy summer camp!) To help me adjust, Meredith has
personally delivered Mother's package of fruit and digestive cookies.

Darling boy,

I hate to think of you consorting with hoodlums while we sip our tea
in the lap of luxury. It just gives me the shudders. Please, Dale Paul,

don't make friends too quickly. Others are not who they seem when
you first meet them.

All my love,

Googie

Despite myself, I laugh out loud. Mother is still worried I will be raped even though I have told her over and over that rapes don't happen in low-security prisons. In fact, not many terrible things happen here. She retorted that terrible things happen everywhere.

I consider telling her that my new home is a caterwauling hub of male noise, a cacophonous racket of men talking too loudly and doors banging shut with a hideous metal clang. *And the heat.* I walk around feeling perpetually clammy, an unpleasant soaked-through sensation. The Bureau of Prisons is unwilling to pay for air conditioners, and the temperature of the buildings, where the men cook and play cards, has been in the high nineties, a lousy portent for the fast approaching summer months. (All right, so there are water coolers and ice machines.) It is even hotter in our shoddy dorms, where everyone sleeps in cubicles or cubes. Each cube has three bunk beds with a desk, and our bunk beds are, just as you'd expect, iron hard.

Then there are endless head counts, including the ones at 3:00 a.m. and 5:00 a.m., when the C.O. shines his flashlight into your eyes. However, complaining will only make Mother fret more.

UNCENSORED
INMATE MAIL
BUREAU OF PRISONS

Dear Mother:

Thank you for writing. Nothing untoward has happened to me and I
don't expect it will. Fortunately, I have been receiving excellent guidance

from my two bunkmates. They are decent fellows despite their crimes: Marvin Bailey Jr. was born in Brooklyn. Derek Williams was born in Yorkshire, England; he is an ex-drug addict who cured himself by taking up yoga. So please don't worry. In many ways, prison is just like boarding school; and, much as I did there, I need friends to help me get through the experience. After all, we are always new boys at something.

Your loving son,

Dale Paul

13

The warden shall allow each inmate a minimum of four hours visiting time per month. The Warden may limit the length or frequency of visits only to avoid chronic overcrowding. The Warden may establish a guideline for the maximum number of persons who may visit an inmate at one time, to prevent overcrowding in the visiting room or unusual difficulty in supervising a visit. Exceptions may be made to any local guideline when indicated by special circumstances, such as distance the visitor must travel, frequency of the inmate's visits, or health problems of the inmate or visitor.

— FEDERAL BUREAU OF PRISONS, *INMATE
ADMISSION AND ORIENTATION HANDBOOK*

THE NEW YORK *Times* has run a front-page story about me going to prison. Its headline reads: "THE PENSION FUND WHALE GOES AWAY FOR TWELVE YEARS." Full disclosure: when the word *whale* is affixed to a financial man, it means someone who isn't afraid to bet large.

The copy of the *Times* is in the law library, where I am writing a long, complaining letter about the American prosecutorial system and its scurrilous practice of throwing every charge in the book at a defendant so they will plead guilty to one or two of them.

Two photographs accompany the story. One features Meredith, Caroline, and me in the prison parking lot, facing down the media cavalcade. The other picture shows two derelict men posing in front of a broken-down car; the passenger door has been left open to showcase the innards of the ancient automobile: sleeping bags, a crumpled assortment of shirts and jackets, along with a small camping stove. The younger man is holding the handles of the older man's wheelchair, and I have to look twice before I recognize Esther's golf caddy, Arnie, and his father, Joshua. The caption beneath the photo quips: "Dale Paul sipped champagne while his clients ate dog food." How can Arnie make up such lies? Ham and cheese loaf, certainly. Possibly ice milk. Arnie ate junk food long before his investments with me went south.

The story of my alleged villainy has been carried over to page fourteen of the business section and prominently displayed above the weather map and a series of stock market graphs. Larded with unconscionable exaggerations, the *Times* compares me with the hustlers in the energy company known for cooking its books and says I defrauded the American military of two billion dollars.

The story also refers to me as a long-ago associate of the media scion Earl Lindquist. *A long-ago associate.* The term must have come straight from the lips of Earl's mealy-mouthed public relations officer.

The final paragraph claims I "managed to fool our veterans and thousands of decent, hardworking Americans." Well, well, Arnie was a veteran, yes. He fought in the first Gulf War and has a limp to prove it. That is the reason I tried to help him. And now the *Times* is suggesting I deliberately talked him into scummy investments, using my reputation for business acumen to convince my pal that my hedge funds were on the up and up.

14

THE FOLLOWING DAY, around 4:00 p.m., I'm startled by the sound of the scofflaws shouting and cheering. Martino is bringing in the mailbag. I hurry over, and he fishes out some letters from his sack and hands them to me. Each letter has been stamped with the Bureau of Prisons seal. The first one is from Sofia Rigby, who has sent me a picture of her son taken several years before Tony's beheading by Islamic extremists, when he was a well-known photojournalist in the Middle East. In the photo, he wears a necklace of cameras, and his mouth is open, as if he is speaking. Sofia's note says:

> *Dear Dale Paul:*
>
> *We have no money to bring our son's remains back from the Middle East, if and when his body is found by our troops, so Ted has taken a job driving North Shore cabs with Arnie. Yes, that's what my husband, the four-star American general, has come to! We're living off the smell of an oil rag, as my grandmother used to say. May you rot in hell!*
>
> *Sofia Rigby*

Living off the smell of an oil rag. Sofia has a flare for Victorian metaphors. When I glance again at the photograph, I realize why she sent it. In the photo, their son looks as if he is accusing me from the grave, uttering a string of blasphemous phrases condemning me to the hell that Sofia believes in. She and her husband are evangelicals. They converted Arnie to their silly faith after I introduced them.

The spelling and grammar in the next letter are appalling:

> *Mr. Paul:*
>
> *I here you are lockedup. I hope it is for good because you fucked things up royelly for me and my buddies who went to Iraq. How can you walk this earth and feel okay? You are the divil himself. I hope you die in prison.*
>
> *Wesley Randall*

Royelly. The divil himself. Now there is a man who isn't afraid of sounding hyperbolic.

15

Tim Nugent

HE HAD COME here for what?
And he must do what?
Kill Roberta? Oh no!

> *And again he lowered his head and gazed into the fascinating and yet*
> *treacherous depths of that magnetic, bluish, purple pool, which, as he*
> *continued to gaze, seemed to change its form kaleidoscopically to a large,*
> *crystalline ball. But what was that moving about in this crystal? A form!*
> *It came nearer — clearer — and as it did so, he recognized Roberta*
> *struggling and waving her thin white arms out of the water and reaching*
> *toward him! God! How terrible! The expression on her face!*
>
> — THEODORE DREISER, *AN AMERICAN TRAGEDY*, 1925

THE WARDEN STILL hasn't returned Tim Nugent's calls, so it was a relief when Meredith phoned and asked him to drop by the inn. He needs the distraction, although he has begun to enjoy the peace and quiet of the village.

He's had time to finish the long-winded Dreiser novel about a murder in the Adirondacks. What an ending for an impoverished Midwestern kid! The boy died in the electric chair after he let his pregnant girlfriend drown so he was free to marry an heiress. Chances are Dale Paul could relate. When Esther became pregnant, his old friend married her in a shotgun wedding, as people used to call those unhappy occasions. Then

Esther had a miscarriage. Everyone was surprised when Dale Paul stayed married to her, and a decade or so later they had Davie.

Around four o'clock, Nugent sets out to see Meredith. He takes a back street and passes the shrubs of dogwood bearing white blossoms outside the country homes; the outside walls of some of the houses are covered in bark. That's Adirondacks style: strips of cedar over everything.

The fresh mountain air makes him want to escape the village and go for a hike. Resorts in the off-season depress him — they exude the sense that real life is going on elsewhere — but he has a social call to make.

Meredith's inn sits atop a small hill overlooking the lake. Tim mounts the tiers of stone steps to its door and cautiously inspects the lobby. The date on its wall plaque reads 1888.

He notes the contrast between his modest motel and the posh inn with its confection of chandeliers and plush carpets. Well, he was never at home in Dale Paul's world. What do those people contribute to the public good? They live off their inheritances and borrow their snooty attitudes from the British aristocrats.

As he peeks into the inn's elegant dining room, he can hear his father's voice in his ear; it was as if Aaron were still alive. *Just listen to yourself, son! You don't have two pennies to rub together! You're a sixty-two-year-old man who has to scramble for money. Who was fool enough to let his ex-wives take what they wanted.*

His father used to send Tim job ads from the local paper when Tim was a boarder at Munson Hall. *If you don't get an education, son, you'll end up a bum* was how he signed his letters.

Aaron disapproved of Tim's marriages and affairs. He didn't understand why Tim preferred female company to the noisy get-togethers of male friends. His father had liked Meredith, so it's possible Aaron would be pleased to see that circumstances were conspiring to pull Tim back into the Pauls' old-moneyed circles. How odd the way life does this. How strange to work hard to escape the world of your childhood only to find yourself drawn into it all over again.

The voices of the Pauls appear to be coming from the second floor, where the inn has set up a private tea room. He stops on the landing to listen. From above his head comes the clink of cutlery against china plates and the sound of people yelling at one another. It isn't like the Pauls to shout. Dale Paul's ex-wife, Esther, is slurring her words, and Tim hears a pleading tone in Meredith's voice. Then a young man cries: Someone wrote *fraudster spawn* on the wall by my bed.

It's Davie, Dale Paul's son.

Hey, that's what they're calling me now. Fraudster spawn! Thanks a bunch, Dad! And they kicked me out of my dorm.

Fraudster spawn is a horrible thing to call you, Meredith replies. But your roommates can't kick you out of Harvard.

The hall monitor said they could ask for a new roommate, Davie replies. No one wants me in the other dorms. Whatever. I'm not going back next semester.

Don't you dare do something self-destructive again, his mother shrieks.

You mean like kill myself?

There is a shocked silence, and then Davie says, Hey, I'm sorry, I didn't mean that. I — I'm okay now. I've got it together.

A housekeeper is coming up the stairs, so Tim chooses that awkward moment to appear. They stare up at him in surprise: Esther, matronly in a baggy pantsuit, and Davie, red-faced and insolent, next to Meredith, who looks alarmed and unhappy. Dale Paul's mother is snoring in a wheelchair. Aside from her stiff 1960s bouffant, Googie Paul is unrecognizable.

Hello, Tim hears his voice boom. Am I interrupting something?

16

Dale Paul

ARNIE AND HIS father have shown up. Somehow, they have got around the red tape forbidding me to have visitors, possibly because Arnie is an Iraq veteran. It is cold and rainy, so I find the sorry-looking pair standing in the visitors' lounge instead of waiting for me in the fenced-off compound by the lake where visits take place in good weather. Arnie's father is paralyzed from the waist down after a malfunction sent his aircraft spiralling to the ground near a Viet Cong village. As if paralysis isn't bad enough, Arnie's father has suffered damage to his vocal cords. Arnie, meanwhile, fractured his pelvic girdle when his parachute didn't open in a reconnaissance flight over Baghdad.

When I come through the door, he turns his face toward me in his hopeful way and I know he is looking for a reassuring gesture, not to mention a promise that I will recoup his lost funds. Unfortunately, I'm obliged to put my old associations behind me. How can someone like Arnie help me now? Yet a display of grace is required: a reminder that Pater has brought me up to walk with kings and keep the common touch.

Arnie's father doesn't smile, although his eyes flicker with an unfathomable emotion when he sees me.

Arnie, Josh, how good to see you both! I exclaim, struggling to be heard above the screams of the tatty-looking children and their frustrated mothers. The visitors' lounge is a vast, airless space that resembles my Anglican Sunday school. The Dead House, I used to call it.

Arnie shakes my hand. The spring has gone out of his step, no question. He has lost a great deal of weight, and a safety pin holds together the frame of his spectacles. He must have gone to some trouble to find a pair of dilapidated glasses so I would feel sorry for him. And, of course, I do, although the last thing I want to discuss are the losses in Arnie's portfolio.

We have something to ask you, Arnie says.

Ask away, good sir.

We're sleeping in Pop's car. And we want to know ... Arnie smiles anxiously. If you can help us?

As far as I know, Arnie's father has been living safely and well in a small apartment the Veterans Affairs people found for him; the VA pays half his rent while Arnie covers the remaining amount. Why they expect a donation from a man in my circumstances beggars belief.

How I wish I could. But you can see the situation I've found myself in. To make my point, I gesture at the visitors' lounge, the perfect synecdoche for my dilemma, and Arnie's eyes follow the movements of my hand with what appears to be desperation.

I know you have money hidden away, Arnie retorts. Esther told me you did.

And you believed her? Arnie, those funds went to my court costs. Hand on heart, if I had the funds I would give you some.

Arnie's father says something in his strange, whispery voice, and Arnie bends down to listen. When he straightens up again, Arnie is scowling. Pop doesn't believe you. He won't forgive you, either.

Forgive me for what? It's me who should forgive you for talking to a *New York Times* reporter.

For a moment, Arnie looks nonplussed. I was only telling the truth, he splutters. He draws himself up to his full height, which isn't very high. Jesus said I am the way. I am the life and the truth you have been looking for.

What version is that? I know the King James: "Jesus saith unto him, I am the way, the truth, and the life: no man cometh unto the Father, but by me."

So you know it, Arnie says. You know it already.

Of course I know it, you fool. I wasn't bored stupid at Sunday school for nothing.

Well, why don't you practise it? Arnie's round, bug eyes, ordinarily so lustrous and bright, turn dark.

You should know better than this! You're a Jew, Arnie, and Jews don't do religious conversions. It's not their style. Look — I did nothing wrong, and the sooner you understand that, the better you will feel.

Arnie's face clouds over, and it strikes me that he doesn't have long to live. He's never been very healthy, and he smokes a pack or two a day. Once, when life was good and he used to come to me for investment advice, we both smoked Silk Cuts. Then, when life was good no longer, I stopped, but Arnie refuses to quit. The nicotine stains on his fingers give him away. Funny, how cigarettes mark you. How they mark your skin and wrinkle it up. Webs of fine lines have spread across Arnie's cheeks and forehead. His skin isn't getting enough oxygen, clearly. Those damn cigarettes.

You've got to stop smoking, Arnie. It's not good for you.

Is that all you've got to say for yourself, Dale Paul?

How are my old friends Ted and Sofia? Are they well?

Ted has cancer of the esophagus, Arnie replies. Maybe you forgot.

I shake my head disbelievingly. Ted with the big C? Perish the thought.

Sofia said she told you about it.

Arnie, this is all very dreary and sad. I think you and your father had better leave. I motion to Martino, who has been watching us with his sleepy eyes. Not all prison visits go well. Nobody knows that better than him.

After the two men leave, I stand at the window and watch my old pal push his father's wheelchair down the pathway to the parking lot. Arnie walks with a slight roll, like a sailor. Is it my imagination or does his limp seem more pronounced? Cradling his father in his arms, Arnie sets him down gently in the front seat of a broken-down car. With a start, I realize it is the junk heap I saw in the *Times* photograph. Then, to my surprise, Arnie turns and shakes his fist at the prison. I assume he is staging a performance for my benefit, although it's hard to see in the rain.

17

ANOTHER DAY, ANOTHER letter. This time from my cousin Meredith:

May 31, 2012

Dear Dale Paul:

I'm back home on Long Island and I wanted you to know that Tim walked in on a family argument. On our last day at the inn, Esther and Davie surprised us with a visit. Esther was ranting drunkenly about Davie, who has been spending his days online. Apparently, he searches the Internet to see if his name is linked to yours. If he finds the two of you mentioned together, he asks for his name to be removed from the website.

When I pressed Davie about going back to school, he said he wished he were dead. Esther and I rushed to his side. (We were thinking about the night he tried to kill himself. Remember?) Thank heaven Googie was snoring away by then. The last thing we needed was her chatter about sundials that record only happy hours.

By the way, your mother has been difficult since you have been in jail — she refuses to let me put on fresh Depends and swears like a trooper when the sticky tabs of the diaper pull at her skin. She also refuses to use her wheelchair, staggering around our suite at the inn gripping the handles of her walker as if it were a wild horse in need of taming.

She seems to be in constant pain, although the doctors can't find anything wrong. I don't really blame her for being cross. If only she wouldn't spend money on things without telling us. The other day a man on the phone talked her into buying a new dishwasher.

Well, enough said. I don't mean to add to your problems. (Okay, let's be honest. Maybe I do.) In fact, I am hoping Essex will be a good place for you to reflect on what you've done. I know your lot isn't easy, but you are a well-educated person with more resources than the other men. So please try to put your time to good use. I can see the

look on your face when you read this, but if you can't do it for me, do
it for Davie.

Love,

Meredith

18

I HAVE HEARD all this palaver before from Meredith, her do-gooder hope that prison life will have a salutary effect on yours truly. She should know better than to waste her breath.

I have a great deal of sympathy, however, for what she is going through with Mother. One afternoon when nobody else was around, I was obliged to look after my parent. As I peeled off her soggy diaper (the ghastly action Meredith mentioned in her letter), a shower of urine wet the back of my hand. Googie pretended not to notice, and I averted my eyes while she lowered herself with steely determination onto the toilet seat. There was a faraway tinkle of water and then she hoisted herself up again using the rubber wall handle. She chastised me angrily as I slid the slacks up her legs and cinched her belt, complaining all the while that I didn't handle her as gently as Meredith.

I am well aware of the difficulties with Mother, just as I can imagine Tim's shock at seeing Esther in one of her inebriated states.

Point being, my ex-wife can't pull herself together; she lives in a salt-box on the main street of Port Washington; its rooms are over-stuffed with the crude pine furniture from Quebec that was sold in Toronto antique shops during the sixties: a beaten-up refectory table and crude rolltop desk with matching captain's chairs. The noise of the traffic outside interferes with social conversations, and it's hard enough to make out what Esther is telling you if she's got into the California wine she likes so much.

Late one night, not long after our divorce, she phoned in a drunken state. I had no idea what she was going on about. Then I understood. Davie had tried to kill himself. Meredith and I rushed over and found my boy lying very still on the bathroom floor. I smelled a coppery odour and saw his bloody wrists. There was more blood on the bathroom mat.

The ambulance arrived just as I was helping Davie to his feet. Luckily, the cuts weren't serious. Hesitation wounds, the medico called them. Practice runs for the real thing.

The unhappy incident turned out to be a one-off.

19

MY LATEST PHONE message from Nugent says he is back in his dreary midtown lodgings. For years I have tried to help him with his unfortunate personal taste, but he doesn't want my advice. Most people don't. In fact, it is extraordinary how satisfied with themselves most people are. What can you do? My old friend has always wanted to be poor.

After my mentoring job is done, I amble over to the ungainly stucco building that was once a residence for Olympics personnel. The prison's computer studio is on the first floor, a capacious lacuna with old-fashioned picture windows that open onto the stand of white pine. I settle myself behind the screen of a newish Dell OptiPlex 760 and start typing. I hope Nugent will find what I have to say helpful.

June 24, 2012

Dear Nugent:

I realize you're starting work on my memoir and that's as it should be. Please note that we prisoners aren't allowed visits or phone calls for the first four weeks. Not until we adjust to our new circumstances. You will need to wait for the warden to approve my visitors' list.

As you might imagine, it was an ominous occasion when I became prisoner number 199421-321. Meredith and Caroline drove me to my new home, and we exclaimed over the derelict buildings in this part of the world. The region's economy is solely dependent on the Essex Federal Correctional Institute. It is located in the national park of the Adirondacks, and the rolling hills and mountains along with the region's small, serene lakes remind me of my grandfather's farm in the Laurentians. The prison staff talks about the weather in the same anxious, hopeful tones as Quebeckers.

And the high, rocky ground is unsuitable for farming. Both areas perch on a cratonic eruption of igneous and metamorphic rock that happened about one billion years ago. The rocks that form the Adirondack dome were created within the past five million years — a relatively recent phenomenon as far as geological time goes.

You'll be glad to know I've made friends with my bunkmates. The name of the black scofflaw is Bailey. (I trust you know the meaning of the word scofflaw, Nugent. It's a Prohibition term for someone who drinks illegal hooch.)

My other roommate is Derek Williams, whose facial tattoos evoke a Maori warrior. If one man can say this of another, Derek is strikingly handsome and very popular here. Apparently, some of the gangsters even go to his early morning yoga classes.

Yesterday, I rescued him from our caseworker, a repulsive cipher who smacks his big wet lips when he dislikes what you say. At the therapy session, Giles taunted Derek about selling drugs at his girlfriend's yoga retreat. Derek explained that he had to save the day because Citigroup was foreclosing on the retreat's mortgage.

Giles immediately accused Derek of "stinkin' thinkin'." Tell us about the three Cs, Giles said. Conditions, cognitions, and choices …

Well, let me see, mate. We needed money … I guess that's the condition …

Giles, the grotesque blovian, smiled and nodded.

Then I … I made a bad choice and started selling drugs again. That's cognition, right, mate?

What do you know? A light is dawning. Giles smirked.

You have no right to mock Derek, I cried. You're a poltroon without an iota of life wisdom.

What did you just say? Giles asked.

I said you are a sadistic blusterer and a popinjay!

The man was so discombobulated he cancelled the workshop. Later, Derek told me he was grateful.

I have decided not to go to another session. Bailey refuses to go too. His hobby is collecting photographs of child stars like Lindsay Lohan and Britney Spears. Do you remember Dana Plato? She starred with Gary Coleman in *Diff'rent Strokes* and she suicided on a drug overdose while Gary, her pint-sized co-star, died of a brain hemorrhage at forty-two. It seems most child stars don't last long. When the guard isn't looking, Bailey tapes up their photos on our dorm wall.

To pass the time, I tell Bailey amusing tales about the celebrities I used to know. For example, Pater and I met Princess Diana when we attended a wedding of one of the minor royals. We were standing with a guard in ceremonial attire when Diana came out of the washroom and told the guard she had dropped her tiara down the toilet bowl. She wanted his sword to fish it out. The guard lent her his implement, and a few moments later Diana reappeared carrying the still-dripping tiara.

Bailey, the idiot, wanted to know what it was dripping with. I wrote up the story of Diana's tiara and Derek emailed it to a friend who sent it on to a website about celebrities' embarrassing moments. It was published under the headline: "PRINCESS DI VISITS THE LOO."

As you can see, I do what I can to encourage my bunkmates. There is something to be said for even the most unpleasant circumstances.

Yours,
Dale Paul

20

OUTSIDE, SEARCHLIGHTS SWEEP the funereal gloom of the yard, but under the LED panels in the Rec Centre, all is cozy and bright. My bunkmates and I are playing cards, and I try not to stare at their ghostly white faces as I deal our hands. It is late June, and they have sprinkled their skin with baby powder to combat the humidity. It's an incongruous sight! Yet they are serious poker buffs, and they've come up with an amusing penalty: whoever loses must drink sixteen ounces of water, a punishing forfeit for older men with a leaky bladder. Luckily, tonight, my fine bunkmates are experiencing a losing streak.

While we attend our cards, Earl appears on the overhead television screen, his odd face with his heavy-lidded eyes radiating authority. At boarding school, Earl would slather on Clearasil to disguise the condition of his leathery skin. His nickname used to be Lizard Man, although he hadn't yet developed the display structures that are part of a male like him.

The scofflaws don't seem to notice anything unnatural about the way he moves his head from side to side, although it always surprises me how often people fail to see the obvious. Possibly, you need to know about his rare condition in order to spot it.

My old friend is getting a reputation for being outspoken on issues like immigration. Only a few days before, a graffiti artist painted an unpleasant verse at the base of the Statue of Liberty: *Flush your tired, your poor, your huddled masses down the sewers and send the losers back to the shit holes they come from.* Earl was quoted in the media as saying the verse should stay up. He said washing it off would suggest Americans couldn't take a joke.

On the television screen, the CNN host mentions a poll that shows Earl is the preferred Republican candidate. How about that? Earl asks, staring at the camera. CNN wants me to run for president.

In the lounge, a few men nearby stop playing cards and high-five one another. Several others shout out Earl's name in rough, excited voices.

Would you vote for Earl Lindquist? I ask my bunkmates.

He be gangsta, B, Bailey says, sounding respectful. Bailey has taken to calling me B, and I go along because I'm told it's an affectionate street term.

He won't get in, mate, Derek replies. He's unpopular.

I wouldn't be so sure, I say as I lay down my aces. Listen. I've got an idea. I point at the television. We'll run a dead pool on old celebrities, and put Earl Lindquist on our list. We could use some of your sad-sack child stars too, Bailey. I'm serious.

B, you never serious!

Derek looks thoughtful. You mean like those dead pools online where you win if your celebrity dies?

When I nod, Bailey asks: How you gon make money on it, B?

The prisoners will deposit a fee in my commissary account. Without the warden knowing.

Derek winks at Bailey. The admin slaps an eight-dollar surcharge on every deposit, mate.

And they don like us puttin' money in another inmate's account neither, Bailey adds. But don feel bad, B.' You jes gettin' acclimized here.

Acclimated, you mean.

Yo! Bailey starts cleaning his oversized prison spectacles with my hanky; it has come back from the laundry badly tattered. He sees where I'm looking and gives me one of his fanged smiles. You wan it back?

It's all yours. My girlfriend can bring me another.

What if the warden finds out, mate? Derek asks.

I'm going to talk to the warden. He'll like the idea once I explain how it will help his boys.

Bailey and Derek begin to hee-haw like donkeys.

What is so amusing, pray tell?

You talking to the warden, Derek says, and they burst out laughing again. Despite their ridicule, I find myself laughing too. There's a sense of the Tao at work in any good scheme. A feeling of flow or confluence, as if the engines that move the universe are coming together effortlessly. It's blue sky from here, as the boys in my office used to crow.

21

The american chestnut tree (*Castanea dentata*) grows to nearly one hundred feet tall and four feet in diameter with a broad, rounded crown. Like you, our saplings have a long way to go.
— A NOTE FROM WARDEN NATHAN RICKARD ON THE
ADMIN BUILDING BULLETIN BOARD, JULY 21, 2012

THE WARDEN HAS sent for me. It's high summer. In his backyard, a cardinal is hovering over a bird bath while marble dolphins playfully spit out frilly geysers of water. Nothing about the Alpine house suggests a prison warden lives there. Nathan Rickard obviously aspires to the grander things in life. A man after my bad, old heart.

At the door, Patti Rickard, the warden's wife, assesses me through a pair of tinted Gucci sunglasses, a hint of frilled panties flashing slyly beneath the pleats of her white tennis skirt. Immediately I feel ashamed of my over-laundered prison sweats. In the days when I was flush with coin, Caroline used to wear Gucci.

Smiling nervously, Patti leads me into a large living room, where the warden sits spraddle-legged in a bulbous Naugahyde chair. He is off campus, so to speak, surrounded by homey comforts — the mountain pottery tea service with its encircling frieze of black bears, the spotless hardwood floors, and the black cooking pots hanging by the hearth.

As she pours our tea, Patti gabs about her work with the Michael Jackson dancers and the politics she was obliged to play in order to copy an arts program from the state prisons. The warden and I listen while she rambles on about the life skills the men are learning, the astonishing drop in recidivism rates among her graduates. The warden smiles and half closes his eyes. No doubt he's heard it all before. At last, he waves his hand good-naturedly, and when she leaves for her tennis lesson, he tells me about his life. His father died young. So he was obliged to drop his idea of becoming a professor of psychology. Instead he began to teach high school dropouts at the army base in Camp Shelby, Mississippi. From Camp

Shelby, he went into administrative work in federal prisons, and now here he is, overseeing the kingdom of the unlucky.

I felt frustrated as a young man, he says in his low, soft voice. Heck, I guess you can understand frustration.

Oh, I know thwarted. It is not pleasant.

I still graduated from college, Dale Paul. So what if it was night school. You ever heard of Bergler?

I say no.

Someday I'll show you my MA thesis. Edmund Bergler had a theory that the gambler gambles to lose, not win.

I sip my tea, waiting.

The pleasures of displeasure, get it?

When I shake my head, his face opens in a smile. Let me explain. As a kid, you learn to like the thrill of being scared … you know the feeling you get when your dad's about to punish you? The worst is about to happen, right? Some of my boys get hooked on that sensation.

Are you trying to tell me something, Mr. Rickard?

Me tell you something! Ha. I'm saying Bergler's theories explain my boys who are into self-damage. He locks his hands behind his head and stares out at the prisoners planting chestnut saplings by the side of the prison road. On the way over, Martino told me how the warden has personally bought the chestnut saplings the scofflaws are planting. Possibly Nathan Rickard is imagining his chestnut trees grown to adult size, the leafy arch of their boughs filtering the afternoon light while the prison vans pass underneath.

Does Bergler have anything to say about recidivism?

He gives me the fish eye.

I hear your prison has a high rate of men returning. Look, I'm not criticizing how you do things. It's just that I think I know how to help your problem.

Oh, yeah? He snorts.

I have an idea, good sir. I'll give a workshop using a fake monetary system involving celebrities. The men will learn how to determine the economic value of something and how to make a transaction based on that economic value ...

How do celebrities come into this?

Referencing popular culture will work at the level of the prisoners' interest. I pause, wondering how much I should divulge. He glances at his watch, so I quicken my pace: The men will bet on which one of the celebrities will die and they'll monitor the health of these celebrities like a stock going up or down. Celebrity dead pools are very popular online.

He breaks into guffaws.

I struggle to keep a poker face. I can feel it coming, the sad dramatic finish to my little scheme.

Heck, that's original! Betting on the death of old celebrities. But, lookit, I can't green-light some hare-brained project just because you have a public profile. He wags his head when he sees my disappointed face. Okay, Dale Paul, I'm aware my boys bet at cards, and I tell the C.O.s to turn a blind eye. But gambling is illegal inside the facility.

I start to tell him about the studies in the law library that claim gambling is able to help prisoners get back on their feet. I cite Brewster's report in 2005 that states leisure experience contributes to rehabilitation, and gambling under the right circumstances is recreational. I also mention Worthington's paper in 2006 supporting Brewster's view, but the warden waves his hand dismissively and rises to his feet, the leather of his massive chair squeaking.

I'll think about your workshop idea, Dale Paul. The boys could use some financial skills. But forget celebrities. It's too far-fetched. How's the mentoring going?

I stand up, too. Well enough.

Good. Patti wanted me to ask you over. She used to follow your stock tips in "Talk Like a Broker."

He is referencing my column for the *Wall Street Journal*, where, before I was unfairly repurposed, I explained financial terms without lapsing into market parlance.

He pumps my hand. But it won't happen again. No special privileges for you or anybody else, understand?

While I stand looking down at the warden, I recall reading something in the *Times* about the aggression of short men: according to the article, it's tall men such as myself who are more likely to lose their tempers and hit you back.

When I leave the room, I bump into Martino, who has been listening behind the door.

Old celebrities, Martino mutters. You gotta be kidding me.

22

THE TERSE WORDS on the postcard Caroline has sent from London send a chill through my bad, old heart: *We need to talk soon, really talk, as ever, Caroline.*

Why is her card so short? Is she planning on dumping me? From Inmate dot com, the term my fellow inmates use for their gossip mill, I know all about the wives and girlfriends who abandon their men when they go to jail. Surely that won't happen with Caroline! After all, she has scribbled an *x* and *o* next to *as ever*. So perhaps I am over-thinking. Possibly I have grown used to things taking unpredictable turns, directions that steer me toward unforeseen disasters that burst into the news and make me out to be the anti-golem of the shareholder, a predatory pariah who bears no relation to the well-intentioned man I know myself to be.

The situation with Davie is more serious still. Will he drop out of Harvard? He hasn't written, so I have no way of knowing what he is thinking, but I have left phone messages urging him to go back to school. My last message said: I know you are upset with me, and my circumstances, and I understand how my situation must seem. I have done many unfortunate things, but I am not a criminal. Please, son, for your own good, continue your education.

I realize the end of my message sounded too forceful: Why won't you call me back? Just you wait, Davie, just you wait until you have a boy of your own.

23

I HAVE SOMETHING to confess. Davie has been unhappy with me since the day he found out about the charges.

It was his twentieth birthday, and my son walked in a few minutes early. From Esther, Davie has inherited blond hair and hopeful blue eyes with something Ashkenazi about his nose and upper lip.

I hadn't seen him since Christmas, and he seemed more sullen than before. I made delighted welcoming noises; then we went into the solarium, where I had set up a replica of the battle at Gettysburg. He walked around the table, picking up the new lead soldiers Dieter had bought on eBay. Years before, Pater had given me a full set — complete with Confederate and Union cavalry officers, the Confederate infantrymen with flags, and Union standard-bearers. The figures I had asked Dieter to order were a little pricier: a Union soldier playing a harmonica and a Confederate soldier firing his musket from behind a very life-like dead horse. Davie picked up the soldier lying behind the horse and turned it over in his hands. He looked quizzically at me and set it down. I knew Davie was worrying about the horses. The subject always came up when we discussed the Civil War. *The hapless slaughter of the animals that so valiantly supported the troops.* I have tried to tell my boy that nobody thought much about animal rights in the days of the Civil War, but I never get very far when we tackle the history of how the horses were treated. Davie is on his computer day and night, rounding up signatures for groups protesting the inhumane treatment of animals.

Unable to wait for the ritual of present opening, I gave my boy his gift, an edition of Ken Burns's series on the Civil War. Davie looked it over wordlessly before I put on the DVD about Pickett's Charge.

Side by side on the sofa we sat, but something told me Davie wasn't absorbing the film's magnificent diorama of General Lee's first major blunder. There was my favourite historian, Shelby Foote, confiding that Lee, the most rational and purposeful of men, had got his dander up. I agreed with Foote's view that Lee ignored common sense that humid July morning when he sent Pickett's men to die on the farmers' fields near Little Big Top.

When we reached the part about Pickett, I heard Davie sigh.

How's college? I asked, turning off the DVD player.

Oh, you know, he replied.

Your mother says you're not enjoying your courses.

I know what you're going to say, Dad. Some barfy stuff about why I need an MBA, so I can be top of my field.

I opened the coffee table drawer where I kept a cache of weed for unsettling conversations. Barfy? I asked. Is that even a word, good sir?

Hey, Dad, no grammar lesson. It's my birthday, okay?

When I lit up, he rose to his feet, and for an uneasy moment, his eyes caught mine; then he turned his back and gazed out at the sound. He didn't approve. Smoking dope usurped a prerogative of his generation.

I considered bringing up what I had done for him. Unfortunately, children, even soft-hearted boys like Davie, don't recall parental sacrifices except in a vague, general way, and I felt sure he had forgotten the hours we spent together staring at Mathew Brady's photographs of the innocent, lonesome faces of the men who had fought in the Civil War. As I sat there wondering how to talk Davie into staying at Harvard, my thoughts travelled back to the day a younger Davie and I had walked down the Gettysburg battlefield while Esther stayed home to nurse a bad case of the flu.

Davie had taken my hand, and we'd trudged together along the neatly mowed path, following in the footsteps of the soldiers. A few minutes later, a spring thunderstorm broke. Davie took off his shoes and ran around barefoot, trying to catch the raindrops on his tongue. Shivering and wet, I thought about the unlucky young men buried on the ridge nearby while my own happy-go-lucky boy was frolicking in front of me. Davie — my one and only son. A kind-hearted man-child with his head of yellow Rumpelstiltskin hair. Yet I had my boy figured wrong. He isn't the happy-go-lucky type at all.

My cellphone rang. It was my assistant, Bip, urging me in a frantic voice to turn on CNN. I followed his instructions, and Davie and I listened in stunned silence while a fuzzy-headed news anchor said I was being indicted on criminal charges, including securities fraud (irresponsible non-sense) and falsifying documents (a load of demented tripe). I clicked off the television.

Dad, Davie cried. Is this true?

Of course not, I snapped. The landline began to ring. Davie watched anxiously while I reached down, grimacing, and unplugged it. Outside, a vehicle was driving along Half Moon Lane, and for one loony, delusional moment, I imagined a squad of FBI agents breaking down the door and swarming in, their guns blazing just as they do in the movies. It was only a grocery van delivering our weekly basket of organic vegetables from a Long Island farm.

24

THE AIR IN the common room is steamy with delectable cooking smells: chicken baking in peanut butter and dessert wraps covered with hot chocolate syrup and granola. For a bunch of shiftless ne'er-do-wells, it is more than a little surprising how many recipes they know. Still others are making chai tea from the hot water cooler. Do the scofflaws worry about their families as much as I worry about Davie? Maybe so.

There is a sudden hubbub; Martino stands at the door with the mail-bag. When I amble over, the men part like the Red Sea, their faces friendly or menacing, and the C.O. hands me an envelope addressed in familiar, loping handwriting. I tear it open, embarrassed by my eagerness.

Aug 12, 2012

Dear Dad:

Please stop leaving me phone messages. You are a taker. Mom and Meredith think so too, although they are too kind to tell you. And there is no point sending me a letter either. I don't want to hear your florid

views on prison life. I think what you did was crap if you want to know
the truth.

David

I sink into a chair, clutching the letter. A taker! Surely Davie doesn't mean those harsh words. Is he trying to hurt me? It's true I didn't see much of my son after the divorce. I was working hard at Quaestus Capital so I could pay Esther child support.

Florid views, indeed.

Bailey sits down beside me, looking concerned. What's crackin', B?

My son. He doesn't want to hear from me.

All boys say mean tings to their daddies. Bailey wags his head disapprovingly. He gon be nice soon.

I hope so, Bailey. I hope so.

The next day, I call Meredith.

Look, calm down, she says. I know it hurts, but David is having trouble accepting your situation. We all are. In her husky voice, she explains that my own child thinks there is something underhanded about my manouevres, a catch that no one can find, unless they are as shrewd as myself.

I take a gulp of air. Can you persuade him to come here?

You really think that will help?

When I don't respond, she groans. Okay. I'll work on Davie. I know how much you care about him.

Meredith, what would I do without you? And will you bring up my brush pens? The ones I keep in the drawer by my bed? I think she answers yes, although I can't be certain because, by then, she has hung up.

25

Tim Nugent

THINGS ARE LOOKING up. After months of waiting, the warden is letting Tim see Dale Paul. The Bureau of Prisons dislikes publicity, and the warden has been suspicious of Tim since the morning the guard learned Tim was a journalist. Tim was asked to submit letters of reference proving he was a reputable writer, and Dale Paul signed a form saying he won't make a profit from the published memoir if Dale Paul is still in prison. Tim isn't sure how long that will be. He's heard that white-collar criminals get fast-tracked through the system because their crimes aren't violent. Chances are Dale Paul won't be in for long, despite his twelve-year sentence.

Tim is travelling north on the bus with Meredith and Dale Paul's son, Davie. Meredith invited Tim to come so he could interview her about Dale Paul. She said it would be killing two birds with one stone. They are going by bus because Davie says that a bus uses less fossil fuel per person than going by car. The son is a more sensitive kettle of fish than the dad, Tim is learning.

He is sitting across the aisle from Tim now. Meredith sits next to Davie. Her eyes are closed and her pretty head has started to loll against the seat rest. Tim isn't sure if she is asleep or just pretending so she doesn't have to talk. She is still awkward with him, and her awkwardness makes Tim uncomfortable. We're a fine pair, he thinks. Two timid souls who prefer to distract ourselves from what we're feeling.

Meanwhile, Davie is engrossed in his laptop; every so often he looks up and catches Tim watching. He hunches over his screen, as if he doesn't want anyone to see what he is typing.

What's Davie up to? Tim wonders. The boy seems shaken by his father going to prison, although Dale Paul has never paid much attention to the kid except as a kind of toy or possession. Dale Paul's father treated Dale Paul the same way, so chances are his old friend doesn't know any better.

As if he can read Tim's thoughts, Davie shoots Tim a frustrated glance, and Tim turns his head away politely and stares out the window. They are far upstate now, passing abandoned factories and forgotten small towns whose outlines shimmer in the late summer heat. The recession has hit hard in this part of the world. American flags hang from the porches of clapboard houses that need repainting. A person could stroll down one of the streets in these places and find nothing to buy except wool socks and chicken feed.

26

Dale Paul

> All visitors entering the institution for a visit will be appropriately
> attired. Visitors may not wear shorts, mini-skirts, sheer or tight
> fitting clothing, excessively short or low-cut clothing, backless
> clothing, halter tops, or sleeveless clothing. Dresses, blouses or other
> apparel of a suggestive or revealing nature may not be worn. If
> the Front Lobby or Visiting Room Officer determines a visitor is
> improperly attired he/she will contact the Operations Lieutenant
> and Institution Duty Officer to determine whether to deny or ter-
> minate the visit.
>
> — FEDERAL BUREAU OF PRISONS, *INMATE*
> *ADMISSION AND ORIENTATION HANDBOOK*

MY COUSIN IS easy to spot in a crowd. She is the only older woman with
her hair in braids. This afternoon, she is wearing a peculiar, drapey outfit
that must have been in her closet for ages, going back to the time when
Mother used to buy Meredith's wardrobe.

As a girl, my cousin didn't like to go out in public because a shard of
glass had made a mess of her right eye, so Mother took over and the
doctors gave Meredith an artificial replacement with a medical name,
ocular prosthesis, and I used to drop the term when someone asked about
her fake eye. That would stop people from questioning her, which was the
general idea.

Meredith is my kister, the next best thing to having a sister. She is also
a devilishly smart woman and attractive enough despite the combination

of a winsome girlish face atop a tank-like body, the full lips and dimpled cheeks counterpoised with the meaty breadth of her arms and chest.

Nugent has come with her, clothed in the drab, ill-fitting schmata so highly prized by his hardscrabble profession. He no longer resembles the fearful, thickset boy who would do anything to get into the good graces of the school prefects. Unfortunately, he still smiles too easily, a nervous tic, and he seems congenitally unable to stand still. He continuously glances about him with his wide doe eyes. I have forgotten his anxiousness and how I used to try to reassure him, although there's no need for me to play his agony aunt now. After all, he has published a well-received book on Harry Truman. Or was it Eisenhower? He waves at me while the guard pats me up and down, looking for weapons; then Nugent walks back up the hill and Davie comes through the gate in his usual hipster fripperies, a dark beret and a wool scarf knotted at the throat. I rarely experience an emotional flutter, but with my son, affectionate feelings seep in all over the place and take me by surprise.

Meredith comes over, looking expectant. What is she hoping for? A sign that says I've experienced a change in my bad, old heart?

She gives me the single hug I'm allotted as an inmate and says she forgot my brush pens.

That's all right, Kis. Where did Nugent go?

He's waiting until our visit finishes, because he's interviewing you for the book.

I see. Well, nice of you all to come and see me in the joint. I wave at the unpainted picnic tables by the lake where groups of dark-skinned men sit talking with their families. *Joint.* I'm poking fun at convict talk, trying to be a good sport about my situation, but Meredith and Davie look down at their feet in embarrassment. I launch into a tirade about the noisy lineups at Chow Hall, the loathsome food so woefully lacking in protein that the men have to live on tins of mackerel sold in the commissary: the ill-mannered rush to the grubby showers, and the poorly paid prison jobs, an absurd parody of real jobs in the outside world.

When I'm through complaining, I pull out the empty pockets of my browns and ask them to buy me a coffee. They don't react. Why are they staring at me like that? Is it so hard to imagine me sans coin? Ah. Bailey has come at us from behind. Fine. All right. Meredith and Davie may stare all they like, but they don't understand that the scofflaws rely on their physical presence to project authority. These men grew up poor and badly educated; their bodies are all they have to work with, in other words. Or, as Meredith might say, employing one of her fatuous politically correct phrases, they are "embodied."

Bailey is my bunkmate, I explain. Immediately, the two of them shake his hand.

He's from Crooklyn, although his mother comes from the islands off the South Carolina coast. Say something for us in Gullah, Bailey.

Out come a few musical, incomprehensible sounds that spring from the slave dialect Bailey heard as a child: We blan ketch 'nuf cootuh dey.

That means, "We always catch a lot of turtles there," I explain. As you can see, Bailey and I have some interesting conversations. Bailey grins, oblivious to the possibility that his filed teeth could frighten my family. Can you say the Lord's Prayer in Gullah for Meredith and Davie?

Bailey winks at Meredith and begins a shortened version of the prayer he says every night before he falls asleep: We Papa een heaben, leh ebry-body hona you nyame cause you da holy.... Fagibe we fa de bad ting we da do.... Keep we from e ebil.... Amen. When he finishes, he drops his eyes shyly. Meredith makes a faint admiring sound in her throat. Davie looks down at his feet again.

Okay, B, I'm gon see da boss. Bailey nods at a tall black woman coming through the gate.

Ah, your mother. Is she the one who gave you The Virgin's Merciful Messages for Unbelievers? I'm referring to the compendium of treacly Christian sentiments that you keep under your pillow, Bailey.

He always like this? Bailey asks Meredith. I never know what Dale Paul gon say.

Neither do I. Meredith smiles faintly. As he walks off, she hisses, I don't think you should have made him talk in dialect. He's not a dancing bear from the circus.

Of course he's not. He's my friend, and he's going to help me hatch a plan to make money. You'll see. I'm going to leave a nest egg for Davie.

My boy turns so pale I can count every freckle on his nose.

I don't care about your money, he cries. And Meredith doesn't care about it either.

Everybody cares about my money, Davie. Even you.

Directing a bad-tempered glance my way, Davie turns to watch the kitschy drama unfolding below us. On the tennis courts, Derek and his troupe of dancers are marching up and down. As the music on the sound system changes to the song "Thriller," the men hunch their shoulders and twist their fingers into claws, the better to menace the warden's wife, who has just joined their dance. She pirouettes seductively, drawing the men in and at the same time pretending she is frightened by the harm they can do.

They begin gyrating around her, jerking their heads and shoulders and twitching their hips until Patti flees in mock terror, the goose-stepping squadron in wild pursuit, their heads rolling and jerking like macabre stalkers, the fluid swivel of their torsos demonstrating demented flexibility. In a matter of minutes, they have her surrounded.

That's the warden's wife. I point at Patti Rickard. She runs a program here called Rehabilitation through the Arts.

I don't believe it, Meredith exclaims. How wonderful the prison will allow something like this!

They do it to cut costs. The men who go through the program tend not to come back. I turn back to Davie. Will you finish your studies this fall?

He shrugs.

You can't drop out. You'll never amount to a hill of beans.

Dad, don't start, okay? I only came to see you because Meredith dragged me here. She said you wanted to apologize for wrecking my life.

Wrecking your life?

A strange, glassy expression comes over Davie's face. Is it panic? Or does the look convey a more unpleasant emotion?

Dad isn't going to apologize, is he, Kis? Davie shouts. You just said that to get me to come.

Meredith blushes. He hasn't wrecked your life, David. He's wrecked his.

Kis, you're a liar, just like Dad!

Don't you talk like that to your aunt! I snap. Apologize to her.

He lowers his eyes. I didn't mean to upset you, Kis. No matter what goes down, you've always been there for me.

Is something going down?

He flinches. Hey, Kis, let's go. I'm so done with this shit.

I put my hand on Davie's arm. He shakes me off and starts walking toward the gate, his head down, the wind lifting his curly blond hair off his shoulders. My poor boy. He isn't the most resilient of creatures.

Meredith mouths some indecipherable sentiment; then she kisses my cheek and follows Davie out. I watch them go. What made me think I can change my boy's mind about staying in school? He is my son, after all. *A chip off the old block.* I sit down at one of the picnic tables and wait for Nugent. I need to think things over. For as long as I can, that is.

A few days later, there is bad news. I haven't been expecting it, and yet perhaps I knew all along what was going to happen.

27

I HAVE BEEN sleeping badly since the story about Davie appeared in the papers. Most of the news accounts say the same thing: Davie jumped off the Brooklyn Bridge.

My bunkmates are doing their best to comfort me. In the next cot, Derek lies reading unaware of the way his lamp is transforming his tattooed face into a Godzilla mask. From above, Bailey's voice rumbles: We sure sorry, B. We sure are.

I nod grimly. I don't trust myself to talk.

In a melancholy fog, I replay the scene: Davie grimacing at the derelict condition of the bridge as he cruised along on his bike, looking for the best spot. My boy never liked New York City, with its smelly air and concatenation of grubby streets, so he likely found the bridge, with its potholes, a shabby backdrop for the grand act he had in mind.

I imagine him placing his bike against the guardrail, trying to ignore the cold air rising up from the river. Maybe he paused for a moment, staring at the ghostly lights floating above the traffic on the bridge. Did he know enough to jump feet first and keep his body vertical? Of course, he didn't. He wanted to die, and that is the position you assume if you want to live.

I picture him taking out the crumpled message: *I can't keep living with a name like mine.*

Oh, Davie. You know how to hurt me. He tucked the note into the bike's tool bag, where the police found it.

A few passersby saw him: A biker whistled past, his sinewy legs pumping hard, the tires of the bike bumping across the metal partitions of the bridge. A man in an old Buick slowed down and asked what he was doing. Davie said he was admiring the view. Maybe he was already thinking about the quick, easy hoist up and over the railing, and the topple-free fall into the river. I have never tried to kill myself, but there must be fear, apprehension, maybe glee?

In the next bunk, Derek puts down his book. You okay, mate?

When I shake my head and shrug, he smiles encouragingly. Go on then, he says.

Slowly, listlessly, I clip my reading lamp onto my notepad and begin to sketch the Brooklyn Bridge using a lead pencil with a soft nib, pressing down firmly again and again in order to darken the greyer shadings. Frustrated, I tear up my sketch. I do another, and then, just as I'm about to destroy it too, Derek grabs it from my hand and hides it away.

The next morning, the reports say Davie committed suicide although his body has not been found. The men are kind enough not to press me for details, although CNN replays what happened ad nauseam. In the common room, small groups of prisoners sit staring at images of Davie on the screen. Their eyes slide away guiltily when they notice me. Only a few have the gall to keep watching.

Caroline has left several consoling phone messages, and Mother called to say she blames what happened on Esther's drinking. Sometimes her unconditional support is hard even for me to take.

It is late in the afternoon by the time Meredith arrives. Her face looks haggard, years older.

I steer her over to two ugly plastic molded chairs, ignoring the families who stop chatting to stare. He said nothing was going down, didn't he? I guess he fooled us.

Yes, he lied. Meredith starts to weep.

I sit down beside her, and for once, I'm at a loss for words.

PART TWO

THE DEAD CELEBRITIES

Dale Paul

MY SON, DAVIE, was born in Toronto on a windy winter night on the ninth of March. Esther, who cleaves to the woolly insights of astrology, said the soft, watery aspect to Pisces made it a confusing sign for a male child. I had no way of knowing if she was right, and I didn't tell her what I'd already sensed, that my child would become more important to me than she was.

And sure enough, by the time Davie was in grade school, I viewed him with awe; my boy was intelligent and generous, a link to the higher self buried inside the flinty parts I need in order to do battle in the world. Everybody has one person whose good opinion of us allows us to feel comfortable with ourselves. For most people it's a spouse or a parent, but for me it has always been Davie. It may seem like a strange thing to admit, but my son was, dare I say it, even a role model?

When we moved to Long Island, Esther and Davie and I were more or less happy. Esther loved our home in the village of Sands Point, although she complained about the smelly summer breezes from the Manhasset sewage plant. She found it difficult to understand why transporting hundreds of thousands of people into the city and back again every day required more attention from the Powers-That-Be than the greening of the planet.

Meanwhile, I floated about in a jubilant daze. New Yorkers welcome men with my talents. I could have been dressed in a gorilla suit for all they cared. Every morning, I rose, took the Long Island railway into Manhattan, disembarked at Penn Station, and strolled to my office, where from my sixty-fourth floor I could watch window washers spider-walking across the glistening spire of the Chrysler Building. I would smile and think, Woo-hoo — I'm really here!

During those years, I felt as if a cape of rectitude had been lifted from my shoulders, as if the official waving me through customs had noticed the heavy cloak I wore and, in a gentlemanly fashion, removed the dreary garment. Point being, northerners such as myself share a unique spatial relationship to America — the sense of looking down in space on that great nation, a sense that goes hand in hand with feeling morally superior. I left that frivolous emotion behind the moment Esther and I began living in Kimberly's old mansion.

On weekends, business partners and clients flocked to our home. Sometimes Tim Nugent came, hoping to get wind of a story. Earl came more often, usually with one of his wives or girlfriends. My new home was big enough to accommodate everyone. Esther painted its sprawl of penumbral rooms eggshell white, and in our backyard she commissioned a landscaper to repair the moon gate, a high stone wall with a circular arch in the middle leading guests to the saltwater pool beyond.

Esther wasn't drinking then, and Mother wasn't interfering in our lives. Then Pater died, and Googie moved into our Long Island home and fought with Esther over who should run the household.

Meredith predicted that a momma's boy such as myself would have trouble with women, and it didn't take long for Esther to fail to meet Mother's standards. Mother claimed that Esther was encouraging Davie's tendency to introversion. Esther realized she'd flunked the grade, and to console herself, she fell in with a crowd at the Plandome Country Club who drank heavily after their golf games.

It was a shock to Davie and me the first night she came home drunk. One day she was a saint in an apron, content to stay at home with her child, and the next, all that changed. The only place she wanted to be was on the golf course or in the bar afterwards.

I had always seen golf as a Neanderthal game where men batted around a tiny rock with a few barky sticks. As a result, I felt a heavy dose of disdain for Esther's pursuit, although I didn't mind talking up the golf courses on

Long Island in order to persuade her to move to America.

Davie became a hacktivist, a vocation completely unlike anything I might choose. I was never really good at math and the formulas; someone at work used to place my stock orders. My technical incompetence led to a great deal of farcical joking at the office.

I can see it all now, how the mystery (mysterious to me) of algorithms resulted in Davie joining the movement that fought for looser copyright laws so ordinary mortals such as you and me could have access to the information that most companies and governments prefer to keep to themselves.

He also took up the cause of animal rights, bringing home numerous stray cats that Esther made him keep outside the house. She worried constantly about the way Davie dropped one cause to take up another. I told her our boy didn't follow through on unworthy projects. If Davie were the hapless kid that Esther said he was, he would never have managed to pull off his disappearing act. Nobody hapless was capable of doing something like that.

2

ONE SUNNY FALL afternoon, Meredith shows up in the visitors' lounge. After we seat ourselves by the picture window overlooking the parking lot and the forest beyond, she produces a note she received from Davie the day he disappeared. It's a message from the grave: *I've gone somewhere where it doesn't suck to be Dad's son. All my love, David.*

Puzzled, I reread his note, and then I'm sure of it. *I've gone somewhere* wasn't a phrase I'd use if I planned to kill myself. Heaven may be real to practising Christians, but my son wasn't a religious person. Meredith, I say. I think Davie is telling you he isn't dead. Don't you see? He says he's going somewhere else ... but that doesn't mean he's flying up to the pearly gates.

You're just trying to make me feel better.

For god's sake. He's not dead. One of these days, he's going to come back from wherever somewhere is and explain himself. To make my point, I insert air quotes around the word *somewhere*.

You're crazy. You think because you want something, the universe will jump to your bidding. You don't have as much power as you think.

Meredith has never called me crazy before, although she is understandably distressed. Nevertheless, it isn't up to me to disabuse her of her conclusion about my son. Instead, I squeeze her hand and say how grieved I feel over losing him. Later on, when she is ready to hear me out, I will help her see the truth.

3

THE DAY AFTER Meredith's visit, Davie comes to me in a dream. As soon as the clock says my workday is over, I rush to the computer studio and start a letter:

September 20, 2012

Dear Davie:

Last night, I dreamt you and I were walking in an apple orchard, and I could feel you as close as air. You didn't notice me, although once or twice you glanced around as if you sensed somebody watching.

The orchard in my dream brought back the blossoming apple trees we passed in late May on my way to prison. In my dream, I was telling you I'd done nothing wrong and you turned around and spat into my open mouth. It was a revolting gesture, intended to humiliate. Yet the force of your spit hitting my throat reaffirmed something I have felt for some time. I believe you are still alive. And when you surface again, I want you to come up to Essex and explain why you have grieved us so unnecessarily. I'll be here waiting.

Meanwhile, my life grinds on in its desultory way. I swim at the prison pool when my jobs are done, and I mentor men who want to get their high school diplomas. My roommate Bailey signed up as one of my students. For a few days, he was my only student. Then a few more signed up, and slowly their numbers have begun to grow.

I tell my students to write about their lives. As a result, I receive many hilarious accounts of scams and heists. A number of these amusing compositions are publishable thanks to the men's colourful way of writing. Certainly, many authors would be pleased if they could render street lingo as well.

The other day I fell into an interesting discussion with my students about why America loves guns.

I explained how the British army went back to England during the colonial winters, and the departure of the soldiers left the colonies on their own for long periods of time. The local militias carried guns to protect settlers from the Indians, and the tradition of bearing firearms was written into the Constitution. The men acted quite interested in what I was saying. Clearly, nobody in their underfunded school system has encouraged the scofflaws to think about American history.

In short, I am finding many of them congenial, although they are, on the whole, a downtrodden and unjustly treated lot. The dreadful conditions of their early years have led them to be warehoused here.

Well, that's all for now, dear boy. You can see that your old Pater is engaged with life inside the BOP. *More engaged than I have any right to expect, but life's sufferings are often not what they seem.*

I miss you. There, I've said it. Your absence washes my heart with sorrow.

Love,
Pater

4

Meredith Paul

SHE IS SITTING on the wrought iron bench on the front veranda of the house in Sands Point. It's an uncomfortable seat for reading, but she doesn't mind. The view of the sound is lovely. Beyond the sound lies the ocean, or what her aunt likes to call the sea, as if the word *sea* implies something more literary and grand than a body of water between continents.

Her aunt, Googie Paul, is sound asleep in her wheelchair. Googie has been sleeping a lot since Davie killed himself. Meredith is worried for her, although she, too, feels like she wants to give up on life and withdraw. At least, that's what she thinks her aunt is doing. First Dale Paul went to prison and now Googie's grandson has committed suicide. That sort of stress takes its toll on an old person.

Of course, Dale Paul will get out of prison — eventually. But Davie isn't coming back, no matter what Dale Paul thinks.

It used to humble her, the way Davie's intelligence didn't make him arrogant; he treated everybody as his equal, and he had a fear of hurting other people's feelings. Meredith had sat with him on planes when he refused to call for the flight attendant because he didn't want to bother her. As a boy, he would listen politely to Dale Paul, who liked to expound on Civil War battles. When Dale Paul finished, Davie would get up from the table and go to his small room and work on his computer. Meredith didn't think much about the amount of time he spent by himself. Not until he became a teenager and began idolizing the young hackers in the Creative Commons movement. In high school he had been invited to one of their conferences.

At first, Esther refused to let him go; then she relented and asked Meredith to accompany him. At the conference, only one room had been left in the tacky American Western hotel outside Cambridge, Massachusetts. Davie slept in the small cot put in the room for children and she took the double bed, worried that he would find their situation embarrassing. He never said a word. She knew he didn't want her to feel uncomfortable.

That weekend, Meredith sat in the audience while Davie discussed algorithms with the middle-aged speakers on stage. Once, in the middle of answering a question about code, he looked over and caught her eye. They both giggled. The two of them found it funny that Davie (who was only fifteen then) was in on a philosophy that would change the world while she didn't have a clue. She felt glad he could giggle over the surreal position he found himself in.

And now he is gone. It is unthinkable, even if Dale Paul is convinced that Davie will return and explain everything. The letters in her purse attest to that. Dale Paul is writing his son and sending the letters to Meredith for safekeeping. A second letter arrived yesterday. Dale Paul asked her to read it and make sure it isn't maudlin. She groans as she picks it up. Heaven forbid her cousin admit to having feelings. If only the world knew his tender side, the part of him that loves his son, and, well, yes, the part that has always loved her too.

Sept 28, 2012

Dear Davie:

This morning I thought of what Shakespeare wrote for the play of his friend, Thomas Kyd: "What is there yet in a son? He must be fed, he must be taught to go and speak. Yet why might not a man love a calf as well?" I am grumbling, son, because you are not available to me, and it pains me to think we are missing our chance to discuss life's important questions.

I don't believe you are dead, so in the spirit of Lord Chesterfield, who tried to educate his son by sending him letters, I have decided to pass on my own whimsical instruction in the art of dealing with life and its horrendous circumstances, knowing that when you come back from wherever you are you might find my words useful.

I want to talk for a moment about what gives value to the things around us. You see, we invest value in what we cherish, and in my case, I have cherished the thrill of outsmarting my fellow man.

Perhaps this is wrong, but I need to compare myself favourably to others. By that I mean I need to feel superior in order to derive a sense of satisfaction out of what I do, and luckily that isn't hard.

I am making a joke, dear boy. There are a few who are smarter than your father, even if I don't know them. (Forgive me another gentle chuckle!) I believe we are unable to function in this world without a sense of superior worth, and others, whether they know it or not, are the backdrop that supplies us with the comparison we need.

Here's what I'm learning: It is not you the world likes, but what you provide, and when the world decides it isn't interested in what you have to offer, it tosses you in the trash heap. That's what happened to your grandmother and her charities. In the 1950s, Googie's Polka for Polio was often written up in social columns. All her neighbours showed up. One year, Maria Callas sang for her guests. Then, as quickly as it came, the attention faded. The social columns stopped writing about society matrons and turned their attention to celebrities.

Alas, most of today's celebrities aren't worth writing about. They're the fools on reality shows who reveal the most idiotic things about themselves because they want to be famous and exposing themselves is the price of their fame. It doesn't matter how vulgar they look, because if what they do or say hits the zeitgeist, the public snaps up what these dimwits have to offer the way children pick Smarties off a cake. However, your Pater is not discouraged. There are always ways to turn an unpleasant event to your advantage, and that is what I'm engaged in here. (More in the next letter.)

Yours, as always,

Pater

5

Dale Paul

IN THE COMPUTER studio, an overweight scofflaw is making a nuisance of himself. He keeps muttering and scowling while Bailey and I get on with Bailey's lesson in English grammar. The man is white. Possibly he disapproves of someone from my background helping a black man. *A pox on his old-timey prejudice.*

In order not to distract the other men, Bailey and I are sitting at the back of the room, several rows away from our thuggish detractor. I am using Uncle Remus's tales of the Old South as my text. If Meredith were here, she would chide me for using these nineteenth-century slavery tales. But Bailey found the ancient VHS tape of the children's stories on a shelf in the chapel, of all places, and if Bailey feels stories by Uncle Remus represent something positive, the summer holidays on Daufuskie Island when his grandmother read him tales from Uncle Remus, who am I to disagree? And if the stories give him a moment of pleasure, a glimmer of something that suggests a literary tradition in his African-American background, why should I turn up my nose at his choice?

Are you ready to write down the dialogue? I ask, and Bailey nods, so I turn up the sound on the video. It shows Brer Fox taunting Brer Rabbit, who is stuck fast in a bed of tar. Bailey has seen the clip several times, and he always laughs when the narrator says, "Clipperty clip, lipperty lip, here comes Brer Rabbit." Animated cartoons aren't usually my idea of fun, but I like watching Bailey get the words right. Yesterday he spelled "How do you do?" without a single mistake.

Can I watch lil' ol' Brer Rabbit too? the scowler yells, causing heads to turn. This is a private lesson.

Oh boy, a private lesson about Uncle Remus. He jumps out of his chair and comes our way. Next thing you know they'll teach niggahs to read comic books.

I rise slowly to my feet and look the man in the eye. That proves impossible. One of his eyelids droops noticeably.

Good sir. I execute a mock bow. Please keep your ignominious comments to yourself.

Ha ha — good sir. What kind of shit is that? Bailey can't read. He glowers. He leers. Then the loathsome creature points at the words on the computer screen. What does it say, Bailey? he asks. Come on, you chomo, read it for Teach. (*Chomo* is prison slang for child molester, and applying the term to someone like Bailey is patently absurd.)

Aldo, B and me busy, Bailey says.

Well, well, aren't you brave now that Mr. Big Shot is teaching you to read. Wait till I tell Mr. Jack.

To my dismay, a fit of dizziness is upon me, and I'm listing like a catamaran on a windy cottage afternoon.

Just who is Mr. Jack? I manage to ask.

Mr. Jack is Mr. Jack, Bailey replies. Ain't nobody like him, but he don care what we doin', Aldo. We straight.

Hell, you straight Bailey? A fuck-up like you? The woodhick sucks his teeth as if he is considering something more malicious to say. Then the lout seems to think better of it and ambles off. When the sound of his footsteps dies away, I ask Bailey why the yobbo called him a child molester.

Bailey shakes his head. You don wanna know, B. You jes don wanna know.

6

I'M IN THE prison pool practising my backstroke when a man with a wide, muscled chest creaks through the door in a low-slung wheelchair. He must have been crippled for some time, considering the natural ease he exudes. He is also someone important because Martino and Aldo are following him into the pool building like a procession of French courtiers trailing the Sun King. Under his arm, Martino holds a small suitcase.

On the pool deck, Martino opens the suitcase and pulls out a pair of plastic calves. Ah, the scofflaw uses prosthetic devices! I watch, careful not to appear too curious as the cripple removes the artificial limbs he is wearing and begins to put on the pair from the suitcase.

As he works, he sees me in the pool and shouts: My swim legs, right-right?

I continue to swim as if I didn't hear, although I sneak furtive looks while Martino pushes the man over to a lift contraption and helps him onto its suspended chair. The cripple must have said something funny because Martino is laughing as he lowers the man down to the pool using a remote-control device. The cripple is laughing too, even though the swim chair is rocking unsteadily under his weight.

When the cripple is just above the surface, he slips off the chair and heads my way, sending up showers of spray like Captain Hook trying to escape the crocodile in *Peter Pan*.

I backstroke as fast as I can, not wanting to be beaten by a man with artificial legs. But soon he is coming in close, unleashing a boiling churn of wavelets and spray. When I look again, he is at the other end of the pool ready to start the next lap while I still have a quarter of the pool to go. I ignore him and keep moving slowly forward on my back, frog-kicking and sculling. The next thing I know the cripple has passed me again, and I have to close my mouth to stop gulping down water. Frustrated, I head for the swim ladder.

Is Mr. Jack too fast for you? Martino asks as I climb out.

He's quick all right, I reply. In the pool, the cripple is still thundering up and down.

Mr. Jack used to swim on his college team, Aldo says. I told you about him, yeah? He grins at the look of recognition on my face. Well, Scooby-Doo, the boss wants to see you tonight.

I'm extremely busy, good sir.

Like I said, Mr. Jack needs to talk to you about something, Aldo retorts.

Good for him, I reply and saunter off.

7

FOR LIFTING YOUR mood, there is nothing quite like the sight of sixty-five scofflaws goose-stepping in unison, their heads turning this way and that, their forearms chopping the air, the percussion drums rolling on the soundtrack while they lip-synch the words to the Michael Jackson song "They Don't Care About Us."

Bailey and I are watching Derek rehearse the dancers. Some of their families are here; the warden must have given them permission to come to the rehearsal.

At a highly suspenseful moment in the song, four white-skinned women walk through the gate into the visitors' section. Their appearance is menacing. Point being, they resemble the scruffy women that Mother refers to as round heels; unladylike rings hang from their noses and metal studs sparkle on their tongues, a salacious prelude to the lewder tattoos that must be lurking beneath their baggy jackets and sweatpants. Possibly, they have family members at Essex. Relatives sometimes rent places in the Adirondacks to be close to a prisoner. Nobody has done that for me, but I don't expect Meredith or Caroline to move up to the hills on my account.

The tarty women stop talking and turn to wait for an oversized black girl pushing a wheelchair. Sitting in the chair is the gangster who swam in the prison pool the day before. He's a handsome man with thick dark hair, and his khaki uniform looks as if it has been freshly pressed. He is *going dancing*, the wry phrase we use to describe visits with our loved ones. In fact, out of his swim trunks, the gangster appears gentlemanly, although to say he resembles Brando in the role of the mafia godfather would be overly charitable. He looks more like Robert de Niro playing the gangster's uncouth younger self. Mr. Jack has the same milky pallor and squinty eyes, along with the same Roman nose and tufted eyebrows, even the very same gelled hair.

Them his runners. Bailey nods at the women. They collectin' his fees. An' they all womin cuz they work for less, he says in his hoarse whisper.

And his legs? I whisper back.

Oh, B, I ain't gon to say nuthin'.

When I press him, Bailey says Mr. Jack lost his legs in retribution for the murder of a Quebec gangster whose corpse was discovered inside a car trunk.

Now the girl stops pushing the gangster's wheelchair, and they both gaze at the tennis courts, where Derek and the other dancers are gyrating around the warden's wife. The black girl stands silently, power-smoking. When the girl catches me staring, she whispers in the gangster's ear; he says something to her and looks back at the dancers.

After the rehearsal ends, we pass Mr. Jack in the line of people leaving the visitors' area.

Dale Paul, you're the man. He fist-bumps me. This is my daughter, Tannie. Tannie, say hello to our friends here.

She looks Bailey and me up and down, her expression masking something I can't identify. Apprehension? Caution?

Yo, she says softly.

I try not to show surprise; Mr. Jack doesn't seem like the sort of man who ventures outside his gene pool. Yet, I underestimated him.

8

THE NEXT AFTERNOON, the pool is full of swimmers plowing through the water with their dripping, hairy arms. Fine. All right. It's time to get out. As I clamber up the ladder, Aldo arrives, pushing Mr. Jack in his fancy-pants wheelchair. According to Martino, the sleek, low-slung wheelchair has been sent over from France.

How's the water today, guy? As warm as the Caribbean? Mr. Jack gives me a charming smile, his eyes glittering with mischief.

You could say that. A tad heavy on the chlorine, though.

It's bad for the skin. Well, we're tough, right-right? The gangster taps his chest, which swells out of his swim trunks like the torso of the genie in *Arabian Nights*. One of these days, you'll take a dip in my saltwater pool and bring along your wife. I'll treat you both to margaritas.

Sounds civilized, good sir.

Good sir? Mr. Jack bangs the arms of his wheelchair. Hey, I think I like you, guy. Call me John, okay? Well, time for my bath. He points at the swim chair with his muscled arm. The impressively thick limb moves in a heavy, singular motion, as if it, too, is a mechanical prop. How about meeting me tomorrow after our jobs are done? In Cat Alley. More private. Will that work, guy?

Yes. The word tumbles out before I can stop it.

9

CAT ALLEY TURNS out to be a little-used lobby at the back of the admin building. The lobby offers a pleasant view of the stand of white pine by the prison, and this afternoon, cats are everywhere at once in the narrow hallway, padding up and down, sitting on the heating pipes, or curling up in headless balls on the green prison blankets that have been placed on the cement floor for their benefit.

A bitter smell evokes the feral cats Davie used to tend in our back garden. If only my boy could see the good-looking, real-life gangster eagerly feeding tins of mackerel to the ragged-looking animals. Several scofflaws open tins and hand them to Mr. Jack when he runs out of food.

I never thought I'd see such a scene at Essex, although I'm told it isn't the only jail where prisoners are allowed to look after strays. Davie would approve!

Mr. Jack must have misread my expression because he exclaims: Do you have something against our feline pals, Dale Paul? He unwraps one of the chocolate cake pops sold in the commissary, along with non-dairy creamer and bottles of squeeze cheddar.

Good sir, I didn't realize you ran an animal shelter! I try not to stare at the wedge of plastic ankle visible below the hem of his trousers.

Are you saying I'm a fuckin' loser? he snarls unexpectedly. What's up with Mr. Jack? The gangster's voice evokes the menace of Shere Khan, the tiger in Davie's favourite Disney movie.

The other men laugh, and then it hits me. Tony Soprano talking to his shrink, Lorraine Bracco? I venture.

Right on. What's her character's name?

Dr. Jennifer Melfi. First appearance: episode one, season one of *The Sopranos*.

So, okay. He says in his normal, more gentlemanly voice. Last appearance, guy?

Episode six, season two.

You got a photographic memory or something? The gangster lofts his eyebrows disbelievingly, and his sidekicks cackle. How about this one? There were the goody-goody people who worked at shitty jobs and took the subway, he says, employing his coarse tone. They were suckers. They had no balls.

Ray Liotta in *Goodfellas*.

He grabs my arm, his grip as strong and solid as his swimming. Holy shit, Dale Paul, you know about the wise guys?

Naturally, I don't tell him any fool could answer his quiz. *The Sopranos* and *Goodfellas* are so well known as to be gangland clichés. Point being, I was brought up in a world where men in bespoke suits worried about blotting their copybooks, so I feel an affection for movie-land gangsters; their aggressive personas represent the sort of heedless male braggadocio that Mother and Pater deplored.

Here's one for you! I say, using a slurred, sluggish tone. I'm gonna get the papers, get the papers.

Jimmy Two Times in *Goodfellas*! He frowns. I went to school with that guy and now he doesn't talk to me.

In the dingy lobby, several tabby cats drift up to the gangster, their tails quivering like antennas. Mr. Jack scoops up an orange tom and begins to stroke its back in the languorous manner of Blofeld in a James Bond movie, stopping every so often to coo a babyish endearment. The poor beaten-up creature crouches uneasily in his arms, blinking its green eyes.

You went to school with Tony Powers? I ask.

Hey boys, Dale Paul knows Jimmy Two Two's real name! the gangster cries.

Mr. Jack's men look my way in surprise.

He smiles. Look, Dale Paul. If anybody gives you trouble, send him to me. Am I right, Aldo? Aldo appears skeptical, and Mr. Jack barks: Answer me, you a-hole!

The harsh sound startles the tabby; it leaps off his lap and comes running over, pressing its thick body against the legs of my track pants.

Watch out! Riley's feral! a man calls.

Hello, Riley, good sir. I fumble in my pocket for some shrimps I'd been saving as an afternoon snack. Bailey smuggled the plump little creatures out of the warden's private kitchen. Needless to say, shrimps at Essex are highly prized. I remove them from a plastic baggie and give them to Riley, who sniffs the shrimp suspiciously; then he begins to chew, glancing up at me with an expression of deep satisfaction.

Possibly, Riley is only feral when there's no food around.

Mr. Jack chuckles appreciatively. Yeah, maybe you're right. Okay, what character does Joe Pesci play in *Goodfellas*?

Tommy DeVito.

You got it, guy. And call me John, right-right?

Thank you … John. I clear my throat self-consciously. What is it you wanted to talk about?

Yeah, boss, Aldo remarks. You're interested in his betting scam, right?

Shut it, Aldo. The gangster shoots him a look, and Aldo turns pale.

As you were saying? I prompt.

Mr. Jack unpeels another cake pop and offers it up, but I shake my head. Martino told me your idea for a dead pool bingo. Death gives each celebrity a sporting chance, right-right?

I'm afraid it was a passing whim. *Dead pool bingo.* The gangster has a way with words.

I'd like to hear about it. And hey, Aldo, get us a coffee? He smiles a slow, lazy, gentlemanly smile. Double sugar for me. Dale Paul?

I like mine black.

He sighs. I wish I had your discipline. He turns toward the men feeding the cats. And the rest of you guys, get lost, okay? Dale Paul and I need to talk.

After the men leave, I tell him about the warden turning down my idea about betting on celebrities, and the gangster rolls his eyes and shakes his head in all the right places.

You have any experience with gambling? he asks when I finish.

I used to play the stock market.

He laughs uproariously, and for a moment I consider telling him about the school lottery I ran at Munson Hall with Earl Lindquist. Then I rescind my notion.

10

Tim Nugent

TIM STANDS UP and stretches. A few blocks away the lights of the Metropolitan Life Tower are still glowing brightly so it can't be very late. Good. He still has work to do. Rolling the kinks out of his shoulders, he walks over to the window and looks out. He is fond of his jumbled view of New York City: the various office towers blinking in the distance like friendly UFOs, the bulky stone apartment complexes with roofs that spout surprisingly old-fashioned wooden towers where the residents' drinking water is stored.

He lives in a one-bedroom at the Carteret, the sand-coloured pre-war edifice near the Hotel Chelsea. He likes its high Victorian ceilings and the wooden dado work framing the windows, but he would never entertain Dale Paul here, not with Charlie the cockroach enjoying the run of the ancient kitchen. He'd made that mistake a few years before, and Dale Paul had left after fifteen minutes. A day later, Dale Paul had phoned with the name of an interior decorator on the Upper East Side, and Tim pretended to write it down. He smiles at the memory of Dale Paul sitting perched on Tim's mission oak armchair with the faded chintz cushion. Tim had bought the chair and the matching desk the year he went to McGill. At least Dale Paul hadn't visited Tim's washroom to see the sink with the hot water stains bleached into the porcelain.

Anything that lacks a view of Central Park would be anathema to his friend. No, he's got that wrong. Anything not on the Gold Coast would be anathema to Dale Paul, who, without knowing the literary history of the place, bought a mansion in the same Long Island village as Daisy, the heroine in F. Scott Fitzgerald's novel *The Great Gatsby*. Gatsby had been on the west shore (known as West Egg), looking back across the water at the green light on her dock. His old friend lived in Sands Point, which was called East Egg in the book.

This morning, Dale Paul has sent him an account of their old game of chance at boarding school. It's strange the things Dale Paul wants to put in the memoir, childhood memories that Tim has forgotten about or, to be honest, wants to forget.

Tim prints out the attachment that Dale Paul sent on the prison computer and begins to read.

11

Dale Paul

EARL LINDQUIST ARRIVED at Munson Hall after Christmas, like an out-of-season hurricane. The other boys had formed their friendships by then, but of course he barged in. One afternoon, during games, he trudged around the school rink flapping his arms and shouting, I'm a U.S. icebreaker, so I'm going to crush you, okay?

That evening, as I was getting ready for bed, I noticed Earl sitting on the floor of the hall outside our dorm. He was wearing the communal wastebasket on his head while Thompson and a few other boys stood in

a circle around him, bashing the metal container with their hockey sticks. They made so much noise I couldn't hear Earl yelling, although he must have been shouting at them to stop.

You're next, Thompson said, and one of Thompson's lackeys advanced my way with a raised hockey stick. Luckily for both Earl and myself, I stood near the fire alarm and with the flick of my hand I pulled the switch. It set off a terrifying racket of bells and whistling sounds. Boys who had been getting into their pyjamas ran out of their rooms. In the confusion, I was able to lift the wastebasket off Earl's head. He stumbled to his feet, his cheeks shiny with tears. Mumbling his thanks, he slunk off.

When the master arrived, I made up some cock-and-bull story about leaning accidentally against the alarm. I was given five detentions for carelessness and not allowed to go home for the weekend, but Earl, who never went home because he lived too far away, snuck out of bounds with me and we spent the afternoon at a bowling alley smoking Camel cigarettes. Not long after, the two of us came up with the game of chance we called About to Die.

To begin: Many strange and memorable things had been done at school in the name of boyish high spirits. There was the boarder who drove the large, black chrome BSA 650 motorcycle off the diving board and into the school pool. There was also the crew of junior arsonists who burned down the hockey shed. The boys covered the shed roof with a blanket doused in kerosene. They lit the blanket with a Zippo, and the flames leapt almost as high as the clock face on the tower. Watching from the dorm window, my heart thundered with excitement. (My young, good heart.)

Their animal rage amazed me, although physical violence wasn't my style. My rebellion started with Mother giving Pater a popular novel at the time, *The Tontine*. It told the story of a group of English people who bet on which one of them would be the last to die. The characters in the novel had purchased a form of "last man standing insurance" and the most unlikeable player was the winner. On the frontispiece of the novel, Mother had scrawled her dedication to Pater, "For Joe, who likes to beat the odds."

I had read *The Tontine* under the bedcovers, and my mind had taken me, as my mind has a habit of doing, to applying a novel idea to my own life, but we were only thirteen-year-old schoolboys, and there would be a long wait to get our money. I thought of our teachers.

My school chums were overjoyed when Earl and I circulated the names of the candidates in our dead pool: Mrs. B., the headmaster's wife, who had been diagnosed with breast cancer; and the geography teacher, old Cootes, who was wasting away with Parkinson's disease. Sixty-year-old Cootes was the odds-on favourite.

Point being, I was a creative, open-minded young man. But until I invented About to Die, the force of my imaginative powers hadn't been appreciated at Munson Hall. Just the thought of what I provoked still makes me laugh.

12

I WAITED ANXIOUSLY in one classroom and Earl waited in another. We had been separated to instill fear. Out in the hall, the shoes of my persecutors were tapping the freshly waxed parquet floor: the headmaster, Rolly Bellwoods, and old Cootes, the scourge of the boarding school, were walking slowly so they wouldn't slip.

In the hall, the footsteps stopped. A door opened, and a moment later, I heard a boyish scream. I counted two more, or was it three? Then: no more bone-chilling cries. Once again footsteps sounded in the hall. They were coming for me. The door to my classroom banged against a wall, flung open angrily, I couldn't help surmising. There was a moment of silence while I waited, shuddering. My cheeks felt hot. Would I keel over in a faint or piss myself?

A voice hissed, Drop your trousers, son.

I had been through this before. Clumsily, I unfastened my belt, my fingers shaking as I found the brass metal clasp. My zipper was next. It seemed to take forever to pull it down, as if I were unzipping the back of Mother's dress when she couldn't do it for herself. I felt the heavy fabric slide down my thighs and fold about my ankles.

Your underwear, a second voice whined. I pulled down my boxer shorts. Now I couldn't move. My ankles were shackled by the cloth of my undergarments.

Bend over, the voice said.

I gripped the backrest of the chair placed in the room for this purpose. Outside the window I noticed the mourners at Mrs. B.'s funeral milling about on the lawn. They were dressed in black suits and hats, and the women's faces under their veils looked sombre.

I bent farther over the chair. I didn't mean for her to die, I cried.

Well, it feels as if you did! the voice replied.

There was a whistling sound, and when the blow came, my head and back jerked upright in an involuntary spasm. The cane stung the childish flab of my buttocks, the back of my thighs, my scrotum.

Hold your balls, my persecutor said.

I wanted to scream and weep and beat my chest, but instead I cupped the vulnerable flesh between my legs and said nothing.

13

AS I DO the breaststroke in the prison pool, I wonder why I didn't tell John Giaccone the story of About to Die and how we campaigned in secret to promote pervy old Cootes so the boys wouldn't vote for Mrs. B. I can see her in a faded floral dress, standing by my bed waiting to inspect the boys' hands before dinner. She positioned herself there to avoid the steaming hot water radiators. Just the same, the sight of her standing near my cot made me feel good.

Let's see what interesting things you have to show me, she would say teasingly as she turned over my filthy paws. She wasn't like Nurse Easto, who sniffed disapprovingly while the school doctor lifted up your balls, checking for bumps and Jeezus knows what other signs of embarrassing sexual diseases.

In fact, it was Mrs. B. who told on Thompson and the other boys for placing a wastebasket over the heads of the new boys, a torture they referred to euphemistically as hockey practice. The headmaster made Thompson and his posse run ten miles around the quad. So that's why I thought of Mrs. B. as our protector. I never meant her any harm.

My campaign against Cootes started during the Easter holidays, when Mother and Pater were in the Bahamas. I had been quarantined in the infirmary with measles, and I could have died alone and unloved in those vast, anodyne rooms. One night, I overheard Mrs. B. talking to Nurse Easto outside my door. At first, I thought they were talking about me, but it was something more serious.

Dr. Wilkes says I have six months left, Mrs. B. whispered. Six months, Clara. I'm still a young woman.

Sometimes doctors get it wrong, Nurse Easto replied.

Well, he says I have the virulent kind of cancer, and the statistics are not good.

You poor thing, Nurse Easto murmured. I couldn't hear the rest of their conversation. After it stopped, I lay staring for hours at the ceiling. What would it be like to know I would never again be heard or seen on the earth? That never again would I buy and sell the preferred shares in General Electric that I received on my birthday? Never again to tramp through the Muskoka marshes, looking for frogs to sell to the fishermen at the government dock near our cottage?

Poor doomed Mrs. B. grew increasingly frail. One morning during prayers, Nurse Easto sat down beside Mrs. B. in the front row of our chapel. The two women exchanged sad looks as our headmaster rolled into one of his boorish pep talks.

The sight of Nurse Easto reminded me of the medical forms she prepared for Dr. Wilkes. Later that day, I stole into the infirmary and scanned the forms that Nurse Easto kept in a drawer in the hall table.

One report was especially enticing. There, in Nurse Easto's cramped writing, was a long-winded description of the nocturnal habits of that crypto-sadist, the prefect Thompson. According to Nurse Easto, eighteen-year-old Thompson still wet his bed, and the prefect had to sleep on a rubber mat placed tactfully under his flannel bedsheets. In Thompson's medical file, there was a pile of old laundry bills with a scribbled note: "Send to Mrs. W.H. Thompson, 42 Forest Hill Rd."

Soon afterwards, an idea came to me about how Earl and I could use Dr. Wilkes's reports to alter the game of chance in our favour. Full disclosure: Mrs. B. had only six months to live, while old Cootes might linger on, the way tiresome and undeserving people often do. If the boys knew the truth about Mrs. B.'s situation, they would vote for her, so it behooved us to improve the odds. Yes, daring was called for, although daring brought punishment. I stole an empty medical form from the drawer in the hall and jotted down in what I hoped resembled Dr. Wilkes's beetle-like scrawl a summary of Cootes and his Parkinson's diagnosis. I used the adjective *terminal* several times and, only once, the damning sentence *Not expected to live out the year.*

Chances are Dr. Wilkes never wrote anything as definitive as "Not expected to live out the year," but my schoolmates hadn't combed through each sick boy's medical form, an experience that led me to appreciate the gravitas of medical terminology. At first, I went overboard forging Dr. Wilkes's report, tossing in phrases like *idiopathic parkinsonism* and *the substantia nigra*, which, after all, is just a harmless region of the midbrain. In the end, I kept in *idiopathic*, meaning no known cause, and threw out the other unpronounceable medical words. My forged report was a *samizdat* document, and I put in just enough snippets of medical knowledge to impress my downtrodden schoolmates.

Earl showed my *samizdat* report to a few of the boys in junior school, swearing them to silence; it was a bargain they couldn't keep. And sure enough, several days later, the boarding school seethed with rumours about pervy old Cooties departing for the big schoolhouse in the sky. Soon the older boys were asking if they could see the damning report, and Earl and I showed it to them after they swore an oath of secrecy. We were especially pleased to offer a peep to Thompson. When he swaggered off, looking like the proverbial cat that lapped up the cream, we knew our ruse had worked.

The report began to look dog-eared. Earl kept it neatly folded under his pillow. Then, just as we expected, it disappeared. By that time, all of the boarding school was betting on Cootes.

When Mrs. B. died first, Earl won the jackpot of $900 and I took an administration fee for the same amount.

The sums appeared in the reporter's story, and in other accounts by hacks in the world's most impecunious trade. Mother cried her eyes out. How did Pater react? He used his own belt to strap me. And when the swelling went down, I felt a tingling sensation that brought with it a sense of euphoria.

14

EARL SAID NUGENT was the one who told on us because Nugent worked as a stringer while he was a student at Munson Hall. Every few weeks, he supplied tidbits of gossip to a Toronto daily that unfairly scrutinized well-to-do families like my own. And it was true that Nugent seemed pleased when I was expelled and Earl was sent to a military college near West Point. About three weeks after I was obliged to leave Munson Hall, Meredith stole into my bedroom and whispered that a R-E-P-O-R-T-E-R was waiting downstairs.

I found the witless scribe lounging on Mother's chintz sofa. The man's head loomed dangerously close to Pater's beloved fox hunting print, *The Master and the Hounds*, and when I pointed this out, the reporter sat forward obligingly as if I were a bona fide truth teller.

Reporter: Some of your friends say Mr. Cootes is overly fond of his students.

Self: We don't take old Cooties too seriously. He enjoys caning us boys. When he applies himself, his hearing aids spring out of his ears.

Reporter: Old Cooties! (laughing) That's a good one. I understand you have something called the zebra award for the most canings.

Self: That is correct. My friend Earl Lindquist has second place.

Reporter: Did you bet on the death of Mr. Cootes because he was disliked?

Self (trying to keep a straight face): We bore him no malice.

Reporter: And the headmaster's wife? Did you expect her to die first?

Self: No. She was thirty years younger than old Cootes.

Reporter (laughing again): All right. I see. Did the boys like Mrs. Bellwoods better than Mr. Cootes?

Self: Mrs. B. took the place of the infirmary nurse on weekends, so she knew which of us had wet his bed. And sometimes she spanked the offender with a wooden spoon.

Reporter: It sounds like you boys felt malice toward her too.

Self: May I kindly suggest that you are missing the point, good sir? Our candidates could have been any one of our teachers.

Reporter: And then Mrs. Bellwoods died.

Self: Yes.

Reporter: Did you go to the funeral?

I lowered my eyes and didn't answer.

Reporter: It would have been a nice thing to do, don't you think?

Self: I guess so.

Mother suddenly appeared with the tea tray. The look on her face suggested she disapproved of the underhanded way the reporter was leading the witness.

Mother: My son's schoolboy prank didn't cause that woman's death. It's time for you to leave.

The reporter stood up quickly. Mother, gloriously disapproving in her designer slacks, ushered the gormless scribbler out while I gobbled down the petits fours.

15

Tim Nugent

THE LIGHTS ARE winking off in the Metropolitan Life Tower. It happens every evening around this time. Yet the sight always affects him. It's as if God in person is flicking the switches.

He gets up and puts on the kettle for a pot of green tea. Tim didn't realize ghosting the memoir meant Dale Paul would include Tim in the stories about their childhood. And now he has written that Tim squealed on his friends. What a jerk Dale Paul could be! If his old friend stopped to think, he would know that squealing was the last thing Tim would do, although maybe he should have told a prefect or a kindly master. Instead good old Pilot kept his mouth shut and watched Earl and Dale Paul rake in the money.

Of course, Dale Paul has never shown much curiosity about Tim or Tim's life outside school. All the Pauls were like that. They assumed the world stopped at the edge of their velvety lawns. For instance, Dale Paul didn't ask about Tim's summers. Meredith did, though, and she was the only one in the family he told about his job as a two-way man on the *North Bay Nugget*, his hometown newspaper, which has devolved into an information rag. He had written for the paper and taken the photographs that accompanied his stories. It was a kind of apprenticeship no newspaper journalist would experience now.

If Dale Paul paid any attention, he would know that unlike Dale Paul, Tim had been brought up to do the right thing. That meant putting the other person before himself. It was the Nugent family ethos. Don't put yourself forward — listen to what the other person has to say. Better to

be a yes-man, to see success as pleasing people ... to stay in the background so others like Dale Paul could frolic in the limelight.

He thinks back to his arguments with his father, who wanted him to
take over the family dental practice in North Bay. Tim wanted to be a
novelist, but his father said Tim had a good second-class mind so he
shouldn't aim too high. Dale Paul's ambitions hadn't been dismissed
like that. And just look where Tim's boyhood training has led him. He
became a journalist, a job that was about making other people look
important.

Of course, he is an author now, which is a step up from journeyman
reporter on the *New York Post*. But ghosting the memoir is forcing him
to remember who he used to be, and he dislikes the picture of the boy
he was almost forty-five years before. Impressionable, callow ... now there
was a Dale Paul word, *callow*. It wasn't a word he would normally use.
Maybe ghosting the book is some kind of reckoning.

He thinks back to the Sunday evening when he and Dale Paul and
Earl had been sitting on one of the uncomfortable wooden benches in
the Munson Hall Common Room. They were talking in lowered voices
about their schoolboy bet, About to Die. At the pulpit, the headmaster,
Rolly Bellwoods, was reading from the Bible, oblivious to how he was
boring everybody. Once in a while, one of the prefects in the front row
would throw a stern look at the three boys, who were conferring about
the best way to circulate Dale Paul's fake doctor's report on Mrs. B.'s
health. The report would squelch the rumour that Mrs. B. was going to
be the first to die.

In his fake report, Dale Paul had declared: "Last week, the problem in
the minuscule duct in Lannie Bellwood's bountiful mammary gland was
resolved by a medical operation. At forty-two, Lannie is a fine figure of
a woman, robust and firm-breasted, with healthy menses. When last
measured, her strapping breasts are thirty-eight inches round following
the circumference of her bra strap ..."

Earl had been interested in her breast measurements, so Dale Paul
had put that last sentence in for his benefit.

What's menses? Earl asked. Tim and Dale Paul exchanged a glance before Tim muttered: A woman's time of month.

Oh, okay, yeah. Earl nodded, looking thoughtful.

Then Tim dropped his bombshell. I don't want to be part of this.

Don't be a goody two-shoes, Dale Paul hissed.

Woman Nugent, Earl growled. Are you going to squeal on us?

Tim's face had turned red and he heard himself say okay, he wouldn't drop out.

IN THE MORNING, Tim carefully puts away Dale Paul's account of About to Die.

I don't think your boarding school story is going to work, he wrote in an email to Dale Paul. So far, the only setting I'm working with is the prison, and although there are certain similarities, it may be confusing for the reader to hear what you did at Munson Hall. He didn't really mean confusing, he meant incriminating, but he isn't going to put that in writing. In fact, there could also be legal problems mentioning the celebrity dead pool that Dale Paul has described to Tim. His editor, Alexis, told Tim to let Dale Paul blurt out his story. The lawyers will worry about its implications later. Alexis also said the same thing about Tim's descriptions of "the condition" affecting Earl Lindquist: We'll fix it — if and when it needs fixing. Alexis is either reckless or distracted, Tim decides, but he isn't going to argue with her.

In an email, Dale Paul writes back that Tim is dead wrong about wanting to keep their schoolboy lottery out of the book. Remember what P.T. Barnum used to say? Dale Paul asks. There's a sucker born every moment and most of them live.

If that's the way you feel I won't stand in your way, Tim replies. It's your memoir.

Well said, Pilot, Dale Paul answers. I'm exceedingly grateful you are such a smart amanuensis!

And there it was all in one sentence, Tim thinks. The insulting school nickname implying that Tim is like a pilot fish that feeds off the leavings of sharks, the insincere flattery and arcane words that camouflage Dale Paul's childish determination to get his own way.

16

Dale Paul

> Blessed with deep pine forests, softly rounded mountain peaks,
> and isolated islands set on quiet lakes, the Adirondacks region
> offers endless days of adventure for outdoor lovers.
>
> — *THE NORTH COUNTRY TRAVEL GUIDE*

THE WARDEN IS as free as a forest ranger in a tower. While I wait in his office, I gaze at his vista. There isn't a house or a church steeple to be seen. The mountains in this vast parkland are treed to the top so the view from his third-floor window resembles a colourful autumnal rug that some woodland troll has unrolled toward the wall of the sky. A confining wall, in my case.

My eyes turn to the warden's bookshelves, which appear to be stacked with texts about rehabilitating prisoners. The books express his benign intelligence. In the parlance of Inmate dot com, Nathan Rickard is known as Mr. R.; the R stands for reasonable because he is a prison apparatchik for whom no outrage is too horrible to understand, a teaching guy warden, who is far and away more desirable than the custody type, who likes to apply the lash of punishment. Nathan Rickard cares about his boys, in other words.

Among the books, I spot a leather-bound MA thesis with the words *Edmund Bergler: Freud's Forgotten Disciple*, by Nathan J. Rickard. Bergler is the name of the psychologist the warden mentioned at our tea. I pull out the thesis and flip through the pages, shaking my head incredulously at sentences like: *The gambler is a neurotic who gambles to lose.*

Behind my back, there is an unexpected susurration, like a hospital door hissing open on its hydraulic hinges. When I turn around, the warden is looking at me speculatively behind the rimless wafers of his spectacles, and I wonder if I am about to hear something unpleasant. Note to self: *No matter what he tells you, Nathan Rickard has a palpable desire to demonstrate that he is immune to your celebrity. But who you are still impresses him. Put his conflicted feelings to good use. Let him know he is your equal, a desire true of any man, any man at all.*

You agree with what this shrink says? About gambling being masochistic? I ask as I stick his thesis back on the shelf.

The warden smiles enigmatically, and from a metal box on the shelf behind his desk, he extracts a letter.

You got clearance for a workshop, he says and hands the letter over.

October 7, 2012

Dear Sir:

We received your request for another new recreational program at Essex Correctional Institute. As you know, Essex already has a dance program and extra costs are involved in the establishment of a workshop on financial literacy. However, we have decided to tentatively approve a workshop for a one-year period. In a few weeks' time, your prison will be visited by a New York City psychologist, Ms. Trish Bales, who will study the afficacy of the program you set up. Please cooperate fully. She will answer any questions you have.

Afficacy. Surely, the BOP official means efficacy. How pleased Bailey will be to know he shares the habit of hideous spelling with the prison admin.

Can you design the program for my boys? Nothing fancy. They will have to relate to what you say or it will be a waste of time.

Good sir, I am honoured by your trust!

Glad to hear that, Dale Paul. The warden strokes the wiry stubble of his Vandyke. Heck, the past few months must have been hard on you. Just as you're getting adjusted, you lose your kid. Maybe it's time to check this out? He hands me a book from his shelf.

You saw my thesis about Bergler? The shrink is out of favour, but he's still got a few things to say. There's red meat about gamblers in these pages.

The title reads *Principles of Self-Damage* by Edmund Bergler. Clearly, Nathan Rickard doesn't understand how much I dislike psychotherapy, that juvenile North American folly. You pay a dollar and buy your way to self-improvement. Pure codswallop. There is no cure for someone such as myself, or him, for that matter.

Okay. I'll level with you, the warden says. His eyes grow sad. My brother played the numbers, and Bergler's books helped me to see why. We grew up in the South Bronx, he added, in case I didn't understand the humble nature of his origins.

I don't know your brother's story. But I have gambled to win and won. Nobody can deny my success.

He stands up and shakes my hand, smiling his odd, secretive smile. Okay, that's it for today, Dale Paul. Report back to me when you have your course designed.

He doesn't need to tell me twice.

·

17

THAT NIGHT, LYING in my bunk, I mull over the celebrities I will put in my dead pool. There's my erstwhile friend Earl Lindquist, who won't return my phone calls, and the Hollywood actress Zsa Zsa Gabor, whose blond hair rides her shoulders in bountiful curls, along with Leonard Nimoy, alias Mr. Spock from *Star Trek*. I doodle their faces using the felt pen I bought at the commissary. It cost five dollars, a horrendous sum for a man living on inferior means. Above me, Bailey is falling asleep counting whatever a man from his background counts while Derek is reading a yoga magazine.

One-two, skip to my Lou, and over you go. The celebrities fly through the air like fluffy sheep.

The next day, after our prison jobs are done, I walk over to Cat Alley, where John and Aldo are grooming the huge marmalade tabby. My new friend is using a large purple comb with the word *Furminator* embossed in silver on its side. Aldo holds the cat by its shoulders so Mr. Jack can comb the mats out of its coat. The sight triggers the sensation I felt on my first morning at Essex, that I have stepped into a prison movie, and what I see in front of me — the handsome gangster stroking the cat in the languid Blofeld manner, Aldo nodding obsequiously at everything the gangster says, the orange tabby stretching and arching its back, its haunches twitching with pleasure under the touch of the gangster's hand — all these actions are tinged with the air of cinematic exaggeration. America is a screen-loving land, after all, and possibly John Giaccone is more talented than I give him credit for being. Sooner or later, when we know each other better, he will drop his guard and initiate me into the charade he performs for the other scofflaws.

We're going to bet on dead celebrities, I announce. To qualify, you need to be in the news and about to die.

The warden approved your dead pool, guy?

In a manner of speaking. But let's not get ahead of ourselves, John. Here's how it will work. The men will bet on which of our old or frail celebrities will be the first to leave the planet. And we'll use handicaps to come up with our list of candidates. Take the actress Zsa Zsa Gabor. I loved her movies when I was a boy. Maybe you remember her?

John nods. Aldo, the ignoramus, shakes his head.

In our handicapping system, she'll get a hundred points minus her age. If she were a hundred years old, she'd get nothing. And if she were over a hundred, she'd lose a point for every year after.

Age determines handicap? Looking skeptical, John unwraps a cake pop.

Age and .health. I'm taking off ten points for an illness or a serious injury. Or a drug addiction. I make a church steeple with the fingers of my left hand, the gesture I use while calculating risk. In a doleful voice, I intone Zsa Zsa's ailments: partial paralysis, the result of a car accident; strokes two years in a row; and a year later a fractured hip followed by a hip replacement; not to mention a hospital stay for high blood pressure.

She's ninety-five. So what's her handicap, good sirs?

The light of understanding breaks across my comrades' faces. The lady is a freaking zombie, right-right? the gangster asks.

John, you catch on fast. Now here's the gist. I hand him a typed sheet with a breakdown of what a celebrity handicap sheet looks like, and I go over it slowly so even a sloth head like Aldo can follow along.

Name:	Occupation:	Age:	Conditions:	Deductions:	Scoring:	Handicap:
Leonard Nimoy	American actor	81	chronic obstructive pulmonary disease (COPD)	-20 (illness)	100-81=19-20	-1

Name:	Occupation:	Age:	Conditions:	Deductions:	Scoring:	Handicap:
Zsa Zsa Gabor	Hollywood actress	95	partially paralyzed, 2 strokes, broken hip etc.	–50 (multiple conditions)	100-95=5-50	- 45
Mickey Rooney	American actor	92	alcohol and sleeping pill addictions	-20 (for 2 addictions)	100-92=8-20	-12

John eats his cake pop as he rattles off the handicaps in correct order: minus one for the actor from Star Trek who is a known smoker along with minus forty-five for Zsa Zsa and minus twelve for Rooney.

I press on: we'll print up paper called c-coins with the ten celebrity names, and the men can use them to trade for prison services, like haircuts or tattoos or sessions with a trainee. Clearly, the oldest and sickest celebrity is a potential winner, but there will be surprises on our deathbed ten.

The deathbed ten! He grins in delight. You didn't get your reputation for nothing, Dale Paul! How are the boys going to pay us?

I was hoping your customers could pay.

So we run two bets? One at Essex, and one at my policy banks?

The inmates will bet for coffee, and your clients outside the prison will pay cash to play. If your people are willing to collect the funds, good sir.

He thinks for a moment. Ever hear about Bitcoin?

As it happens, Bip, my assistant, wanted me to invest in Bitcoin, a new digital currency. I turned him down, even though I admire how Bitcoin works. Imagine that you design a currency; you put it online and give it a name; next you set an initial price for it and talk your friends and family into using it. Soon you are working with an online network that moves money around the world without using the banks. It's as if one thousand small accounting firms have joined forces to compete against Deloitte.

Dale Paul, you're going to love Bitcoin John says. The guys who record the transactions don't post the identity of the people making the deposits.

The account holder is anonymous?

Yeah, nobody knows their name, right-right? That's why you get a Bitcoin account.

What if Bitcoin drops in value?

We pay the difference. But, hey, do I look worried? The value of Bitcoin keeps going up. You know how much it's worth today? Twelve dollars and forty cents. I'm betting it'll hit five hundred — maybe a thousand for a coin. And that means our jackpot could be huge.

I'll need to sleep on it, good sir.

Take your time. He winks knowingly. Make sure it feels right.

18

THE NEXT AFTERNOON at the pool, I tell John I'm in favour of Bitcoin, and he does a jig on his hollow legs. Aldo, the slimy yobbo, has had a brain wave.

There's these fuckin' categories, see? The Selena if your celebrity is capped by a fan. Not nice. But death is death, yeah?

Who on earth is Selena? I ask.

The Puerto Rican singer who got clipped, John says in his gentlemanly voice. Go on, Aldo.

There's the Sid Vicious category. Yeah? He fuckin' cut up his girlfriend and let her bleed out in a New York hotel room.

Ugh. How gruesome, I exclaim.

Yeah, brutal. John catches my eye and winks. Some of us older guys remember Sid Vicious. What else, Aldo?

Well, there's the Owen Hart category. You know who he is, right?

We shake our heads.

He was a wrestler. They put him in a block and tackle and flew him over the ring. He was going to drop down on his opponent, yeah? But the block and tackle broke and he got popped.

Ouch, John says. The Owen Hart. Well, what else?

The JFK. Aldo smirks. You guys know it already. Then there's Bruce

Lee's kid. You know Brandon? He was shot on a film set. Some goof didn't know the gun was loaded.

What is it about Aldo? Even when he tries his best, he is loathsome.

19

DEATH IS A useless state. Aside from the fortunes that undertakers have made for centuries, death is not productive in any shape or form. It is a wasteful business. A pointless predicament that's rarely fruitful, no matter how you look at it. Or so I tell myself as I sit in the computer studio compiling the list of celebrities for our deathbed ten.

We are considering a deadbeat hockey player from the Detroit Red Wings, a crippled British physicist, as well as Leonard Nimoy and Queen Elizabeth, whose coronation Meredith and I watched on television. Mother bought us hats designed like the Union Jack, so we resembled the thousands of other cheering schoolchildren we saw on the screen. We liked the ermine-lined capes worn by the lords and the shiny, black-tasselled helmets of the horsemen guarding the Queen, whose gilded coach crawled through the crowded London streets like a giant golden spider with spindly legs.

With some reluctance, I am voting for Queen Elizabeth, along with Leonard Nimoy and my old boarding school friend Earl Lindquist. Yes, Earl, who used to come home with me on Sunday afternoons when none of the other boys at Munson Hall would invite him to their houses; Earl, who gulped down Irene's delectable turkey with chestnut stuffing while Mother and Pater watched in alarm; Earl, who wouldn't stop swilling our Portuguese rosé like a veritable drunkard. Earl, the grubby Brooklyn schoolboy who won't return my phone calls; that Earl belongs on my dead pool, too.

Someone calls my name. Derek is heading my way with John Giaccone.

Hey, guy, John says. What about Tony Gandolfini, I hear he has a bad ticker.

Are you sure about your information, good sir?

Hell, yeah.

Mmm … May I suggest instead the Duchess of Alba? They look baffled, so I explain that the Spanish duchess is distantly related to English kings and queens. Point being, Dona Maria del Rosario Cayetana Fitz-James Stuart de Silva whined to me once too often about being ignored by the American media. The last time Caroline and I suffered through one of her stilted dinner parties, the duchess wouldn't shut up about it.

If you want a spic, let's go with our guys. John looks thoughtful. There's Rita Moreno, right-right?

When I shake my head, he confers with Derek, and then John exclaims, looking hopeful: Hey, guy. Here's the solution. What about a mystery celebrity? Derek will come up with the celebrity's name. He won't tell us who it is. He'll put the name in an envelope, and the warden will keep it under lock and key. John stretches out his muscled arms, palms up. Maybe some suckers will get lucky.

What a good idea! I reply and they grin boyishly.

Ah, the joys of c-coin! At the door, more men are coming in, brushing snow off their army parkas and waving at me. It's the third week of October. Winter comes early in the mountains.

Ordinarily, we aren't allowed to use the Internet, let alone gamble, but help has come unexpectedly from Trish Bales, the English woman doing a BOP study on my workshop. She is a timid creature with a moon-shaped face and discoloured teeth. (Why do well-to-do Limeys like Trish avoid the dentist? The state of their choppers is a national disgrace.)

To my surprise, she agreed with me that a teaching tool with references to popular culture would keep the prisoners interested. Her view convinced Nathan Rickard, who has let us use the names of real celebrities in our dead pool. And thanks to Ms. Bales, the men can go online for one hour every day and work on our private website, the one with a flashing daisy logo and cartoon image of feet pushing up daisies.

In a back corner of the room, Trish Bales sits bent over some questionnaires while Martino and a new C.O. named Bowles walk up and down, inspecting the men's screens to make sure they aren't watching porn.

Outside the prison window, snow is falling chastely, as if the world has been rinsed of dark motives. As if I, too, am rinsed of dark motives. There you have it: The falling snow. The scofflaws in wet boots and parkas. The handicaps. The spreadsheets. There is a word for what I feel, but damned if I can bring myself to say it.

20

WORD ABOUT THE dead pool spreads through the prison, and the scofflaws pester me with questions about the deathbed ten whether I am in the chow line or playing cards in the Rec Centre. Their excitement matches mine, and I am having trouble sleeping at night so Derek has talked me into joining his yoga sessions. He says the yoga will calm me, and now here I am at five-thirty in the morning, heading out of our dorm with the prayer pillow he has so kindly given me. He nods at me and smiles his grin distorting his facial tattoos so he appears ludicrously sinister.

I follow him down the stairs of our dorm. It is the only time of day when the prison is free from the macho posturing of the scofflaws and their noisy bickering over nugatory trifles.

Another snowstorm is expected. In the mountains, winter is already a dead white fact. This morning, wind screeches about the prison building while inside one of its depressing hallways, three inmates are placidly mopping the floors; the sharp odour of freshly applied cleaning fluid hangs in the air.

The men engage me in animated chatter about c-coin until Derek waves them off, and we stride purposefully on to the common room where John sits on the floor with the other men, his eyes closed, his lips moving in some private incantation. In the darkened light of the room, he, too, appears unfamiliar, like a rough-looking boover boy lacking any sign of his gentlemanly charm. Perhaps I am foolish to trust someone like him. But all of us have moments when we notice the avarice and deceit in other people, and there is nothing to be done except acknowledge what you have seen and move on. Point being, I am a betting man.

What is John doing here? I whisper to Derek.

It helps his back pain, Derek whispers. He gestures for me to sit on the floor, and that's how I find myself sitting cross-legged on my pillow with the other scofflaws, my fingers cupped awkwardly on my knees. In a rumbling voice, Derek intones Om and so begins his spiritual intercession with the Grand Panjandrum of the Spiritual World, whomever he, or for that matter she, happens to be.

The earth turns, the seasons change, and we follow our breath, Derek murmurs. Feel the sensation of air striking the skin inside of your nostrils ...

Oh Lordie. *The sensation of air striking the skin of my nostrils.* Why did I agree to listen to such gobbledygook? Me, of all people, who hates rising early?

Now Derek is leading us through a sequence of exercises involving flailing arms and legs. And then we are back sitting on our pillows, trying to meditate. It is difficult to concentrate; from the television room comes the syrupy babble of Robin Meade's voice on *Morning Express.* Today she is ridiculing the high school principal who won't let girls wear winter leggings. Robin's comments are followed by explosive giggles from another female newscaster.

Fine. All right. Ignore Robin and her coquettish friend. As I sit there trying to concentrate, a door creaks open and Martino comes tiptoeing toward us, his flashlight throwing beams about the darkened room. The C.O. bends down and whispers something to Derek.

Derek mumbles a thank you and the correctional officer walks off, the halo from his flashlight once again bouncing up and down. All well and good. Then I blink. And blink again. Miniature waterfalls of golden light froth in the air by Derek's chest and the chests of John and the other men, and before I know what is happening, passages from the New Testament fly into my head, and I hear my Anglican Sunday school teacher whispering in my ear: *And these shall go away into eternal punishment, but the righteous into life eternal.*

Is this a trick? The men sit motionless on their pillows, their eyes closed. Perhaps the tiny shimmers of light come from Martino's flashlight, although the C.O. has left the common room.

Then, as suddenly as it began, the air stops sparkling like someone has short-circuited the electrical system, and my bunkmate leaps off his pillow, flexing and un-flexing his tattooed arms. He is a veritable rubber man lacking spinal vertebra. Feeling somewhat discombobulated, I haul myself to my feet. The lights have come on and outside the window the blizzard has started. Snow is falling in long, whirling veils of white, shutting out the forest near the prison.

John wheels his chair over to Derek and me. How did it go, guy?

I'm at a loss for words.

Ha ha. Well, that's a good sign, isn't it, Derek? Okay, sauna time. Last man there gets to buy me some cake pops. John smiles broadly and heads for the exit, beckoning for me to follow.

21

THE SAUNA IS a nightmare. John and Aldo compete over who can withstand the hottest temperature and throw bucket upon bucket of water on the crib holding the sauna rocks. Martino has come to supervise, and the scene in the wide L-shaped room resembles a tableau from the infernal regions. Other men sit on the wooden benches or stand nearby, while pinkish chunks of arms and heads appear and reappear in the steaming clouds.

Back in our dorm, as we sip Derek's morning brew of spicy ginger tea, I tell him what happened.

You won't believe this, Derek, but I saw — uh, some lights in the air.

He gives me a maternal look as he sits turning the cracked prison mug round and round in his tattooed hands.

Maybe you can read human energy, mate, he says finally. Some people have the gift. When things are in balance, it can happen.

When things are in balance. Leave it to Derek to spout spiritual bafflegab, although I know he is only trying to make me feel better. I have wracked my memory for a scientific explanation and come up with zilch.

22

SNOW LIMNS THE roofs of the prison buildings and the warden's frail chestnut saplings; it clings to the links in the cyclone fences and rises like pale hats from the tops of the guard towers down the road.

By the door of the admin building, the tacky prison fountain is still tinkling away. To my delight, the broken ice by its bubbling spout has formed itself into the shape of the letter *C*. Good for c-coin. Good for me. I am nature's golden boy.

I dust the snow from my jacket and rush through the door. On the blackboard a scofflaw has scribbled the quote for the wintry November day: *Money is the root of all evil. 1 Timothy 6:10.* The accurate quote is, *For the love of money is a root of all kinds of evils.* Fine. All right. Let the scofflaws blame the evil of the world on an abstraction like money — if that is their inclination.

The visitors' lounge is packed, and the screeching male voices convey their excitement. Bailey and Derek are sitting with Aldo and John Giaccone. On their laps, they balance cartons of c-coin. To showcase the idea, the warden has allowed Derek to print a limited run of five hundred c-coins from a copy shop in the town. These c-coins have been reproduced in full glossy colour on a 2.5-x-6-inch lightweight card stock that feels more substantial than regular paper; these are the thickness of a paper bookmark. The other two thousand and five hundred c-coins have been rubber-stamped on the paper surface of our old commissary receipts. We would have printed all the c-coin in the same fashion but for the warden's restricted budget.

I follow the diagonal of yellow tape directing me to a dais at the front of the room and sit down next to Nathan Rickard.

As soon as the men are quiet, he rises to his feet. Today, you are getting the chance to learn money skills from our resident expert. He looks startled when the men shout my name, clapping enthusiastically.

And now I'd like to introduce the nice lady who is doing the study on our financial literacy program. Ms. Bales will ask you to sign consent forms, okay? She'll be handing out questionnaires too, so please, no bullshit answers.

Ignoring the hungry stares, Trish Bales gets out of her chair. She is not eye candy exactly, but inside a men's prison every woman is a goddess. Silence descends on the feverish room; the men shift restlessly in their chairs, their eyes fixed on her breasts beneath her shapeless blouse while she nervously explains what she's done to get her study approved. As far as I can make out, the ethics of her work had to be approved by dolts at something called the Institutional Review Board.

Her talk soon devolves into a long-winded explanation about her approach, a technique she calls the mixed method. It means questionnaires for the four hundred men in my workshop, followed by interviews with a smaller group.

Just as she seems to be winding down, she spends twenty more unnecessary minutes spraying around sociological terms like *recidivate* (an unfriendly Latinate word), *capture* (an absurdly trendy verb), and *carceral* (I rest my case).

My turn. KISS. *Keep it simple, stupid.* I mount the dais and stand behind the ancient wooden lectern that someone has dragged in from the chapel. My name is Dale Paul, I begin. And today I am going to talk about a club of specially selected celebrities, and you are going to bet on their lives.

A few of the men hoot in derision, but the rest of my audience looks genuinely interested.

I've come up with something that will teach you how the financial markets work, I say. And slowly, carefully, I explain c-coin, going over the handicaps of the celebrities and rhyming off their illnesses: Mickey Rooney, the former child star who takes drugs and drinks too much; Zsa Zsa Gabor and her list of Job-like ailments; the ancient *Playboy* magnate Hugh Hefner, rumoured to be studying the science of cryonics; Queen

Elizabeth II and her intermittent bouts with the dangerous norovirus; Stephen Hawking, a victim of the disease that makes fast work of its victims. We've also added Earl Lindquist, whose notoriety and advancing age make him a suitable candidate.

I imagine I hear a shocked intake of breath at the mention of Earl's name but when I look again, most of the men's faces are lit up with smiles. How could I forget the way losers detest the winners among us? How fiercely those who fail long to pull down those of us who prosper? Possibly, envy of the rich and famous is worse now than at any other age in history; certainly, the animosity I sense to Earl and most of the celebrities is a revelation. It explains the resentment I experienced when I made a fortune selling hedge funds.

The rest of the names are on the admin bulletin board, I add, and I remind them they can also bet on our mystery celebrity.

To my surprise, they clap loudly when I point this out. John clearly knows our clientele. The noise makes it impossible to talk, so I hand the scofflaws in the front row some c-coins. They erupt in disbelieving laughter at the c-coin with Leonard Nimoy's name. Their faces sunny with glee, they pass it on to the bug-eyed men sitting in the next row.

How does c-coin work? a man shouts.

Everything depends on how you trade it. If you want to win, you need to pick the celebrity who is going to die first. That means you will be checking our weekly bulletins on the health of the deathbed ten. Their health will change, so the value of your c-coin will go up and down. Like American currency, or a Chinese banknote. I pause. Of course, we won't be giving out health reports on the mystery celebrity. Then they wouldn't be a mystery, would they?

The men laugh. John Giaccone catches my eye and smiles. I square my shoulders, blow out my cheeks.

Winners will get five bags of coffee from Starbucks. And we'll give five tins of mackerel to the runners-up. So, let's have a hand for Mr. Nathan Rickard, who has graciously supplied our jackpot.

The men cheer, and the warden gives me a pleased look.

How many winners will there be? a scofflaw yells.

It's hard to say. Maybe two. Maybe fifty. Mr. Jack will work out the percentages in your stake, depending on how many of you end up with the name of the celebrity who is the first to go through the pearly gates.

It beats trading postage stamps, a man cries.

Dale Paul, my man! someone else shouts.

The lounge grows so quiet I imagine I am able to hear the snow falling outside the windows. Now I'd like to invite Bailey and Derek to come forward. I point at my bunkmates. Our tellers will let each of you randomly pick twenty c-coins.

This is quite the experiment, Trish Bales calls amid the rumble of chairs. Are you worried how it will turn out?

Good lady, I expect there will be glitches.

Oh, you will know how to fix them, she replies, widening her eyes. The admiration in her voice stops me dead. Surely she isn't interested in an old croc such as myself, a penniless man with a lame excuse for a heart? I give her a fatherly smile and walk off.

23

FLUSH WITH MY triumph, I am writing a letter to Davie in the computer studio, where several men sit staring silently at their screens. I want to humblebrag about c-coin. When I am satisfied I won't be interrupted, I begin to type.

November 15, 2012

Dear Davie:

I am writing to you in good faith and with the hope that you'll read my letter when you come back from wherever you are. In the meantime, the warden has given me permission to teach financial skills to the men at Essex. I'm sure you'll be glad to know I am doing something to help the other prisoners.

In order to explain the basic principles of economics, I'm using a fake currency called c-coin. Each man has been given twenty c-coins to trade with the other prisoners, and each coin bears the name of one of ten old or sick celebrities. As the health of each celebrity changes, the worth of each c-coin also changes — its value going up or down like a junk bond on the stock market.

The symbol for our currency is the stylized letter c sprouting dollar signs. We have hand-stamped the c-coin symbol on the receipts we get from the prison store. In my workshop, the men will trade these slips of paper for sessions with a trainer or haircuts.

Of course, I am aware that c-coin may sound bizarre or ugly to you. Nothing could be further from the case. C-coin gives my comrades something useful to do after they finish their tedious prison jobs. And for the first time in months, I wake up each morning eager to get on with my day. I don't mean to imply that I am a different man from the one you knew. I am still the same old Pater who loves you.

I add a postscript:

When you come back from wherever you are, you may continue to hear unpleasant things about me. Please shut your ears to the evil that others say. Everything I have done has been for you because I wanted you to have an inheritance. I still wish it for you. That is why I am going to redouble my efforts inside the BOP so I can return to you what the Department of Justice has stolen from me. One day you

will receive the funds to which you are entitled. And then perhaps
you will think more favourably of your old Pater.

Naturally, I long to confide that John has encouraged the inmates to tell their families to bet on c-coin. The only difference between the bet in the prison and the bet on the outside is the jackpot. The winning scofflaws will be given bags of Starbucks coffee while John's clients will get a sizable share of our Bitcoin account.

However, Davie might not understand that gambling is creative play, a life-giving distraction that contributes to your well-being just as the academic studies in the law library have pointed out. And, in the end, if all goes well, Davie will draw a modest dividend from the scheme.

I fold up the letter and put it in an envelope to send to Meredith. It is important to maintain the conviction that Davie will read it one day when he returns from where he is living, fruitfully, I hope, and well. For now, it is enough to jot down my thoughts so my boy will realize I don't deserve to be where I am. Yes, sooner or later, Davie will come to understand that if you don't go for your shots, you're not going to win.

PART THREE

HOMECOMING

1

Tim Nugent

TIM HASN'T HEARD from Alexis in months. She has a reputation for going MIA on a writer, although she has never disappeared on him before. It makes him feel demoralized. Doesn't she know what her silences can do to the self-esteem of wordsmiths like him?

She's like a famous brain surgeon, a writer friend tells him. There's a lineup a block long to get into her office but once you're there, she'll shine a light on you that will make you feel like the most famous writer in the world. So, chum, the wait is worth it, the friend adds. Or did the friend say *chump*? Writing a book remains one of the few long processes in modern life. Like giving birth to a child, or making a film, another friend says. Tim has never had a child or made a film, but he finds this advice comforting. As if he is participating in an ancient mystery school that does secret, valuable work.

He opens a new email and starts to read Dale Paul's latest installment.

Dale Paul

A furlough is not an entitlement. Neither is it a reward for good behavior or successful programming, nor a means to shorten a criminal sentence.

— FEDERAL BUREAU OF PRISONS, *INMATE ADMISSION AND ORIENTATION HANDBOOK*

I HAVE NEVER thought much about Mother dying. Her death always felt like a distant event, the way I used to think about graduating from college when I was a boy. But she is sick with Creutzfeldt-Jakob disease, a degenerative neurological illness. There is no cure. The warden has given me permission to go home for two days because she is at the crisis stage.

Martino is driving me to Long Island, and the four-hour trip will give me the chance to reflect on what lies ahead. Time to think and fret about whether my friends and family will greet me with god-knows-what vengeful thoughts in their hearts. There is Meredith, who will be looking to see if I have repented. And Caroline. (What am I to make of her infrequent letters and phone calls?) There is also Esther, who hasn't seen me since Davie disappeared, as well as Dieter and Irene. Yet they are all minor hazards, and Meredith and Caroline can be brought around. The person I dread seeing again is none other than my neighbour, General Theodore Rigby.

He isn't the sort of fellow you'd expect to be a four-star general, even though he came from a long line of military men. A tall, mild-mannered man with a grey Hitlerian tuft beneath his nose, Ted served in Afghanistan under General Petraeus, who relied on him before Petraeus's affair with his biographer became public.

I met Ted the night Esther invited our neighbours home, along with several lifeguards, from the Plandome Country Club. She told Irene to throw white crème de menthe into the blender along with cracked ice and my best brandy. Ted's wife, Sofia, a dark-eyed flinty matron, and Ted, tall and reedy and wearing his weary, pained expression, sampled a few before I poured Ted a Laphroaig in my study and didn't correct him when he congratulated me on attending the Canadian equivalent of West Point.

More than a century and a half before, Munson Hall cadets fought against a group of American Fenians who wanted Britain to give Ireland its independence. When I mentioned the battle, Ted egged me on. In the army, he had been known as the listening general. By that, I mean Ted gathered information for his superiors. So that night, I found myself talking non-stop about the Battle of Ridgeway near Niagara Falls.

Ted smiled his pained smile. And the battle tally, he asked.

Seven dead and twenty-one wounded, I replied. One of the dead was a Munson Hall student.

By then, Ted and I had moved on to Armagnac, and he was explaining how the army tried to placate him after the failure of his promotion under Petraeus. When he retired, he was made director of the army pension funds. His official title was deputy CFO. He managed the stocks with two other senior military people, and their low returns brought him a great deal of dissatisfaction.

How on earth could they make a good return, he wanted to know, when they weren't allowed to invest in stocks that yielded more than three percent? The other two board members were unconcerned. Their lack of receptivity, the failure of their imaginations, these attributes greatly troubled and irritated me, although at first I didn't say so. I let Ted complain without offering a solution. Years before, Pater had told me it's better to hear the other person out before you jump in with your ideas on how to fix things. They won't listen otherwise.

We took our drinks outside and sat on the patio. I was feeling mellow. Fireflies glittered in the humid ocean breeze blowing through the rose garden, where Meredith was pushing Mother in her wheelchair. They had gone there to gather a bouquet for our dinner table, while in the kitchen Esther was force-feeding brandy stingers to her lifeguard pals. In a lowered voice, I began to tell Ted about the money I was making. Ted seemed astonished. He'd never heard of a fifteen percent return. Of course he hadn't. Not when he was dealing with low-yield government bonds. Naturally, he asked for my help.

Good sir, isn't there a rule against investing in high-risk stocks?

I haven't mentioned this to anyone, but there may be a loophole. Cone of silence, Dale Paul?

Cone of silence, I agreed. I'd sown the seed. Now it was up to Ted.

3

I MET THE other members of Ted's troika, and they were just as I feared: sloth heads, slow thinking and suspicious. They were the American version of the boys I met at Munson Hall. Quick to scoff and disapprove. Slow to grasp the brilliance of a new possibility, too suspicious to open their minds to the inevitable. You have no idea how much they depressed me.

Ted told them I had gone to a military college in Toronto, and that it had lost a cadet or two defending the honour of British Canada. The military men sat up and listened; after all, they'd seen me on CNN talking about the bailout of AIG.

Ted's loophole was the clause telling the troika to maximize investment income. The troika had failed pitifully in this regard, so they agreed to let me try something more enticing. It would take two to three years for the auditor to question our investments. And by then, our stocks would have done so well the army would be glad they had given me some wiggle room.

There's a lot more I could tell you about Ted and his trusting nature. I'm not sure additional details will be helpful. What you need to understand is how much everyone resents government. How oppressed and overwhelmed we feel over the way government takes our hard-earned dollars. Ted is no different. He'd already experienced a bump with the General Petraeus affair. And between us, he was never good at managing money. His wife, Sofia, who worked for the FDA, had been left a modest inheritance, and she used it to buy the handsome mansion a few doors down from us on Half Moon Lane.

I admire Sofia's taste. She sets her standards and lives by them — just as I live by mine. Ted is another matter. He is an unlucky person. Yet let it be said that Ted tries hard, although it is always someone else's fault if something goes wrong.

4

I'M JOLTED OUT of my half-slumber by the sudden glimmer of Long Island Sound. I am back on Half Moon Lane and there's my house on a tranquil grassy slope. *My home, my refuge.* I take in its wraparound veranda, the blackened hydrangea blossoms in Esther's old flowerbeds, the dull twinkle of late November sunshine on the glass of the solarium. The only thing I disliked about the property had been the asphalt road in front cutting our lawn off from a sand beach.

It was a minor flaw, and minor flaws aren't worth trifling about when your grounds evoke Mrs. Rockefeller's country garden.

Martino pulls into the driveway, and my cousin hurries out the back door and down the stairs, her maidenly braids flying. She calls out a greeting while Martino uncuffs me, his vacuous eyes fixed resolutely on the ground. When I point out that prisoners in transit are obliged to ride shackled, Meredith's mouth falls open, and she gives me a hug, her substantial body sagging against my chest like a dead weight.

Well, you're home now, she murmurs.

Soon I'll be an orphan like you.

I know, she replies.

She treats Martino to a polite smile and makes the necessary social noises when I explain he'll be my escort for the next two days; then she half turns and grins at someone. Caroline is hurrying through the moon gate, a bouquet of Mother's late-fall sedum in her arms.

Dale Paul, you're terribly thin! She exclaims as she hugs me.

While I stand in a half-swoon, over Caroline's shoulder, I notice the For Sale sign on the lawn. *My house is being sold! And nobody consulted me.*

Meredith shakes her head sadly when she sees where I'm looking. Malcolm de Vries said we had to pay off your legal costs.

That dimwit told me the house would be secure. Why doesn't Caroline's brother pay you what he owes me? When I think of the money I gave that mouth-breather …

Now really, Dale Paul, Caroline says. Charles is broke from paying his medical bills.

Oh, don't bother Charles right now. Meredith sighs. We'll muddle through somehow. Maybe we can borrow from Googie's trust.

Meredith, I would wait on borrowing money.

You don't understand how hard up we are, Dale Paul. She levels a stern look my way. Your mother is upset. Losing her home is hard for an eighty-six-year-old woman! And I've had to let Dieter and Irene go. Don't you want to say you're sorry about our situation? I suppose you think it's like crying over spilled milk.

Something like that. I smile vaguely. One day there will be discoveries made. The discoveries will be discombobulating, and the known unknowns will come leaping and bounding out of their hiding place and shatter those near me. *One day but not now.*

5

CAROLINE SQUEEZES MY hand as we stare down at the old woman thrashing about in her sheets. Who is this strange, irrational creature trying to free her arms, which appear to be tethered to the aluminum guardrails of her hospital bed? And where did my own mother go?

For god's sakes, do you need to keep her trussed up like that? I whisper.

At the sound of my voice, Mother lifts her head and fixes me with a weird glassy stare. Her beautiful curls hang in greasy strings.

Joe? She asks. Have you come to take me home?

Mother thinks I'm Pater, I whisper.

Play along, Meredith whispers back. That shouldn't be hard for you. She smiles.

I shoot Meredith a warning glance. Yes, Mother, it's Joe, I reply, feeling ashamed of myself.

Thank god, Joe. I've been waiting so long for you. Mother grabs my hand, drool spilling from her mouth. Meredith leans forward to wipe my parent's chin with a Kleenex. That girl there ... that girl ... Mother jerks her head away angrily. That girl doesn't know how to look after me properly.

Mother, behave yourself. Meredith is being kind to you. I pat her hand, and she rounds her eyes and smiles as if she is seeing me for the first time.

You came, after all, she murmurs, sounding like her old self. And here's Caroline. How lovely. Did Joe bring the two of you?

Yes, I mumble. Caroline smiles obligingly.

That's what I like to hear! Mother fixes me with her hollow-socketed eyes and mutters something about Pater's old Cartier watch. Alas, I'd been obliged to give it to the guard at Essex for safe keeping, although I don't say so to Mother.

There's a whispered conversation between Meredith and someone at the back of the room, and a nurse in a white uniform marches over to Mother's bedside. She glances at me dismissively, and in that quick disapproving stare I understand she blames me for the poor state of Mother's health. I want to tell her how wrong she is, but the woman's manner stops me from uttering a sound.

The nurse gives Mother a shot of morphine. Immediately, my parent stops her terrible tossing and turning and lies very still, her mouth wide open. Meredith nudges me forward and I force myself to kiss Mother's forehead. Her skin feels hot, feverish.

As we leave the bedroom, Meredith says in a wondering tone: Maybe Googie really saw Uncle Joe standing by the bed. Maybe the dying see things we can't.

Yes, maybe so, Caroline agrees.

My poor, ailing mother dies several hours later. Meredith says Mother felt she could let go now that I am home.

6

I AM WAITING for Caroline, safe and sound in my old bed, the pine four-poster with a canopy that Esther bought years before. The bed is a reproduction like the pair of Queen Anne chairs that someone, likely Dieter, positioned in front of the gas hearth. Anticipating the lovemaking to come, I pick up the framed photo of my sweetheart on the bedside table. Draped in her bright swimwear, her lanky form floats against a backdrop of Paradise Island's long shore of pinky sand.

I went there with Mother and Pater when the place was called Hogg Island after the wild pigs that pirates had set loose on its sand dunes. And, soon after Pater died, in a fit of nostalgia, I bought Surf Song, one of its neglected beach houses.

My beach house perched on a lot between a yoga camp and a handful of clapboard houses belonging to old white Bahamian families, although the weather-beaten homes were slowly being replaced by new four-storey villas that financial men such as myself were building.

Caroline and I met there on New Year's Day, 2006. Meredith and Davie had set off to look for the green flash of the sun before it was swallowed by the heaving turquoise sea. On their walk, they saw a crowd from the yoga camp dipping buckets into the ocean. When they stopped to find out what was going on, Meredith ran into an old friend Caroline Worsley, who worked in a London publishing house. Caroline had flown in the night before with Charles, her half-brother, who resembles the actor Albert Finney. She told Meredith the retreat had run out of fresh water: its toilets were overflowing, and the food was being washed in seawater. Charles was sick with kidney cancer and she'd taken him there for a rest. Meredith immediately invited them to stay with us.

Meredith and I watched Caroline and Charles come down the beach, dragging their suitcases across the sand. Caroline glanced apprehensively at Charles, who swayed and lurched as if the hundred or so yards from the yoga camp to our beach house were a marathon.

I sent Davie off to help, and I was struck by the starry expression on my son's face when he rushed back up the wooden steps to our patio, carrying their bags. He couldn't stop staring at Caroline, whose large beautiful eyes were as blue as Valium capsules, and that day, she did look especially lovely even though her fair English skin was sunburned and sweat as thick as olive oil glistened on her lovely cheekbones. She hung on to Davie's arm and surveyed the grounds. Following the direction of her gaze, I was appalled by the salt-rusted lock on the sea gate and the shabby beach umbrella made out of greying palm fronds. Sand had blown into the cracks between the coral flagstones, and the old wooden loungers needed replacing. Until Caroline appeared, I hadn't realized how much the place needed a makeover.

She caught my look of dismay and said, What a charming cottage. I am sure we will be very comfortable here.

Sis and I adore derelict places, Charles declared and began to laugh uproariously. She gave him a fond smile; they were obviously sharing a private joke. Later, I found out that Charles had been referring to their strange childhood, when Caroline's blueblood father had installed their family in a farmhouse in the north of England, a wreck of a place without heat or running water.

Esther chose that moment to emerge from behind the hedge of sea grapes. She had been drawn by the high-pitched sound of English voices. Take a moment to picture Esther, will you? Her frizzy blond hair, the features of her gentle face blunted by alcohol, her plump stomach an oval-shaped ball of the sort you might see on one of Caroline's Buddha statues.

When she saw Charles sitting on our patio, she staggered over and started gushing about Hollywood films. To my horror, I realized she had mistaken him for Albert Finney.

This is Caroline and her brother, Charles, I said. Esther's face fell slightly, but she let me lead her by the hand to one of the loungers, where she sat until lunch, criticizing the yoga camp in a loud, aggressive tone, her eyes never once leaving Charles's face. Oh, where did she go, I wondered, the shy woman who used to laugh at my jokes?

Charles explained that acting in British commercials kept him rolling in dough, and I made some mocking retort, lofting my eyebrows to let him know how pretentious I found him, but nothing distracted the lout from his spew of loquacious babble. Talking in an absurdly plummy accent I couldn't understand, he helped himself to another rum punch whenever he refilled Esther's glass. By the time Irene called us for conch salad, the pair were as drunk as lords. When she tried to stand up, Esther fell down, knocking over the patio table.

As I bent down to help Esther up, Caroline threw me a consoling look, and my bad, old heart knocked with happiness; the unfamiliar sensation was as sharp and clear as the sound of a pebble ricocheting inside a dried-up desert well.

That afternoon, Meredith helped me put Esther to bed, where she stayed for the rest of the day. Charles disappeared after pleading exhaustion, and, freshly liberated, Caroline plunged into the ocean, splashing and frolicking with Meredith while Davie and I played volleyball on the beach. It was the first time in a long while that Davie seemed genuinely happy, and on several occasions, Caroline looked over at us and smiled. We were all in a mellow mood, experiencing the giddy release that comes after handling something unpleasant.

Meredith made dinner that night, and afterwards the four of us sat on the patio listening contentedly to the thud of the ocean waves hitting the sand, the security light occasionally picking up the gleam of white foam. Davie hated anyone seeing his mother drunk, and Caroline sensed his distress. She told him about the work she did rescuing albino Great Danes and how she found new homes for the animals because interbreeding had resulted in great numbers of these dogs being born congenitally blind and deaf.

(Alas, the subject of Great Danes became a sore spot between us. I felt it wrong to keep the poor beasts alive, and Caroline thought it was better they live even though they suffered. It was the sort of recurring squabble couples indulge in, a humdrum clash of opinions that get exhaustively argued and never resolved.)

After Meredith went to bed, the conversation turned personal.

Hey, Caroline, Davie said. It's cool how you help your bro. He's in pain, right?

I started to say that Charles enjoyed posing as a drunken movie star, but as soon as Davie spoke, I realized Charles had been suffering physically and hiding how he felt behind a gabby bluster of rum-soaked noise.

Then, to my chagrin, Davie asked Caroline if she thought his mother could be cured of her drinking.

She'll have to want to be cured, Caroline replied. We can't do it for her.

Davie sighed. I wish I could.

He sounded so miserable I wanted to throw my arm around him and say everything was going to be all right, but he would accuse me of reassuring him with a false picture. I knew that about him because I am the same way myself.

Caroline made a comforting maternal sound. You love your mother and she feels your love. That is the best any of us can do.

Afterwards, when Davie went to bed, Caroline confided that her ex-husband had been an alcoholic so she understood what my son and I were going through.

It's not Esther's fault, I replied. She and I were never compatible.

Are you sure about that? Caroline gave me a knowing glance. I suspect her drinking gave you a good reason to stay at your office. After all, nobody likes coming home to a drunk.

That's not what I mean, I retorted.

Isn't it? I could feel her eyes on me in the darkness; she was silent, as if reflecting on a memory, and I was sure she could hear my bad, old heart.

Then she stood up and said she was going to bed. I walked her to the door of the sleeping cabin, where she gave me a hug, pressing her round, firm breasts against my chest. For an awkward moment, I didn't know what to do, and to my surprise, she grabbed my hand and pulled me inside. Once again, I noticed the appalling household neglect. Cobwebs hung off the headboard of the ancient bed, and the windowpanes were smeared with crusts of salt blown by the ocean winds against the glass.

This place hasn't been used for a while, I said. Does the plumbing work?

It works perfectly. She smiled and began to undress. When she turned to face me, she looked so lovely I dropped my eyes. She helped me undress, and to my embarrassment I felt myself tremble as she trailed her fingers feather-light across my chest.

I've always wanted to see what the Antichrist of capitalism looks like in his boxers! I'm not disappointed, Dale Paul.

I wondered what she meant. I still have all my hair, but I'm no prize at the poultry show, as Pater used to say. Yet Caroline sounded sincere. Drawing me over to the bed, she lay down on its quilted cover, generously offering up her body. And so I came to the fear that no man says aloud: Can you satisfy the woman you desire? How will you address that wild honey pot of thrills, the creamy mounds of breast waiting to be caressed, the mysterious thatched delta you are obliged to fondle as if its secrets are second nature to you?

Alas, I hadn't the slightest idea what to do. Esther and I used to go without making love for shockingly long periods of time.

Caroline gently pulled me down beside her, kissing my lips and the rubbery skin of my ears, and when her head moved south to salute my nether regions, I tugged her hair and whispered, It's … it's not nice down there.

She giggled. I don't believe it. You're shy.

Unable to utter a sound, I lay as passive as a Victorian bride while Caroline began. *And began and began.* And when she finished, she began once more until both of us lay in a satiated stupor. Point being, Caroline showed me my body was more than just a fleshy pedestal that kept my head from hitting the floor.

The next day, Charles took a turn for the worse, and Caroline and her brother flew back to London. A few weeks later, she wrote me a sweet thank-you note and said there'd been good news. Charles's cancer was in remission, and she invited me to look her up in London, where I had opened a branch of Quaestus Capital. Ablaze with lust, I wrote back saying I would. Even so, I had to send her several hundred dollars' worth of Shropshire Lass roses before she would agree to see me, and then she made it clear she didn't date married men. All that changed when Esther moved into her rented house in Port Washington.

7

THERE'S THE SOUND of footsteps in the hall and Caroline appears in the doorway still dressed in the suit she wore earlier. (A dismal portent for our nighttime pleasures.) I pat the side of the bed, and she shakes her head.

I've just come to say good night. I have menstrual cramps, darling.

Oh, *quel* shame. Tomorrow then?

We'll have to see. She smiles apologetically.

I try to pull her down next to me, and she cries out teasingly: Don't be a bad boy!

She means what she says. As far as she and Meredith are concerned, I am a child who bears watching, an overgrown adolescent who listens stony-faced while they hammer away at me with the battering ram of their good intentions.

Oh well. Sinking into the generous allotment of down pillows, I pick up the Q and A that my cousin wants me to check for errors. Nugent was the interviewer, and I imagine Meredith looking embarrassed as he fiddled with his tape recorder. Nugent is good with women so he would have made jittery small talk, trying to coax her out of her shell while she must have sat, her good eye darting about anxiously, not wanting to look at him.

Did they discuss the criminal charges against me? And deplore the way nobody takes my economic forecasts seriously now? More likely, knowing my cousin, they reminisced about our school days.

On weekdays, Mr. Eric, the family chauffeur, brought Earl and me a cache of Irene's peanut butter and banana sandwiches so we weren't obliged to eat the noonday slop the school fed its boarders. Once in a while, Nugent came along, but Meredith was there almost every lunch hour. Mr. Eric parked Pater's limo beneath the shady maples in the school lot. Sometimes, before Earl and I had to go back to class, we read *Classics* comic books. *Ivanhoe. Treasure Island. Gulliver's Travels.* My cousin brought any comic I asked for; she borrowed them from friends at her day school.

I sat in the front seat with Mr. Eric and boasted about my investments in Quaker Oats while Earl and Meredith sat in the back. If you bought a box of its cereal, you received a coupon that entitled you to a square inch of land in the Klondike. Nobody knew the lots were worthless then.

While I yakked on, Earl would pretend to listen, all the while mauling poor Meredith, who, for a while, encouraged his attention.

One noon hour, I happened to glance into the limo's rear-view mirror and noticed Meredith's school bloomers down around her ankles. Earl was the obvious culprit; one of his hands was hidden up to his elbow under her school tunic. I berated them both while Mr. Eric's face assumed an eyes-forward expression, and my cousin quickly made the necessary repairs.

I had tried to warn Meredith about Earl's credo: *Any port in a storm. Just put a bag over their head and go at it.* She didn't listen. Nugent was smoother than Earl; he appeared interested in what girls were saying, and I suppose his charm has come in handy with getting Meredith to help him with his research. The day she lost her eye would always be on her mind, although she wouldn't refer to it. People from our background are like that. We don't talk about the elephant in the room. We assume everyone knows, so what's the point?

Tim, before we start, I don't want any questions about what happened that day in the woods. Can you promise that? (Ah, she slips by it so cleverly. Good girl. Nicely averted.)

Fair enough. I don't really want to discuss it either. Let me begin by asking you about your childhood.

You mean after my parents died … when their bush plane crashed near Bear Lake … you know this, don't you?

Yes, but I want you to tell me in your own words.

All right. After the plane crashed, Googie and my uncle, Joe Paul, adopted me. They were living in Toronto at the time because Fairfield had just opened a branch there. Remember the Pauls' furniture chain? Uncle Joe worked for it before it was sold. The day I arrived, Dale Paul called me a poorhouse orphan, and Uncle Joe threatened to wash his mouth out with soap, so I told him Dale Paul was too young to understand what he was saying.

Ha ha. You were always the Paul family conscience!

Oh, I don't think so. I was too in awe of them. Their money came from Googie's American relatives, and I didn't know then that a woman could be richer than her husband. My father made a pittance selling his oil paintings in Toronto, so I went to St. Clemens on a scholarship. I have a few memories of my parents' postwar bungalow in Toronto, and the image of a kind woman, likely my mother, pushing me on a park swing. But over time, my years with the Pauls made it hard to believe my parents were real.

Were the Pauls a happy family?

Googie was happy, but not Uncle Joe. Googie's father wouldn't let her marry an academic with a modest income, so Uncle Joe had to stop working on his PhD in history and take a job in the family firm. He didn't do very well because his heart wasn't in it. As for Dale Paul, he inherited Uncle Joe's interest in books, but my cousin was always headed for business, and he certainly never doubted his self-worth. When he was a child, he insisted on being called two names, like the Pope.

He still does, doesn't he? [Am I being paranoid or do I detect unpleasant laughter here?]

Remember the day he read out our future bios from *Canada's Who's Who*? He was pretending, of course.

You mean when he said we were going to be famous?

Yes, famous and rich. All of us. I was going to be a famous scholar like Simone de Beauvoir. He said you were going to star in Hollywood movies, like Tab Hunter and the other actors we read about in *Modern Screen* magazine. Dale Paul predicted he would head up the New York Stock Exchange. And Earl — I can't remember what Dale Paul said about Earl.

Dale Paul said Earl was going to be mayor of Chicago. Ha! What a joke.

Let's not talk about Earl. But listen, Dale Paul works hard. He's not lazy like some of our friends who inherited money.

Ouch! I hope you're not thinking of me.

Of course not! You're a working journalist.

8

SHAME ON YOU, Nugent! For a fact-finding journalist, you are dead wrong about my predictions. I said Earl was going to be mayor of New York.

Point being, Earl's success has always been astonishing, considering he used to be the boy who thought an oyster fork was the right utensil to use on Irene's Thanksgiving turkey. However, it's true I assumed Meredith and Nugent would be famous too, and instead they have turned out to be ordinary Joes, to borrow Pater's term for the losers among us.

Suddenly, I think of my brush pens. Sure enough, they're still in the drawer in the bedside table. I test one of them out on a notepad. The ink in its cartridge has remained fresh, so the pen makes a clear, flowing mark on the page. Brush pens, in case you don't know, are used in Japanese and Chinese calligraphy, and those eastern scribes have a few tricks up their sleeves, sleights of hand that remain out of reach for a western amateur such as myself.

9

I PICK UP the Q and A again.

Was Dale Paul a difficult kid? Bear with me, Meredith. I need you to tell me everything as if I'm not familiar with any of it. Okay?

Okay. I think I told you Dale Paul was angry when I came to live with them. He wasn't used to competing for attention with a sibling. Googie put pressure on him to be nice. Googie used to recite a nursery rhyme when he was being difficult. It's a verse by A.A. Milne about the English King John, who had been forced to sign the Magna Carta:

"King John was not a good man — He had his little ways. And sometimes no one spoke to him for days and days and days." Dale Paul could anticipate what Googie was going to say, and he would throw his head back and shout, "Har dee har har!" That was our way of saying LOL, remember?

I do.

He had his little ways, as the rhyme says. Uncle Joe liked to tell Dale Paul he was the boy who said the dog ate his homework. But Dale Paul was always kind to me. He and I used to play-act Queen Elizabeth's coronation. I was the queen. Dale Paul played the Archbishop of Canterbury and he placed the royal sceptre and the rod of mercy in my hands. Sometimes Uncle Joe came in to watch. When Dale Paul set the cardboard crown on my head, Uncle Joe prodded me to say, "I hereby give my life to my subjects!" By the way, we didn't use real sceptres. Dale Paul carried brass fire pokers, one slightly thicker than the other. They were also quite heavy, and Uncle Joe was cross the day Dale Paul dropped one of the pokers on his foot.

The Q and A ends with Meredith talking about the novel experience of being interviewed. (Novel for her, perhaps.) My cousin is wrong about the poker, though. She is the one who dropped it on Pater's toes. Meredith was a clumsy, big-boned girl, always tripping over her own two feet.

10

Meredith Paul

MEREDITH FOLLOWS DALE Paul and Caroline up the steps of All Saints Episcopal Church, trying not to look at the prison guard walking a few paces behind Dale Paul. It feels humiliating to come into her aunt's church with such an escort. The humiliation has nothing to do with her, of course, even though insensitive people suggest she is implicated. Unfortunately, her cousin has begun to babble about the history of the church; how it was built with stones from the nearby fields because his old friend's maternal great-grandfather, who sat on its board, wanted the Long Island church to resemble a rural English parish. Thankfully, Caroline puts a finger to her lips and hushes him.

Unexpectedly, her cousin comes to a halt and stands gaping at a bearded young man sitting in the back of the church. Meredith looks too. There is something familiar about the young man, although for the life of her, she can't say what. Is he the child of a neighbour? All at once she knows. But how could it be? Davie is dead. For one breathless moment, the young man looks their way, then he turns his head and she can't see his face.

Hey, you two! Caroline hisses. Meredith nods and she and Dale Paul follow Caroline down the aisle to the family pew. The Pauls' ancient aunts (whose names Meredith still confuses) avert their eyes at the sight of her cousin being escorted by a prison guard. Only the oversized woman with a rolling chin and frizzy hair gives them a welcoming smile. At first, she doesn't understand the meaning of the pitiful, half-strangled sounds Esther is making. Then she realizes Esther is talking about Davie not being there.

Above their heads, the minister plays his old-timey part in his white surplice over his black cassock, his liver-spotted hands tugging at his long ecclesiastical scarf. We have brought nothing into this world, he drones. And it is certain we can carry nothing out …

Trying to follow along, Meredith opens her prayer book, and that's when Tim reaches over and takes her hand. Startled, she looks up and catches Dale Paul glowering at them. She glances quickly away. So now he knows how she and Tim feel about each other. Despite herself, she shivers. Surely, Dale Paul can't ruin that too?

11

Dale Paul

THE SERVICE IS nearly over. The congregation sings, "There Is a Green Hill Far Away." Meredith and I used to sing our own version, mouthing, "There is a green still far away," and we giggled while Pater scowled down at us. The next thing I know I am shuffling out of the church. I look around for the bearded young man, but he must have left by the side entrance. Feeling discombobulated, I send Nugent off in a cab while I climb into my time-honoured place, the passenger seat next to Meredith. We make an awkward social grouping; Martino is in the back seat with Caroline. Everybody sits stiff as fence posts, feigning interest in the streets of Manhasset, whose motley shops and skuzzy restaurants flow past the car windows.

I give up on small talk and look out the window too, and there, in the doorway of the unsavoury Greek takeout place, stands my former client, Gyro George, as the girls in the office called him. His correct name is Giorgios. Gruff and kind-hearted, Gyro George stands smoking with his waiter, a scrawny pickup artist named Spiro, who likes to offer his smelly Greek cigarettes to the customers: Assos for the men, Karelia Lights for the ladies. I wave, and the two men look startled; then Giorgios and Spiro both give me the finger and hurry inside.

From the back seat, Caroline puts a consoling hand on my shoulder, and for the first time, it strikes me how well Gyro George is doing. Of course, I, too, did well once.

How I loved America then; the best thing about it was how easily people believe what you say, not like my northern brethren, who lack the ability to appreciate the art of the pitch. A person who lives north of the border is too skeptical to understand the vision you need or the benefits that accrue when someone like me, who believes in what I'm saying, can inspire confidence in someone like you.

Do you know the story of the American customs official who asks a man to declare his nationality? I have a dual passport, the man exclaims. I am both Canadian and American. The guard isn't satisfied, so he keeps questioning the man until finally the guard asks: If your country went to war, what would you do?

It depends on the war and why it was being fought, the man replies. The customs official goes all smiley-faced. Now I know, the guard says. You're Canadian, and the man with the dual passport nods warily.

I ask you truly, what can be done with such people?

12

NOT MANY GUESTS come to the wake for Mother. Most of her old friends are dead, and the others don't want to share a drink with me. When Aunt Georgia arrives in her Cadillac Escalade, I rush to help her: Don't you touch me! she hisses. Your poor mother! How could you sell the house out from under her?

I catch Meredith's eye, and she throws me an understanding glance from the back porch where she stands greeting our guests. The service must have leeched away my cousin's strength because she doesn't hurry to my rescue. Nugent stands beside her, his round brown eyes grave with concern. Every so often he shoots her a quick, reassuring grin and she smiles back.

Nugent has always admired my cousin who seemed more sophisticated than the knock-kneed girls our own age. She used to read racy French novels like *Bonjour Tristesse* and she would opine on the merits of free love as casually as if she were talking about the health benefits of fresh orange juice. So once, as a favour to my old school chum, I persuaded Meredith to take him to her school dance. They were doing the polka when he twisted her around so recklessly he stepped on her crinoline; there was an ominous rip, and it fell onto the auditorium floor. For a terrible moment, her under-garment lay there, limp as roadkill. The other dancers stared in shock while her girlfriends stood shoulder to shoulder pinning the crinoline back on my blushing cousin. I watched from the sidelines, feeling awkward. She and Nugent have certainly had their ups and downs.

And now they are enjoying a détente while I am *persona non grata*. Nobody wants to talk to me, or if they do, they don't want the others to see.

I turn my back on the demented gabfest and set off down Half Moon Lane, the breeze from the sound burning my cheeks. I want to smoke a joint I found in the pocket of an old coat. Looking around for the right place, I spot the For Sale sign on the Rigbys' house. So they are selling their place too. Never mind. It is too late for anyone to do anything now. I head for their pond. Wild turkeys and indigenous waterfowl once frolicked there amid plants native to North America. Other flora and fauna weren't allowed.

It takes me a moment to understand I'm not alone. The bearded young man I saw at the back of the church stands half-hidden in the phragmites, a plebian grass that grows by our local rivers. I start toward him eagerly. When I am almost at the pond, I feel a prickle of recognition; it's the same skinny frame, the same slouching slope of the shoulders.

Is that you, Davie? I call. The young man sees me and runs as fast as he can down the lane. It was my son. I'm sure of it, but who will believe me? Feeling adrift, I walk home and peer through the living room window. Arnie, my ex-wife's caddy, inclines his noggin with its high flat-top toward Esther while Arnie's father, Josh, sits staring into space. Esther is talking earnestly about something, and Arnie appears to be agreeing.

When in doubt, avoid, ignore and evade, my boyhood version of I came, I saw, I conquered, Julius Caesar's stirring pronouncement after vanquishing Gaul.

Turning my back on the crowd, I hurry off to the potting shed. I built it for Mother the year she came to live with us. No one will search for me here. I lock the door and light up the joint. A pair of Mother's ancient secateurs lie flat on a trestle table, as if she put them there only moments before. Mother and Sofia liked to plant indigenous sedge in the spots where my ex-wife wanted ornamental African grasses. Esther would go into a tizzy watching them from the living room window. She'd invite them inside for coffee, and a few minutes later they'd be back outside digging up more of the exotic grasses until Dieter gently tried to stop them.

To my dismay, the pot is making me feel light-headed. And now, another shock: Martino's sleepy face in the shed window. He bangs on the door. I bury the evidence in a flowerpot and step outside. He eyes me distrustfully.

You trying to shake me?

I can't smoke inside.

Yeah, okay. The register of Martino's voice slips into his usual affable tone. Together we walk back across the lawn to the house.

13

OUR GUESTS HAVE departed; even the serious boozehounds like Esther have handed over their drink glasses like employees tendering their resignations. Through the doorway into the kitchen, I watch Meredith finish tossing a green salad. Before I went to prison, that would have been Irene's job, yet Meredith looks extraordinarily happy to be doing it.

Absently, she pats her braids, which have been wound in an elegant fashion around her head. Now she is coming through the door toward me, carrying a portable phone. The new hairdo is not unpleasing. Mother would have been delighted to see how Meredith smartened herself up for the funeral.

Nugent follows my cousin through the doorway, pushing a glass trolley with our lunch: the freshly tossed greens and a dish of shrimps on a bed of long-grained rice. My old friend must have been cracking one of his asinine jokes because the pair are laughing and smiling at each other. I feel a jealous twinge.

Where on earth is Caroline?

At the store buying groceries. Meredith gives me a tight-lipped smile and hands over the portable phone, her hand clamped across the receiver. It's Esther, she whispers. I think she's drunk.

I take the phone into the den. At first, I don't absorb what Esther is saying. Then it hits me: she wants a funeral for Davie. I tell Esther about the two sightings, the first at the church and the next by Ted and Sofia's house. Esther says I am talking nonsense.

You don't understand! I bellow. Davie is alive and well.

She hangs up. My ex-wife can be remarkably obstinate. I put the phone back on its hook and go off to eat lunch with Martino.

Half an hour later, I slip out to the patio to catch the sea air and find Nugent putting used drink glasses on a tray. When he sees me, he smiles shyly, and for a moment he turns into the timid boy I knew at school. Then the moment passes and he changes back again into the burly older man whose soft brown eyes nest in his face like a vestigial echo of our youth. We sit down on some wrought iron chairs, and for the first time I feel myself relax. After all, not many of my old friends are speaking to me.

14

I'M SORRY ABOUT your mother, Nugent is saying. You've had two big personal losses. And the news hasn't been kind lately — do those stories in the media bother you? He is referring to a blast of unfortunate publicity about Thomas Schroeder Limited.

Not at all. I can't take responsibility for what Schroeder did.

His smile dips slightly. But Schroeder was one of your companies.

It was, indeed. And its method of evaluating pensions is a standard in the industry, although you realize, don't you, that when Schroeder started, the average citizen lived ten years less than they do now?

He frowns and I consider telling him about the morning Marcia Gallagher, my director of investor relations, charged into my office with the news that our pension funds were running short of money. I promised to look into it, and when I did, I was given the same answer Schroeder gave to anyone who asked: *Yes, the growth rate has stopped, but there is no reason to worry because the growth rate in pension funds goes up and down and one day it will start going up again.* Except that the growth rate of pensions didn't go anywhere but down.

He looks at me curiously. Well, you always liked to push the river.

Are you saying I court danger unnecessarily, good sir?

Let me put it this way. You create drama wherever you go.

Maybe so. Now I have a question for you, Nugent. Was it you who told the headmaster about our game of chance at Munson Hall? You can tell me now. I don't mind.

He looks off at the sound, where sailboats are jostling for position on the starting line despite the fact that sailing season is over.

I told you years ago it was the prefect Thompson, Nugent says irritably. His father owned the newspaper.

Ah, I'd forgotten Thompson was the villain. I beg your pardon. How can I make it up to you?

Well, there is something. I'd like to interview you for the *New York Times Magazine*, he replies, taking me by surprise.

Really? Will readers find an article about an inmate amusing? I build a steeple-fingered pyramid in front of my face, aware I'm being coy.

I'll talk about how you're doing a financial workshop for the inmates. It will be early publicity for your book.

I think for a moment. All right — provided you don't rehash my case. I've already told you how I feel about that dreary subject. And now I have a question for you. What are your intentions toward my kister?

We're just friends, Nugent splutters. Okay? She's been helping me with my research.

A likely story.

He looks at me in surprise, and I smile broadly.

15

I AWAKE FROM a nightmare, my skin unpleasantly sticky with perspiration. Caroline has come and gone, permitting me liberties that no gentleman should divulge, but without her usual ardour, and so I failed to perform in the way I hoped. After she fled, I lay for a long time, wide-eyed and desolate. And then, when I at last fell asleep, I dreamt about pleading my court case before Arnie, Sofia, and Ted. They wore black judges' robes and sat perched on the horizon line. I had to look twice to make sure I wasn't seeing things. They were a doleful group if ever there were one.

Dear friends, I exclaimed in my nightmare. I am not a felon.

My male accusers flew about, screeching inanely while Sophia pecked savagely at her feathers. Why didn't I notice the feathers before? My old pals had turned into crows. Or were they magpies? (I was never very good at identifying birds).

Birds — jailbirds. My tawdry unconscious has been making a joke at my expense. While I implored them to listen, Sofia and Arnie flew off, their dark robes flapping. Only Ted stayed behind. Dale Paul, I forgive you, he cackled. When I regarded him stonily, he ducked his head under his inky wing and began to weep. That's how it ended. With my amiable, forgiving pal sobbing his heart out.

16

I PUT AWAY thoughts of Ted Rigby and leap out of bed. Thank god I am a free man for a few more hours. In a state of mild ecstasy, I shave with my hard-edged razor, running it over my facial zones — up my neck and across my cheeks until my skin tingles. Luckily, Meredith hasn't packed my things, so my aftershave lotions are right where I left them. Not for me the cheap unguents in the commissary. Oh no! Inscribed in fine print on the side of the squeeze bottle is my organic shaving soap with quaint messages from its founder: *Full truth our god, half-truth our enemy; we're all one or none*, and so on and so forth. And then the delightful choice of two shaving balms: toner from Giorgio Armani if I need soothing or Thayer's Witch Hazel to pep me up. Today I choose the witch hazel, patting it on lavishly before I emerge ruthlessly shiny and clean-shaven, only to find Meredith and Caroline glaring at me from my doorway.

Can we come in? Meredith asks. What choice do I have? I am about to hear one of the tiresome pep talks my cousin gives her students, the type of well-meaning litany that ends in promises I will be unable to keep.

I'm going to come right out with it, Meredith says after I usher them in. We're holding a funeral service for Davie. We don't care what you say, do we, Caroline?

Caroline's condescending smile makes me wince. I have thought this over carefully, Dale Paul, she says, and I believe a funeral is the best course of action right now, even though you may harbour the conviction that Davie is alive …

Stop right there. What do you mean *may* harbour? I saw him at the funeral!

Esther said you claimed to see Davie. But you have no proof it was him. Meredith frowns. It was probably just a boy who looks like Davie.

You see, darling … Caroline pauses breathily. Denial isn't really helpful at this moment. Your family is suffering from the loss of two of its members.

You don't know what you're talking about! Either of you! And I don't want to hear anything more on the subject.

Suit yourself, Meredith says huffily. But don't say we didn't tell you about it. She turns to Caroline, who throws me a worried look, and they walk out the door. Meredith will get over her hissy fit. Point being, she lacks the tenacity for a long-standing feud. And if she is the same old Kis I know and love, she will apologize for making me feel bad.

17

Tim Nugent

TIM SHAKES ESTHER'S hand at her front door, feeling awkward. Did he accept the invitation to the family powwow to impress Meredith? Oh, he knows the answer to that one.

He is getting too involved with the Pauls, and woe to the ghost-writer who takes sides against his subject! But it's hard not to support Meredith, who, for too long, has been the neglected member of the family. So here he is in Esther's home helping to plan a memorial against Dale Paul's wishes. Meredith told Tim about the boy in church who looked like Davie, but she has decided it was a coincidence. If it was Davie, Meredith thinks he would have declared himself to them.

Esther is a plump woman with the same wild, fair hair and pale, freckled complexion as her son. She lives on the main street of Port Washington in one of those Yankee houses with two storeys at the front and one at the back. In the front hall, Tim notices the Yousuf Karsh photograph of his schoolmate. Karsh has captured Dale Paul's deep-set eyes under their imposing brows and the way his old friend's glossy black hair fits the contours of his large head like the pelt of mink.

Doesn't he look creepy? Esther asks when she catches Tim staring at the portrait. She steers him into the comfortable living room. I wish I'd never met him.

Oh, Esther, Meredith says as she follows them in.

Esther and Dale Paul had been an unlikely match, Tim thinks as he sits down on the Montauk sofa next to Meredith. It feels good to be by her side. Natural even. He is five inches shorter, almost half a foot, but as he often reminds himself, he is broad and fit enough to take on any man or woman.

Esther sits across from the two of them, apologizing because she doesn't have money for a real fire. The brick hearth, Tim notices, is stacked with faux birch logs. She begins to complain about the traffic noise outside, and moves on to a heating bill that Dale Paul is refusing to pay. Tim feels himself twitch with impatience.

Dieter appears with a silver tray and three mugs of tea. Meredith has told Tim that Dieter and Irene share Esther's modest quarters, but her house isn't humble, in Tim's opinion. Esther must have some money or she wouldn't be able to afford household help. He thinks of his old arguments with Dale Paul. You can't alter the fact of your family or your skin colour, Tim would tell his school friend. But we can change our sense of entitlement. These conversations would end with Dale Paul shouting at Tim that he wasn't going to apologize for his family's wealth.

Remembering their disagreements makes Tim frown.

Dieter notices the scowl on Tim's face and gives him a friendly smile as he heads off to the kitchen. Davie killed himself for a reason, you know, Esther says the moment Dieter leaves. He wanted to get back at us.

He was angry with his father, Meredith replies. He has been for years. I don't think he was mad at you. My guess is no.

I can't say he was very nice to me toward the end.

He may have felt ashamed of himself, Meredith says. That he caused you to worry.

It must be nice to have all the answers, Esther retorts.

I have no answers. Meredith shrugs. But I do teach young people. You learn a few things from them.

Esther turns to Tim, her face flushed and irritable-looking. You could have saved Meredith from teaching those silly girls, you know. I always thought you two should have got married. What happened that day wasn't your fault …

Tim throws Meredith a helpless look. Should I leave and let you two discuss the memorial?

To his horror, Esther begins to sob. I know you don't like me, Tim, and Meredith thinks I'm a bad mother, but I never expected Dale Paul to go to jail. And then my son ... it's all so horrible ...

Meredith doesn't meet Tim's gaze. Esther, I'm so sorry, Meredith says. It truly sucks.

18

Dale Paul

IT'S TIME TO leave. I avoid looking at the packed boxes of Meissen china in the dining room and the Sheraton chairs that Dieter has stacked as a favour to my cousin. I have already kissed Meredith and Caroline goodbye. Caroline lowered her eyes when she saw me in my prison uniform.

Outside, Martino apologizes for shackling me. I look back at the house. Meredith and Caroline are watching from the kitchen window. They look sad. I smile faintly and nod, and Meredith points at a dented Volvo cruising along Half Moon Lane. The car slips out of sight behind a hedge. When I glance back at the house again, Meredith and Caroline are gone.

I climb into the front seat with Martino's help, and we drive slowly up to the handsome twelve-foot gates, which open at the right moment, thanks to my cousin pressing the release switch at the house. Suddenly, Martino begins to swear; the Volvo that passed us on the road is parked across my driveway. Before I can tell Martino who they are, Sofia Rigby helps a crippled old man out of the car.

I take a breath.

The human wreck standing in my driveway is Ted Rigby, the last person I want to see. I haven't talked to him since the summer night he hustled me anxiously into his office. There, spread across his desk, I spied the financial statements about the retirement community in Laverne, North Carolina.

What am I going to tell the others? Ted asked.

The truth, I replied. Our funds aren't doing very well right now.

You don't understand, he retorted. I've lied and said our investments are taking off. I had to keep them off my back, Dale Paul. And now this! Ted groaned as he gestured at the papers on his desk. Maybe we should tell them we've invested in high-risk stocks.

A wheelchair squeaked outside Ted's study. Mother. Sure enough, the door opened and she poked her head in.

Darling boy, she said. I'm tired. Can you take me home? She noticed Ted's face and asked, Is something wrong?

Your son and I are worried about a financial matter, Ted replied.

Well, if anybody can fix it, Dale Paul can. He's a wizard, you know. She locked eyes with Ted. I don't have to tell you that, do I?

No, you don't need to tell me that, Ted replied generously.

Mother's faith in me touched my bad, old heart. The next day, I doubled down on gold. What with so many countries devaluing their currencies, gold was a no-brainer. It could rocket up to six thousand five hundred, maybe ten thousand dollars an ounce. Then the price of gold dipped unexpectedly. We lost everything.

19

SOFIA MUST HAVE wanted me to see Ted in his full cancer regalia, because my old friend is without a coat to protect him from the wind. A breathing apparatus covers his throat, and a sinister-looking plastic sack has been hooked in an ungainly fashion onto his belt.

When she is satisfied I've taken a good look, she starts pulling something out of the Volvo. As Martino and I watch, stupefied, she holds up a large framed photograph of our sons by the Plandome Club pool. The sight of Davie's face makes me feel light-headed.

She walks briskly forward while poor Ted waits by their Volvo, looking mournful.

You want to talk to them? Martino asks. I nod yes, and Martino rolls down my window. I'm sorry about everything, I shout, thankful Sofia can't see my shackled hands. She looks up at me in confusion. In the background,

Ted is making horrible croaking noises, and I have to listen carefully to understand what he says.

You see, Sofia, Ted chides. He didn't mean to hurt us.

She pulls a face at her husband and turns towards the van again. Dale Paul, take a good look at our boys! She holds up the framed picture. You ruined their lives!

Beside me, Martino asks, You okay with this?

I shrug. Martino climbs out of the van and walks over to Sofia, who is clutching her photograph like a vampire charm. Martino takes her arm and says, Ma'am, I have to get my prisoner back to jail. If you will move your car …

She pushes his hand away and tries to climb onto the front of our vehicle.

For a long, dread-filled moment, the vehicle bucks and heaves. Is she off her rocker? Martino hisses through the open window. I am shocked and cannot answer. Ted is staggering toward Sofia, his plastic tubes flying. In what must have been a rare burst of adrenalin, he manages to pull her off. Martino waits until she struggles to her feet; then he climbs back in and guns the accelerator, driving across the lawn to avoid their vehicle. From beneath the van's wheels comes the tinkle of breaking glass. We have run over her photograph. When I look back, she is bent over the shattered portrait while Ted stands staring after the van, an expression of disbelief on his face.

20

BACK AT ESSEX, I can't stop thinking of Ted's face as we drove off. Naturally, I feel unhappy about his distress, but what can a jailbird like me do for a man who is dying? Should I offer up the usual platitudinous guff to a battle-worn general who fought in the Middle East and downed gin highballs with Esther and myself on hazy summer evenings? Who watched our boys gambol about the pool in wet bathing suits? Possibly yes. I begin a letter to him:

Dear Ted:

There is so much ground to cover I don't know where to begin, but I am sure you must know how downhearted I feel over the news of your illness ...

I tear up my letter. There is Sofia to consider. Why did she bring poor ailing Ted to see me? And then, to act as if I were the sole reason for their troubles! I did not cause Ted's cancer or talk him into the investments we made together. He asked for my help and I gave it, and then he went out of his way to make our plan work, so why, pray tell, is it all my responsibility when I was doing what I could to help? People like Sofia don't understand there is no gain without risk. They assume the stock market is a rainbow with a pot of gold at the end. That's their problem. She and Ted loved me when I made them money and despised me when I didn't.

21

Tim Nugent

TIM HEARS THE rumble of the voice first, then he sees the back of the strange hairless head: Earl, his school chum, is crouched on a stool at the airport bar in Nassau. Earl's hooded eyes catch Tim's in the overhead mirror, but Earl looks away quickly and Tim hopes they can get away without saying hello. The day before, Tim flew down with Meredith and Caroline for Davie's memorial service in the old chapel on Paradise Island, built out of coral by Dutch settlers in 1784. Esther had flown down with one of the Paul aunts, but Esther and the aunt left the same afternoon.

After the ceremony, Caroline and Meredith and Tim stayed on at Dale Paul's beach house. Around midnight, Meredith came to Tim's bedroom. He wasn't sure what to do until he saw her look of anguish, and then he held out his arms. After she fell asleep, Tim stayed awake until the sunrise lit up the tops of the palm trees. Now they're leaving Nassau, going back to their lives, and Earl is not a person they want to see. But Earl has slid off his stool and he is walking their way, lumbering along with his strange side-to-side motion. Tim has never known what to make of Earl's condition. It was said to be the result of a malfunction in a tiny genome in human DNA, a rare microscopic event. Tim has read a study that claims something in your genetic coding can go awry, resulting in an abnormal physical difference that has never appeared before. The study suggested that global warming is causing these accidents to occur more often, but the link to environmental damage hasn't been proven and there are times when Tim thinks "the condition" is a scientific put-on that Earl uses to manipulate other people.

Nugent, Earl cries just as a calypso band on the PA system breaks into "Yellow Bird." You're limping. Got a gimpy leg?

Tim can feel himself blush. He had thrown his right leg over Meredith's thigh to gain purchase on her longer body and now his groin muscles are painfully sore.

Okay, don't tell me. Too much tennis? Earl gazes at Tim with his cowled eyes. And you're with the lovely Meredith. What are you guys doing here?

We came down for a memorial service. For Dale Paul's son, Tim replies.

Oh, yeah. That's horrible.

Yes, it is, Tim says. Did you stay in town?

Atlantis, Earl answers. A hell of a place. All those sharks in aquariums. Dale Paul still own that shack on the beach?

He's selling it, Tim says.

Too bad. And look. You got Dale Paul's beautiful girlfriend with you. How are you, dear?

I'm well, thank you, Caroline says coldly. Like Meredith, she has no time for Earl.

Earl's friend stops watching the overhead television and turns toward Tim. A big man with a thick neck and genial, wide-open face, he is often in the news discussing the need for cuts to federal prisons.

Tim offers his hand. Tim Nugent.

Oh, I know who you are, the man snaps. You're a friend of that guy who ripped off our vets.

Tim, Meredith interrupts. We need to catch our flight. Giving Earl a severe look, she nods at Caroline and the three of them start the long walk to their departure gate.

22

Dale Paul

I'M IN THE television lounge, watching Oprah interview a guest, when I realize the overweight codger sitting next to her is Mickey Rooney, one of our deathbed ten celebrities.

Mickey, as America's most famous child star, you've had a longer career than most people in show business, Oprah says, smiling. What helped you to ride the ups and downs?

No comment. He smirks, and for a moment I see the cocky kid in the Andy Hardy reruns that Davie and I used to watch.

Well, I'm glad it worked out for you, she answers suavely. You've been married eight times. Can you tell the audience your secret?

Stupidity, Rooney replies. You gotta keep hitting your head against the wall.

Oprah laughs obligingly. You're ninety-two. How does that feel?

Just dandy, Oprah. He squints at her through his close-set eyes. I got diabetes. My house is a worthless shit hole. And I am a victim of elder abuse. Maybe you read about me testifying to the senate committee about my relatives? Looking suddenly aggrieved Mickey Rooney starts playing with his coffee mug. He appears to be trembling from rage or sorrow.

Oprah gives him a worried smile. Mickey, can you tell the studio audience what your stepson did to you?

The camera lingers on the actor's squashed nose, his warthog cheeks, his puffy body in an unkempt track suit, and suddenly Rooney is on his feet yelling. Something has gone awry. Then Rooney seems to remember where he is and shoots the audience a look so paranoid it sends a chill down my spine. That's when I understand: he is high.

Rooney stumbles toward the camera, his piggy eyes opened wide, and the screen suddenly switches to an insurance ad for elderly drivers.

Having a larf, mate? Derek puts a hand on my shoulder. He drops down beside me, and I tell him about Mickey Rooney.

Was he shaking? Derek says.

I think so, yes.

He's chasing the dragon, mate. Maybe he'll be the first of the deathbed ten to pop.

23

IN THE LAW library, I look up the term *chasing the dragon* in the dictionary of American slang. As far as I know, crack and heroin are versions of the same thing, but it seems chasing the dragon refers to inhaling vapour from heated morphine while crack comes from the cocoa bush.

The dictionary also notes that crack addicts often overdose by accident. The thought of Rooney taking an overdose distresses me. My boy and I spent wonderful hours watching his old Hollywood movies. Davie especially loved Mickey Rooney in *The Simpsons* episode "Radioactive Man." Shutting down a little voice that says, Don't do it, you fool, I set off for the computer studio to write the actor a letter.

Dear Mr. Rooney:

You will be surprised to know that I am writing you from inside a prison. I am here because, well, let's just say I've had financial troubles. I won't bore you with the details. But your appearance on television this morning compelled me to write and introduce myself.

I'd like to encourage you to stay away from drugs, although I realize this may be a tiresome thing for someone to say to a man of your age and position. Unfortunately, an addiction is hard on the people who

love you. My own son was not above taking the occasional beta blocker
when he felt stressed …

I stop typing. Should I tell Mickey Rooney about my hunch that Davie
is still alive? I press Select All and delete the letter.

I begin again. Without mentioning Davie, I write almost word for word
what I said in the first letter. Then I add:

Mickey, I hope you won't hold my concerns about your health against
me. I assure you I do not often write fan letters. Please be good to your-
self. I loved your acting in Boys Town *with Spencer Tracy and it would*
mean a lot to me to know you are doing well.

I reread the last sentence. *It would mean a lot to me to know you are*
doing well. Do I really mean that? It seems I do. Hand on heart, I am aware
of the perils of treating a celebrity as a friend. Clearly, they do not know
you as well as you know them, but I can't help myself. I want the actor to
take charge of his life. After all, he hasn't lost his old spunk. I return to
my letter.

I realize I ought to offer you an explanation. The police think my
son, David, jumped off the Brooklyn Bridge. And the public believes it's
my fault …

I stare at the sentence "And the public believes it's my fault." Better not
to get into what happened with Davie. I delete the last two sentences and
start over once more:

One of my best memories of being with my son is watching your
film It's a Mad, Mad, Mad, Mad World. *Of course, I saw every one of*
your Andy Hardy films when I was a boy and I identified with the way
Andy never gave up. You said as much on Oprah's show, although you
described it as hitting your head against the wall …

If by any chance you want to write, I would be very glad to hear from you. I can be reached at ...

I keep my letter to Mickey Rooney in my locker. Then, one chilly December afternoon, when the prison feels cold and inhospitable, I look up his agent and mail the letter to the Los Angeles address.

24

JUST AS NUGENT promised, his story about me appears in the *New York Times Magazine* along with an unflattering mug shot. There is also an aerial photograph that shows Essex the size of a Lego set safely tucked away in a pinewoods. A bone of reassurance for *Times* readers.

At least Nugent did what I asked and omitted Earl's name. Putting Earl on the dead pool has been revenge enough; I don't need to draw his ire too.

Nugent starts with the usual rundown: "Dale Paul, known among his financial cronies as the Pension Fund Whale, was convicted of three charges laid by federal prosecutors. These charges included a willful miscalculation of pension contributions; cross-trading that involved his companies buying from each other; and forging documents and investing in gold without permission, with the result that untold billions in U.S. military pension funds were lost.

"He was acquitted of seven other counts, including the misuse of corporate perks, such as taking the company plane on holidays with his British girlfriend, Caroline Worsley."

In a highly sarcastic tone, my old friend remarks: "Fraud isn't a black-and-white crime like robbery or murder. Instead, there's always the question, Was the crime intended to be a crime? That's why a hedge funds manager like Dale Paul believes he's innocent. Furthermore, his belief in his innocence is bound up with rage over the U.S. justice system's plea-bargaining practices. The prosecutorial game of overwhelming a defendant with charges so that he or she admits guilt whether guilty or not — these practices keep Dale Paul awake at night. He claims the charges aren't true."

Thank you, Nugent, for pointing out that fraud is open to interpretation. But why did my old pal use the phrase *he claims*? Is Nugent hinting the charges were just? And why skip over the way money managers like myself help capital flow around the world? If you are a maker of widgets, you can't do without our help. Who else but a lord of liquidity will give you the cash to get your business off the ground? Few banks or investors have the courage to take a chance on your enterprise.

Toward the end of his article, he touches on the way the scofflaws revere me: "In a world of endless head counts and starchy meals, financial wizard Dale Paul has adjusted to prison life by teaching the convicts financial skills, and they appreciate it."

And then the treachery of his final sentences: "Is there life after fraud?" *Fraud* — the word is my proof. Nugent believes I am guilty.

"Even though his work in prison won't make Dale Paul rich, it does make him a felon worth reckoning with — an unlikely crusader who is helping his fellow man."

Felon, indeed. There it is again: the taint of guilt. At least he was kind enough to say I was helping my fellow inmates, although I didn't set out to help others. Helping the scofflaws arose from my plan to help myself. Isn't that the way the world works? Everyone is self-interested, and nobody is more self-interested than I am.

25

MANY JOURNALISTS HAVE called the prison about Nugent's magazine piece, but the warden has forbidden me to call them back. He is angry with me for doing a media interview without his permission, so he has docked my swimming privileges. Then, out of the blue, a message arrives from a relative I've never heard of. Intrigued, I dial the number and say hello.

Don't send me any more letters, a wheezing voice says. I read about your dead pool in the *Times*.

I think for a moment. You are … Mickey Rooney?

Fuck, yeah. His voice cracks as if a winter storm has blown out his windpipe. Are you the infamous felon?

They say I am, but it's not true. We don't have time for me to go into what happened.

Geez, too bad. Is that stuff about c-coin true? Are you betting on my death?

It's a joke, good sir. You're going to outlive the others. In fact, I'm counting on it.

Yeah, well, your joke ain't so funny, Mr. Convict. People don't understand how crappy it is to be famous. What you're doing is nasty, okay? I mean, somebody like you oughta know better.

I'm not sure I do. Don't you have a sense of humour?

Maybe you don't remember who you're talking with here … He wheezes again and then comes a noise like a sigh. A lotta people have forgotten me, he says in his raspy voice. He sounds so sad I feel a twinge in my bad, old heart.

Before I can utter some reassuring words, the line goes dead. As I put down the phone, a cloudlet of dark and soggy thoughts floats into the space behind my eyes. *Somebody like you ought to know better.* Those were Mickey Rooney's words. Should I take him off the list? I run through several scenarios: Bailey and Derek will grouse about finding another celebrity to replace him, and the warden will dislike changes to the dead pool that might affect Trish Bales's study on my workshop.

Alas, Mickey Rooney doesn't understand that my own fame is news I have never fully absorbed; I have been too preoccupied with shutting out the vicious way others have blamed me for my success. Point being, I used to read the hateful letters and emails that Bip, my assistant, reluctantly showed me, so I am more sympathetic to the old thespian than he might think.

PART FOUR

TROUBLE

1

Dale Paul

Quote of the day from Mae West: *"Between two evils, I always pick the one I never tried before."*

— THE BULLETIN BOARD AT ESSEX FEDERAL
CORRECTION INSTITUTE, 2012

I'M AT THE lectern. Four hundred scofflaws look up at me like expectant schoolchildren. I blow out my cheeks, bring on the simpleton logic. What you are doing is no different than traders on the stock market, I tell my students. And the odds are ten to one for each celebrity. Or let me put it this way: if one celebrity has a ten percent chance of winning, then ten candidates (ten times ten) have a combined chance of winning of one hundred percent.

The men laugh and clap. After the round of applause subsides, I move on to Zsa Zsa Gabor, my sentimental favourite. When I was a boy, Mother was often mistaken for Zsa Zsa, I explain, but like Humpty-Dumpty, Zsa Zsa has had a bad fall. And at her age, a fall spells trouble. But, as you know, the handicaps of our celebrities go up and down like a junk bond. That's why you must read the reports that Derek posts on our prison website.

Yo, Big C, a scofflaw yells. (C is for c-coin. Everybody who is anybody here has a nickname.) The place rings again with enthusiastic noise. There is nothing I can do wrong, it seems. Nothing at all. C-coin is a hit. Think of a giant Mexican piñata filled to the brim. Think of a fiesta guest breaking the piñata open so our commissary receipts flutter down on the heads of the prisoners. Think of men tossing c-coin into the air like Uncle Scrooge in a Donald Duck comic book. That will give you some idea of the carnival atmosphere that c-coin has created.

Encouraged by the men's smiling faces, I move on to the law of supply and demand. It doesn't take long. The men understand the economic principle intuitively because our dorms are a hive of black-market activity — everything from liquor distilled out of candy to sessions of tattooing to bargaining for chicken patties stolen from the food warehouse to the selling of drugs and cigarettes — all these entrepreneurial schemes comprise the hundreds of small businesses going on right under the warden's nose.

Satisfied they've understood, I turn to the naughty derivatives that created the financial crisis in 2008. Now we're going to discuss option contracts, I tell the scofflaws. Obviously, you don't want your children to follow in your footsteps.

Good. The men look puzzled. Prefacing a tricky financial explanation with "obviously" eliminates awkward questions. Most people won't admit they don't understand what you've said.

So obviously, I continue, you and the mother of your child hope to pay no more than one hundred fifty thousand dollars for your child's food, housing, and education until the child is twenty-one. I have put that figure together for you after factoring in the statistics for the sex of your child, your socioeconomic background and family history, not to mention my projection of inflation and the first round of IQ and psychometric testing.

So obviously, I repeat. Obviously, you hope your child will be drug-free and without a criminal record when he or she turns twenty-one. So obviously, I have to charge you a premium of fifteen thousand. This modest sum may result in thousands of dollars for you later.

A bout of whispering and coughing breaks out. I glance around the room, looking severe, and the noise dies away.

I pick up my thread: I realize the sum of fifteen thousand could be a stretch for some of you, but let's imagine you have the funds, and by the time your child is twenty-one, he or she is healthy and crime-free. Obviously, our option contract has zero value, and you get no money back from me. But say your child has health problems and you have doled out more than one hundred and fifty thousand, or say he or she needed a lawyer to fight a drug charge. Obviously, that is going to cost you seventy thousand. So you are obliged to hire a second lawyer, who wants another seventy thousand to fight another drug charge ... Shall I fill in the dot-dot-dot?

The scofflaws dutifully shake their heads.

Okay, you get the picture. After paying for food, clothes, and legal fees, you have forked over more than one hundred and fifty K. Obviously, you're in luck because I must pay you the difference between the one hundred and fifty K and the huge sum you've been forced to spend on your child. Sound fair? Obviously, yes. I wait for them to give it up. Instead, raucous grumbles erupt from every corner of the room and I'm obliged to cut the workshop short.

They file out, looking relieved. It was too soon to get into the messy history of collateralized debt obligation. *Obviously.*

2

NOBODY COMES TO see me over the Christmas holidays. Meredith is too busy closing the sale on the house. In the chapel, the scofflaws lustily belt out "Hark the Herald Angels Sing" after receiving lame toiletries and two bags of chips. The scene is hopelessly maudlin: the men mouthing sentiments I deplore, the tawdry Christmas fir weighted down with ancient necklaces of yellow popcorn, the kernels shrunken and stained like the teeth of a corpse. Equally preposterous: the large sleigh hand-carved by the scofflaws and pulled by gauche-looking wooden reindeers.

On Boxing Day, Bailey and I are ordered to clean the C.O.s' washroom, an unpleasant task that requires face masks. Aldo is responsible for stocking our sanitary cart with bottles of cleaning agents, brushes, sponges, mops, industrial vinegar, giant rolls of cheap toilet paper, and the jugs of bleach that can burn a hole in your nostrils. Every so often, we stop our work and silently accept the supplies the woodhick hands us, doing our best to ignore the ill-mannered jests from the C.O.s who have dropped by to see me mop the bathroom floors. The washroom is filthy because the guards don't care about the mess they make.

Hey, the chomo missed something! Aldo points at the windows on the shower doors. Guess Bailey don see too good, huh? Aldo sniggers.

The light bad in here, bro. Bailey glares at Aldo through his oversized prison spectacles.

You mean you can't see, Four Eyes! Aldo shoots back. The C.O.s guffaw.

While Bailey sulks, I spray a huge circle of foam on the tiled wall. I drizzle in a face, adding an overhanging eyelid on one of the eyes. The resemblance to Aldo is striking. I pull down my face mask and bow. Look like anybody you know?

The C.O.s laugh again.

Don't fuck with me, Dale Paul, Aldo snarls. Or I'll get you sent to the hole.

Aldo wants to send *me* to solitary confinement! I contort my features in an ape-like grimace. An idle threat from a slack-jawed hominin!

The C.O.s laugh harder.

You cocksucker! Aldo cries. What did you call me?

I called you a hominin. It means human. Not to be confused with hominid, or ape. I begin to rinse the soap off the tiles, furtively moving the hose close to Aldo. Feigning a look of surprise, I pretend to lose my grip and douse him; the water from the hose makes a large, gratifying stain on the crotch of his pants.

He jes pissed hisself! Bailey chuckles.

Aldo's face crumples. To my astonishment, he looks as if he might cry, and I feel as if I've been caught tormenting a child.

You all fuckin shut yer mouths, Aldo yells. While the C.O.s applaud, he storms off, his face teary, his filthy track shoes splashing through the puddles.

3

I AM TEACHING Bailey English grammar in the computer studio.

With some encouragement from me, Bailey has dropped Uncle Remus for a video of Malcolm X, the dead Black Muslim spokesman. He is too young to know the civil rights leader, but he likes the idea of Malcolm X having been a convict, too. I press play and turn down the volume so other men won't hear Malcolm X's voice. In the video, the black leader is discussing his problems with a rival who has fathered children with teen-aged girls.

I nod as I press pause, and Bailey begins scribbling down what Malcolm X is saying: "I have no fear whatsoever of anybody or anything."

I press play again.

"If my followers go against my preaching, they are acting out of religious sincerity," Malcolm X adds. And on and on it goes: pressing play then stopping the machine so Bailey can write down the words. At the end of the tape, Bailey opens his notebook and shows me several neatly written pages of dialogue. In each paragraph, he's recorded what Malcolm X has said in faultless English.

B, I always could read some, he says when he sees my look of surprise. Member those postcards my daddy sent?

He is referring to the postcards from his father with bright, glossy images of Seattle, Washington, or Anchorage, Alaska. The message on each card was always the same: *Maybe one day you'll see this place, Marvin.* Or: *As soon as you're older, you'll come here too.* Bailey took each card as a paternal promise, a veritable oath.

Eventually, Bailey noticed all the postage stamps had been stamped in San Francisco, and his mother admitted that his father was incarcerated in Alcatraz so she had sent packages of postcards to his father and one by one he had mailed them back to Bailey.

I am moved by the tale of Bailey's father and his postcards. After all, I, too, hope to open my boy's mind to life's possibilities.

B, I kin read all the words on my daddy's cards now, Bailey crows.

Without warning, the clammy herald of unpleasant things creeps up my back. Anxiety isn't the only emotion that brings on tachycardia. Joy also sends blood pumping crazily through the antechambers of my bad, old heart. Then — wouldn't you know? — Aldo appears, afire with menace. He points at my bunkmate and draws a line across his throat.

You see that, B, Bailey whispers as Aldo saunters off. Aldo goin' git me.

Nonsense. The cretin is only trying to scare you.

4

THE NEXT AFTERNOON, I'm obliged to use the washroom kept open for Food Service workers. Nobody is there, but I sense a presence, and I stand as if frozen to the washroom floor. Through a haze of steam at the far end of the shower stalls, Bailey is dangling by his heels from a showerhead. His prison sweats are soaked through, and his sopping dreadlocks hang over his forehead like shrivelled bulrushes. A shudder passes through me.

I step cautiously into the shower room, hot steam assailing my face. To set Bailey free, I have to navigate the rest of the showerheads spewing scalding water.

Cut me down, B, Bailey yells. Quick, quick, I gon faint.

The faucet on the first tap singes my fingers. I grab a towel and use it to shut off the tap, closing my eyes to avoid the stinging mist. Somehow, I disengage two more faucets and then, *quelle surprise!* The water is tepid. I'm drenched from head to toe, and no harm has been done. I turn off the fifth tap easily and leave the rest.

I pull at the strips of prison T-shirt used to bind Bailey's ankles, blinking back the spray from the showerhead. The soaking cloth falls apart in my hands, and Bailey plunges downward. Panicking, he wraps his arms around my waist, causing me to stagger backwards on the slippery tiles.

Did Brer Fox get caught in a trap with Brer Rabbit? Aldo stands in the doorway, smirking.

Did you do this to Bailey, you skunk-faced vermin? My grip on Bailey's waist loosens, and he slips gently to the floor.

What the fuck did you say, Dale Paul? Aldo cries.

You heard me. You yellow-bellied miscreant. Now get out of here before I …

Before you what, Mr. Big Shot? You throwing a punch at me, asswipe?

Bailey lurches to his feet, his wet T-shirt flattened against his chest. Yo, we straight, Aldo. Nobody gon snitch.

You better watch it, you chomo, Aldo says. Next time, I'll toast Brer Rabbit good.

When I start after him, Bailey grabs my arm. You chill, B. Today was nuthin'.

He turns out his forearm, flattening it to expose the scar that runs from his palm up to his elbow. That muthafucka did this, okay? When we were muscle for a club in Jersey. They brung in Serb girls, an' Aldo kept this lit thirteen-year-old in his room so he could, you know. I tol' the manager. She was a happy lit thing before he started on her.

He accuses you of molesting children because you championed a thirteen-year-old? I didn't know Aldo was so cunning.

Man o' man, don get it twisted. Aldo so stupid he smart. And he be the eyes in Mr. Jack's head.

I laugh disbelievingly. Why didn't you tell me this before?

Don go stickin' your nose in bad places, B. It be bad for you. I gotta protect you because you got a big mouth. No point you knowin' bad things, is all. You too innocent.

Me, innocent? Nobody has accused me of that before.

5

LIKE THE COMPUTER studio, the hallway named Cat Alley faces the forest surrounding the prison. On sunny winter days it is a pleasant spot despite the hideous smell of cat urine.

Speaking softly, I call Riley's name, and a bundle of rough-looking marmalade fur emerges from the assembly of sleeping cats. He blinks his green eyes at me as he sniffs my scraps of overcooked chicken. Riley knows me well by now, but each time we meet he still takes his time making sure I'm not dangerous, which is clever, seeing as danger is something we humans do extremely well. Satisfied I am still the same old Dale Paul who always brings him a tasty tidbit, Riley gulps it down.

He's favouring his back leg, I call to John.

Riley got in a fight, John answers. He won't let anybody touch him. Toms, right-right?

As John and Martino watch, I move my hand cautiously down the cat's back and gently pry a large burr from the lumpy fur around the animal's hindquarters. The cat holds stock-still, his scabrous frame quivering.

It's all right, Riley. I won't hurt you, although it's clear some numbskull once did you appalling harm.

The cat rubs himself against my arm and scurries off.

Make them depend on you and they'll be loyal forever, right-right? John grins good-naturedly.

Loyal forever. Who is like that? Not Caroline, who rarely writes, or Meredith, who is too busy being lovey-dovey with Nugent. John misunderstands the nature of dependent people; when you aren't there, they find someone else to lean on.

I heard you have a beef with Aldo? he asks in his regular voice.

It is startling the way John turns his coarse gangster manner on and off, although I'm beginning to understand the scofflaws burnish their personas as regularly as Dieter once polished Pater's brass collection. Some of the men, like my friend and ally, consciously reference the thuggish roles they see on television. Point being, the scofflaws are unabashed image queens, acting out their personal destinies inside the frightening opacity of American prison life, a rugged existence that happens far away from the eyes of the public. They perform their parts with astonishing verve, like some of the famous people I used to know.

Those showers cut the hot water off after a minute, guy, he says. So forget about Aldo. He doesn't like blacks to ride in his car. That's all. But you're different. How come? You and Bailey close? He studies me curiously.

He's a colleague.

A colleague. That's a good one. Okay, I get it. Know what I say when the boys complain about you? Dale Paul has class so shut the fuck up! He beckons me closer. Look, guy, I get it about Aldo. He's not the brightest bulb. And he's a pussy too. Make a crack about his weight … and his eyes start to leak. Right, Marty?

Martino fixes me with his dullard's gaze. If a C.O. don't see Aldo do it, nobody gives a shit. You gotta let them work it out themselves.

I understand Martino to mean that we shouldn't interfere with the purity of Aldo and Bailey's native passions, the wild thrust and parry of their animal instincts. I am out of my depth. The world inside the BOP is light years apart from the unrelenting civility of the land I come from, that daunting muddle of lakes and mountains above the American border.

Okay, that's enough shit about Aldo, John says. Listen, guy. We've got problems with our dead pool. He flicks his eyes at Martino.

You told Martino about our bet?

We can talk in front of Marty. He's my first cousin.

The C.O. smiles sleepily. You guinea, I'm your second cousin.

See, guy? John punches my arm. Marty used to work for me. He took a job here when I got sent upriver. Now don't freak out. We need some muscle in Admin.

My mouth falls open. *Martino knows about the bet outside the prison.*

Hey, Dale Paul. Relax. Marty's one of us. He wears the Bitcoin insignia. Show him, Marty.

The C.O. extends his hand like a bride showing off her wedding ring. On one of his fingers, there's a gold signet ring with the Bitcoin design on the face of the band.

Give it to him, Marty. John nods at Martino, who hands it over.

See the inscription inside the band? That's the password to our Bitcoin account. Only Marty and me know it, and Marty won't snitch. Clearing his throat, John declaims: The greatest thing in life is never snitching on your friends.

Henry Hill in *Goodfellas*, I reply. The two greatest things in life are keeping your mouth shut and never ratting …

Okay, already. He throws me a deprecatory look. Marty's a miner … you know the guys I mean? The ones who record transactions on the blockchain? Every week he's going to bring you and me a statement from our Bitcoin account, so there's no funny business.

Glancing at Marty's ring with its incomprehensible list of numbers and letters, I deploy the grave, look-here voice I offer to dissatisfied clients. So what's the problem then?

The celebrities aren't dying fast enough. He looks gloomy. Players get frustrated and drop out. There are state lotteries now. They cut into business.

Yeah, Martino says. But those guys pay income tax on their winnings. Maybe we can help one of the celebrities to croak?

John laughs and opens his meaty hands, palms out. Shut your trap, Martino. No dumb jokes.

The good health of the deathbed ten is just bad luck, good sir.

Don't give me any shit about bad luck. You need to figure out a way to make it pay faster or I'm outta here. John is back in his gangter role, treating me to the same menacing register he uses on Aldo. I mutter something noncommittal; then, to my relief, the whistle blows. As we head off to our dorms for the head count, I find myself experiencing the bewilderment I feel after an argument with Caroline. Of course, John is a meta-riddle, a real gangster playing an actor playing a film gangster. It's much like the Shakespearean actress who played a man playing the stage role of a woman. But one way or another, I need to get him back on side.

6

LO AND BEHOLD, a few weeks later, John Giaccone, Trish Bales, the government shrink, and I are riding to the maximum-security compound in one of the prison vans. Martino sits behind the wheel. He helped me make the case to Nathan Rickard, and our warden has talked to his counterpart, and now here we are, speeding along the service road, which slopes uphill slightly, offering, with every twist and turn, an unending view of the round, snow-covered hills. From this height the forest exudes a menacing ambience; it could be a game preserve, where big game hunters track John and me down like wild animals.

As we bump along in the prison van, Ms. Bales offers us her pack of Kools. John takes a cigarette. When I refuse, she smiles apologetically, exposing her unfortunate teeth. I have the warden's permission, don't I, Martino? she asks. The C.O. shrugs as he opens the window, and for a moment, I see the glint of the Bitcoin insignia on his ring.

You know, I can't figure you two out, she says, flicking her ash into the old coffee cup that Martino has passed to her. I wouldn't have pegged you for friends.

John's eyes fly open above the half-moon pouches on his cheeks. You saying I'm a loser? he asks churlishly. She looks at him aghast.

Don't lie to me, girl. You think I'm a loser. And maybe you think I'm funny too. But funny how? Funny like a clown?

No, no, she replies in a frightened voice. I mean, your backgrounds are different. That's all.

Yeah, different. He wiggles his tufted eyebrows at me. Hey, do you think Trish is old enough to remember Letterman asking Joe Pesci if he's funny?

Alarmed, I shake my head.

Sure she is, pal. You know how Pesci answers? He says Letterman has a funny face. Letterman's the guy that's funny ha ha, right-right? See, he breaks Letterman's balls! Okay, I get it, little lady. He winks at her. You have a hard-on for me, don't you, Trish?

She turns a mottled shade of pink, and for the rest of the drive we sit in an awkward silence while John puffs away, looking contented. I pull out my notepad and begin to doodle, my mind buzzing with anxious thoughts. Will the criminals in maximum security listen to my talk about financials? I have my doubts, although I haven't said anything to John.

We pass through the same stands of birch and white pine that bracket our own prison. Some C.O.s are walking German shepherds between fences made of concertina wire. At the guardhouse, Martino tells a C.O. that I am giving a talk on money skills and he waves us through. A few minutes later, the warden marches through a tall stone archway to greet us, and it is clear from his massive shoulders and small, cruel eyes that Joel M. Cody is a far less amiable creature than Nathan Rickard. After shaking our hands, he leads us down a forbidding hallway with four sets of double doors. The cascading set of inner rooms and hallways evokes the claustrophobia of a submarine, where the hatches are designed to stop the water from flowing in, although the design works the other way around here: it keeps the population of felons from getting out.

At last we come to a cafeteria, where ten C.O.s and six scofflaws sit glumly waiting. The sight evokes the old show business proverb about stopping the performance if there are more actors on stage than audience members.

I glance at Cody for reassurance, and he nods his hideous bald head. Note to self: *Drama depends on stagecraft so play your part. Your life may depend on it.*

Some people think betting on the health of old or frail celebrities is in bad taste, I begin. However, death is a wasteful business, aside from the fortunes that undertakers have made for centuries. I wait for the laugh. Silence, absolute and total. I blow out my cheeks, start again: The answer to all problems is monetize, monetize, monetize.

Another leaden silence. I have miscalculated. Their leering faces suggest that for them death provides a healthy revenue source. I try again: Say you have five dollars to your name and need to buy some peaches. Three baskets are on sale at three prices: six dollars, five dollars, and four dollars and fifty cents. What happens if you buy the five-dollar basket?

In the front row, a prisoner the age of my son doubles over in a fit of bilious coughing.

The six-dollar basket of delicious peaches costs too much. But the peaches selling for four-fifty are of poor quality. However, if you buy the five-dollar basket, you don't have money left over. So what do you do? I ask the cougher.

He glances up at me with panic-stricken eyes and then down at his battered sneakers as if the answer lies there.

You have to wait, I explain. The next day the basket of six-dollar peaches is all that's left, so you can buy these succulent beauties for four-fifty and still have fifty cents left over. That's how c-coin works. You trade to get the best deal. Any questions?

Nary a one. In the seat next to me, Ms. Bales sits writing in her notebook, pretending she doesn't see the evil sidelong glances from the scofflaws. She is likely thinking the same thing I am: When can I get out of this frightful place?

It is all over in twenty minutes. One of the oversized C.O.s blows a whistle and the six men are hustled out of the cafeteria, shuffling their feet. I have never seen such a miserable bunch of ne'er-do-wells.

I expected more players, I hiss.

It is what it is, John growls.

It is what it is. A useless phrase. Provincials deploy it when they're trying to sound wise, but it can mean anything. *That you need to be careful of over-thinking. Or that you need to accept your circumstances, as in, "It will be what it is."* Never mind. I put on a good face, but neither John nor I are surprised when my workshop at maximum-security is cancelled for lack of interest.

7

WE HAVE NO chance now of expanding our dead pool to a second prison. Worse, we are in the midst of a celebrity drought and there is nothing to be done except wait it out. In a phone conversation with Nugent, I explain the problem.

Let me get this straight, Nugent says. You have a bet with real money going on outside the prison. That's in addition to the bet for coffee in your workshop?

That is correct, and our bet outside the prison is going well. The prisoners tell their families who to bet on, and John's runners collect five dollars every two weeks from his customers.

Does the gangster have other customers, Nugent asks.

He has over nine hundred clients, maybe more, and their money goes into our Bitcoin account. It's a genius stroke.

Ah. So there are really three bets. You are betting that Bitcoin will increase in value?

Precisely. But John says the celebrities are taking too long to die. He is accustomed to the numbers racket, where his customers bet on a random group of numbers, like the published daily balance of the United States Treasury.

You need to get out of your dead pool, Dale Paul, Nugent exclaims. You're doing business with a gangster. What if something goes wrong?

Nugent, I've been dealing with gangsters all my life — they happen to run the financial markets.

They aren't the same!

They are to me, I reply, but by then he is no longer listening. Never mind. Nugent was always a scaredy-cat. John may be frustrated with the healthy celebrities in our dead pool, but by and large I am pleased at how things are unfolding. I admire the gangster's set-up — his runners collecting the fees from his customers and bringing the money to the bookies at John's policy banks in New Jersey; customers dropping in on the bookies to collect our latest bulletins about the well being of our celebrities or requesting updates by email.

All businesses operate on faith or the stock market would collapse; my partnership with John is no different. What's more, I know he isn't cheating me out of my share because every week Martino shows me a printout of a document that resembles an online banking statement. The statement never fails to pitch us about buying more Bitcoin, and well it should because Bitcoin's value has been rising steadily since I've been in prison. One coin used to be worth twelve dollars and fifty cents. Now it's one hundred dollars a coin. The jump in its value has made John impatient, and he never misses the chance to grouse about the length of time our bet is taking to cash out.

Maybe you're losing your nerve? How do guys like you put it? You get risk averse, like scared girls. We've got to make the bet go faster, Dale Paul.

I nod and smile as if I agree, and he gives up and changes the subject. You get the gist.

8

OPEN YOUR MOUTHS, you fuck-heads, Derek says as we lie prone. Stick out your tongues and roar like a lion.

John and I compete to see who can make the loudest bellow.

I win.

Before our exuberant roaring, there is cross-legged sitting with several long minutes of intentional breathing, exhaling and inhaling through nostrils that are repeatedly covered and uncovered, and all the while my eyes remain firmly closed in case I see the lights flickering near the other men. Once or twice I glimpsed a dull glow around Derek's head, although I haven't mentioned it to him. Nor shall I. I admit to a superstitious feeling that speaking about the experience will open a portal into a disagreeable dimension. So I say nothing, and Derek, good man, never asks if I've seen the lights again.

This morning, Derek and John and I set off to the sauna for a redemptive blast of steam. Aldo must be in the washroom, or possibly the lout is gorging on stolen Doritos back in his dorm.

We are sitting together, chatting amiably, a trio of glistening wet Buddhas on the wooden benches; then John throws too much water on the rocks, and he and Derek rush out laughing, leaving me alone. Billowing grey clouds roll my way, obscuring the tiled walls. Is my imagination playing a trick, or does a door open? I hold my breath and listen, but all I hear is the hissing steam. Is anyone here? I call. If someone *were* there, they would laugh uproariously.

From the far corner of the sauna comes the creak of footsteps on the moist floorboards; then a hair-covered body emerges out of the scalding mist and a long arm stretches toward me, a thingamajig grasped in its thick-knuckled hand. When the arm disappears upwards into the hot, roiling clouds, I suddenly understand.

9

I LIE ON a cot in the prison infirmary, a thick surgical bandage covering the wound at the back of my skull. Bailey and Derek are by my bed, expressions of consternation and alarm on their faces. What trustworthy comrades! To comfort me, Bailey has brought a can of iced tea from the commissary, while Derek gave me a sketchbook he pinched from the supply warehouse. Derek and Bailey think my assailant used a tube sock stuffed with gym locks. It seems the cretin exchanged five Zsa Zsa Gabors for six of my Stephen Hawkings, which I had left in the pocket of my browns.

To comfort myself, I spend my afternoons drawing. Although it is generally dismissed as frivolous fare, there is a great deal to be said for doodling. You make a mark on the paper, and you respond to that mark. Yes, you make a mark and you exclaim: How dandy! I was the one who did that! And after a while you begin to think that nobody else can do it the way you do and you fall into a swoon over what you have done. And sooner or later, when you have drawn enough, you become the master of your doodle the way a factory worker gets the hang of screwing on a bolt.

10

WHAT HAS MEREDITH done? She has cut off her braids and dyed what is left of her grey hair an unsightly aubergine. She has also lost weight, albeit not a great deal of poundage, but enough that the counterpoise of her small, feminine head with the broad frame of her body looks more in balance, as if she has been redacted to the tall, big-boned girl I knew growing up.

She stares in horror at the surgical bandage I am sporting. You've hurt yourself!

Someone mugged me in the sauna. I pause. For five bags of Starbucks coffee.

They attacked you over coffee beans? She looks incredulous.

In here, good coffee is rarer than cocaine.

How odd. Are you sure you didn't do something to upset them? Now that Googie is gone, it seems you are guilty in the Paul family until proven innocent. No dollops of grease for the squeaky wheel, in other words. The noise of the squeaking wheel sets them agin' you.

I affect my best jocular smile and kiss her cheek. You look different. Where are your glasses?

She waves me away. I use contacts now. And you and I have important family business to discuss.

Her ominous tone suggests I should be awash with remorse, and yet I have no reaction. How I wish I could feel something beyond the pressure of her wishing I would.

With a sigh, I bring out my pen and start doodling. I'm not thinking about composition; I'm simply following where the pen is leading me. It is enormously satisfying to create logic out of randomness, to follow up on the possibilities the first doodle offers you. Doodling is pattern making, after all, and pattern making is how thinking works; you feel a sharp, ecstatic jolt when you come up with a new motif.

Point being, when you blacken a page, you are learning how to work with paper, whether it's the smooth sort used in a printer or a material like rice paper that deteriorates over time. At first, the paper is inert and inflexible, and what's more, it doesn't speak, and then *voilà*! You give it a voice. Indeed, you are fashioning something out of an inanimate material … and that makes you a sorcerer who works beyond the bounds of logic.

Meredith's voice breaks my concentration: Why are you drawing? Please put down your pen and listen!

I explain that I listen better if my hand is busy, but nevertheless I set down the pen. Satisfied she has my attention, she pulls out a piece of typed paper and dons a pair of bifocals that match the colour of her zany hair.

Dear Dale Paul, she says, reading. Last week Malcolm told me there is no money left in Googie's trust fund. For a few days, I despaired. This is the first time you have deliberately hurt your own family members. I tried to understand the reason for your behaviour, so I looked at an old YouTube clip in which you discussed your rules for making money. *Number one: Take action. Number two: Learn to sell — selling is a transfer of emotion …*

I had to shut down my computer because I couldn't listen to your lies.

You mustn't jump to conclusions, Meredith.

Not so fast! I wrote down what I have to say so you can't con me.

When I protest, she shakes her head and continues her cousinly obloquy:

I used to think you were a better person than the man the public saw in the news. And when you were charged with fraud, I felt if I could understand what was stopping you from being honest and fair, I could help you learn to be less selfish. I'm a teacher, after all, so I'm inclined to keep reaching for knowledge, even if it means I get hurt in the end.

I'm inclined to keep reaching for knowledge, even if it means I get hurt in the end ... The ease with which my cousin is able to describe her feelings puts me at a disadvantage. My own emotions are not always available to me.

Well, do you have anything to say for yourself? Meredith asks.

I showed you the photographs of my retirement community in North Carolina ... the unfinished streets, the fire hydrants and gravel side roads sitting idle and unused ...

She looks puzzled.

I told you I needed funds for this development, and I didn't hear you say no when I said I was going to borrow from the trust. Did you? Admit it.

She gives me the stink eye and picks up where she left off:

I have absolutely no idea how you could spend all of Googie's money on business projects. Malcolm de Vries claims you had the right to do so because my aunt had given you power of attorney over her property. He says this document meant you were effectively Googie, and any purchases you made in her name were legal, so there is nothing, absolutely nothing, we can do to reclaim that money. How could you have been so reckless?

She frowns as more puddles appear on my piece of paper. Depending on your point of view, puddles are material in perfect repose. Or mass with potential. Today, my pen is making one otiose blob-like shape after another.

Puzzled, I add some dots to see if that improves matters. Hmm ... not so much, so I draw a few more blobs, a variation on the theme.

All right. Have it your way. Meredith regards me over the tops of her bifocals. Let's hear your excuse.

I realize you were counting on getting money from Mother, but I'm working on something that will bring in cash. I can't talk about it right now.

You can't talk about it right now … Of course you can't. Because you're probably up to no good. Do you remember telling me the money from the family trust would be my retirement pension?

Well, I thought … I hoped that was the case. Look, I'll make the money back because I care about you. My childhood would have been lonely without you, Meredith.

Her good eye softens. Now that she is without her unflattering glasses, I can see her other eye, the fake eye, clearly.

Good old Kis. You *are* my ally, aren't you?

Well, you were so fond of me you ran through all the money that Uncle Joe set aside for my old age. Were you too cowardly to tell me what you had done? Or maybe you just don't care. You don't seem to suffer, Dale Paul, but everyone around you does. We pay your price.

Oh, I think I am paying the price now.

Are you? I wish that were true. Nothing gets through that thick skull of yours. She stuffs her nasty letter back in her purse. Do you remember the way you acted when Earl assaulted me?

I feel myself stiffen. Kis, why bring that up?

See, there you go denying things! When Earl tried to rape me, you said it wasn't important.

Her po-faced air takes me back to our childhood — my cousin has always put on a sad expression when she wants me to agree with her. Fine. If only I could. But I've been down that route before — surrendering my will for a set of false promises to satisfy my cousin's notion of how men ought to behave. Before she can make further accusations, I tell her I need to visit the washroom and walk quickly away, the shoddy parquet floor dipping slightly under the weight of my footsteps.

11

WHEN I RETURN to the visitors' lounge, Meredith is weeping into a tissue. I well up. Doesn't she know how much it hurts me to see the childish pout on her lips, the depressing way her broad shoulders slump? Perhaps I have gone off on the wrong tangent. We should be talking about how I'm going to provide the family with the money I have lost. Point being, I need to reassure her that things will turn out well.

I sit down beside her and start over. Meredith, I disapproved of Earl's behaviour that night. You know I did.

She puts away her Kleenex and makes her fussy *tock-tock* noise with her tongue. Oh, don't pretend to be concerned. You don't care what happened to me. You are indifferent to other people.

Kis, I always want the best for you.

She laughs a harsh little laugh. You make me think of something I read once. Never trust a man whose first name could be his last.

That's not funny, Meredith. Tell me. Have you seen Davie? I'd rather he didn't know about the trust.

Davie is dead.

I know otherwise.

She gives me a disbelieving look. Please, Dale Paul, not that again.

All right. I make an attempt to smile. How is Nugent? Are you still helping him with his research?

Tim and I have been seeing each other. She starts putting on her coat.

You're not leaving, are you?

She nods yes.

I see. Then please congratulate Nugent. He always wanted to know what you were like in the sack.

If you cause us any more problems, I will never speak to you again.

Hand on heart. I won't let you down.

Oh, go fuck yourself, she says and hurries for the door.

12

Tim Nugent

THE LIGHTS WENT off hours before in the skyscrapers near Tim's building, but Tim is still at his desk, making notes on Meredith's account of her visit with Dale Paul. Imagine having the gall to doodle while your cousin tells you the bad news about the family trust! He was there when the lawyer told Meredith the money was gone, and the sight of her face tore at his insides. He might as well admit it: he has started to loathe Dale Paul. The lies — the lies are constant. It was Dale Paul, not Tim, who stepped on Meredith's crinoline at the dance. Dale Paul did it because he was in a bad mood and he wanted to make sure someone else felt miserable too.

Dale Paul's dismissal of Earl's assault on Meredith takes the cake.

It happened years ago on a Canadian Thanksgiving. Tim and Earl had gone home with Dale Paul for the holiday. The Pauls lived then in a comfortable stone mansion a few blocks from the boarding school, and Dale Paul had his own apartment inside the house; it was a bedroom suite that had been built for the previous owner's invalid father, and Mrs. Paul had installed brand new Danish furniture for her son along with a full set of beer glasses, a dishwasher, and a Coca-Cola machine.

Meredith slept next door to Dale Paul in a cramped bedroom that had once belonged to a servant. She jokingly referred to it as The Garret; the wall by the door sloped halfway down so you were obliged to stoop to look out its tiny window. That weekend, Tim had slept in the bedroom next to hers.

The Thanksgiving meal started off badly. Tim had watched in shock as Earl jabbed Irene's roast turkey with his oyster fork.

For god's sake, young man, Mr. Paul cried. Were you born in a barn?

Earl exchanged baffled glances with his friends. He had used his hands to slurp down the oysters, so the oyster fork was the first implement he saw by his place setting.

Dale Paul handed Earl a proper dining fork. This will work better, Tim remembered Dale Paul saying.

Okay, I thought maybe Canadians used miniature cutlery, Earl said, colouring up. They do in some countries, right?

Golly, how backwards do you think we are? Meredith giggled.

After that, there were no more gaffes by Earl. Dieter poured them all glasses of Portuguese rosé and they made short work of Irene's turkey and pumpkin pie with hand-whipped cream. When they finished, Mr. Paul rose to his feet and hit his water glass with his spoon. It made a surprisingly loud tinkling sound.

"My flesh is clothed with worms and dirt; my skin hardens, then breaks out again." Mr. Paul's voice sounded soggy with Scotch.

Meredith looked embarrassed, while Tim and Earl stared up at Mr. Paul in slack-jawed wonder.

Job, chapter two, verse twenty-eight, Dale Paul responded.

Life is a tale …

A sorry tale of pain and suffering, Dale Paul answered.

Vallis lacrimarum, Mr. Paul prompted.

Life is a vale of tears. Psalm 84:6 refers to the valley of Bacca where rain filled the pools.

Thank you, son. You often get what you want.

But it comes with a twist, Dale Paul replied. Pater, of all your bromides about suffering, I dislike this one the most. The twist reminds me of the dismal ending in a Grimm fairy tale.

Mr. Paul snorted. When you grow up, son, you will discover the truth of what I'm saying. And look here! He pointed at Earl, who was pouring himself another glass of the rosé. One of our young buckaroos is drinking us out of house and home! Good sir, will you put down that glass and listen to your elder?

Dale Paul reassured his father that Earl had absorbed every word, and Earl made a sideways movement of his head suggesting agreement. Soon afterwards, the teenagers fled to Dale Paul's apartment, where they smoked a pack of Players that Dale Paul had stolen from his father.

Several times, Tim caught Meredith laughing at something Earl said. She seemed to be enjoying Earl's attention. Tim excused himself and said good night.

Later, he was awakened by the sound of something large and heavy crashing against his bedroom wall. Alarmed, he threw on his bathrobe and rushed to wake Dale Paul. When they opened Meredith's door, the party dress she had worn earlier was lying on the floor, and for the first time Tim saw her panties and snow-white bra whose cups had been memorably sprinkled with Shasta daisies. Her dark braids hung in dishevelled strands down her shoulders. She appeared to be panting.

A look of relief swept across Meredith's face when she saw them. She shoved Earl with all her might, and he half fell to the floor. He let out an outraged howl, and, grabbing her by the shoulders, he threw her against the wall — so that was the cause of the strange noise.

As Dale Paul and Tim stood, too shocked to move, Mr. Paul marched in. He seized Earl by the ear and led Earl out into the hall. Before shutting the door, he yelled at Meredith: Don't stand there cringing! Cover yourself up. Didn't I tell you not to invite boys to your bedroom?

Meredith began to cry, and her tears seemed to make Mr. Paul angrier. Goddamnit, Meredith. Get ahold of yourself. None of this would have happened if you had acted more ladylike.

The next morning, Mr. Paul talked Meredith out of going to the police.

You don't want to make a fuss, do you? he asked in a scolding tone. People will think you're unhinged.

As if that wasn't bad enough, Earl said he wasn't sorry about what happened because Meredith was only Dale Paul's cousin.

It had been a cruel thing to say. Meredith longed for the Pauls to think of her as one of the family.

13

Dale Paul

MEREDITH'S QUESTION ABOUT my attack in the sauna haunts me. *Did I do something to set someone off?* What if she has put her finger on the truth? What if somebody somewhere in the bowels of this dreadful place wishes me harm?

To avoid encountering my assailant again, I no longer take a sauna with the others. And sometimes I wonder if Derek and John left me alone that morning on purpose. Yet surely Derek wouldn't do something so underhanded. What possible reason could he have for betraying me?

Perhaps my imagination is working overtime, but someone followed me from the pool to my dorm late yesterday afternoon when the shadows were growing long between the buildings. Curious to discover the identity of my stalker, I waited behind the industrial garbage bins near the kitchen. A few minutes later a large man wearing a hoodie and gym pants walked my way, twisting around as if he was looking to see where I had gone. I stepped out of my hiding place, and he fled.

I swear I recognized the back of the dullard's head; but, if it was Martino, he had vanished by the time I reached the admin building. There was no one around except for the C.O. at the main gate.

I stood for a moment, listening to the light March wind stirring the boughs of the pines. The grass in front of the admin building was still winter brown, but here and there, some yellow crocuses had sprouted, although soon enough the scofflaws will trample them down.

Suddenly, a furry orange shape came barrelling toward me.

I bent down and patted his fuzzy head. Fixing me with his round green eyes, he licked my hand with his sandpaper tongue. Riley, my boy! I exclaimed. What will become of us?

PART FIVE

DEATHWATCH

1

Tim Nugent

MY APOLOGIES FOR being out of touch, Alexis writes Tim in an email. I'm sorry it hasn't been easy working with Dale Paul.

Under the terms of the contract you signed with us, the author has total discretion regarding the contents of the book, its copyright, and its disposition. As a ghost, you are bringing your craft to the table, not your ego. However, there is an escape hatch. The clause in your contract gives you the right to withdraw your name from the cover if you're unhappy with it. In fact, publishers prefer one name with the title. None of that "as told to" business to confuse the reader! Of course, I hope that doesn't happen in your case.

Tim smiles at the emoticon she uses to sign off: Alexis :). If only she knew what hard work the book has turned out to be! He's too proud to tell her. Not yet, anyhow. He will let it go a few more weeks.

What he has been dealing with is something unexpected: Dale Paul is convinced a prisoner wants to kill him. Tim has weighed the possibilities without coming to a conclusion. There's no doubt that Dale Paul antagonizes people, and his old friend hasn't been behind bars long enough to be aware of all the inmate protocols. Or maybe Dale Paul knows and doesn't think their rules apply to him.

Tim has read about murders in prison, although these crimes usually happen in maximum security, so the best solution is to wait and see. However, Dale Paul's paranoia has left Tim unsettled. His old friend recently smuggled out two letters to Tim rather than trust the prison's internal email system. That tells him something.

2

Dale Paul

Monday, April 29, 2013

Dear Tim:

*I am well aware this may sound melodramatic, but every morning
I awake to the horrifying thought: someone wants me dead. I no longer
rush through my duties with the same zesty élan, exhibiting the combination of persistence and mental acuity that compels the scofflaws
to sit up and listen. And the situation with the dead celebrities bet
depresses me too. It's been over six months, and not one of our deathbed ten has gone to eternal rest.*

*One small victory — my doodles have become freer. My aim is
always to achieve the cartoony look of a comic book, but these days I
feel less constrained by rules. In short, I have discovered the un-mined
joys of the amateur, a role that imbues those of us who doodle with
hidden power. Into my sketches go all my old familiar executive pleasures, like the satisfaction that comes with problem solving. What's
more, I'm under no obligation to charm sloth heads like Ted Rigby and
his military troika. No more second-guessing how I'm going over when
I'm making my pitch.*

*Recently, I've started making magician's handkerchiefs, and on some
of these drawings I write arcane messages, the meanings known only
to me. Thoughts on how logic drifts to the place where it is no longer
logic. Secret, private thoughts that remind me of the daydreaming
I used to do as a boy. And hand on heart, gratitude overwhelms me*

when I think of people like Derek taking the time to view my drawings and say they like what they see. Derek is particularly fond of the sheep with halos.

He often asks what the images mean, but there is no obvious rhyme or reason to the doodles, and that's what I like about them.

Alas, my stalker has taken to following me down the ancient staircase outside our dorm. The stairs are leftovers from the days when this part of the prison was a sanitarium. The door to the stairs is kept locked because the stairs are unsafe, but it's easy enough to unhook the latches on a screen window overlooking the landing, and that is what we do in warm weather when we we're in a hurry to get to Chow Hall. Last week, when I took the shortcut, someone's long shadow on the stairs behind me seemed to merge with mine before separating again. Perhaps it was a trick of the light, but I hurried down the steps as fast as I could.

And now I always take that route in the hopes of catching him. The stairs are wooden and rickety, and I do my best to hold tightly to the railing, also wooden and also rickety. The slant of the late-afternoon sun through the pines creates frightening patterns around four o'clock, the time of day when the cold mountain air stings your cheek.

It's then that I glimpse the shadow of my follower on the steps behind me, and my bad, old heart begins beating crazily. It is all I can do to stop myself from toppling over in a faint. I don't turn around. Instead, I rush to the bottom before my follower has the chance to exercise his nefarious purpose and throw me over the railing.

I know what you're thinking. So why use those stairs? There are other ways to the Chow Hall. All right. Here is the answer. I am determined to find out who is following me. But each time I am possessed by a wild fear that turning around is exactly what he wants, and that if I stop long enough to see him, he will strike me dead with the lethal tube sock he used in the sauna.

Of course, it is absurd to choose to go down the stairs and then not to turn around and face whoever it is behind me, and each afternoon when I climb through the window onto the stairs, I think, This time you will catch him, Dale Paul! Yes, this time you will stop and see who it is and dare them to strike you. Yet that isn't what I do. My courage fails at the very moment I need to be brave, and I flee down the last wooden steps as if the hounds of hell are pursuing me. It would be mortifying if it weren't so preposterous.

Derek, my bunkmate, laughed when I told him about my stalker.

Even paranoids have enemies, mate, he said. But that sounds loony-tunes.

I suppose Derek is right, although I know what I saw with my own eyes.

Yours,
Dale Paul

Wednesday, May 7, 2013

Dear Tim:

My lawyer, Malcolm de Vries, has gone AWOL, so thank you for investigating the possibility of a transfer to another prison. I would prefer Butner, where the Ponzi King is locked up. Or Otisville or even Morgantown, which Derek says is fairly decent. As a last resort you could try Pensacola, an old and ugly prison where the prisoners work at low-paying government jobs on a nearby naval base. Butner doesn't offer government jobs like Pensacola. Or the cushy perks of a prison like the Milton Hilton in New Zealand, which supplies everything from rugby fields to heated floors in the winter months. As we used to say at school, beggars can't be choosers, and I will be grateful for anything you can do.

In fact, knowing you are looking into a transfer has been extremely calming. Derek and his yoga sessions are helpful too. He and I have been spending a great deal of time together, hashing over problems with the deathbed ten.

When the singer Richie Havens died of a heart attack last month, my friend Mr. Jack (the gangster) berated me for leaving Havens off our dead pool until Derek had to tell John to stop.

Few of the younger men remember Richie Havens. Nevertheless, "Here Comes the Sun" boomed out of radios in some of the dorms, and a group of older prisoners lit votive candles on the quad. Then they traipsed back inside and traded c-coin like there was no tomorrow.

Now Zsa Zsa Gabor has been suffering respiratory problems. In his latest bulletin on the health of the deathbed ten, Derek noted that she is experiencing the type of heart congestion that only women get. Despite our need for a celebrity death, the news made my spirits sink.

Zsa Zsa possesses the same cat-like eyes as Googie, and I associate her with more innocent times, when I spied on Mother at her makeup table applying her crimson lipstick and gooey mascara. Tilting her head this way or that, she would blot her moist red mouth with Kleenex. Then, administering a quick pat to her blond curls, she would spring to her feet and swish out the door, making it clear to us that her real lover was the heavenly reflection she saw in the mirror.

Tim, I have written the aging actress a letter and sent it off to her agent. (I fear what my interest in her suggests about my psychological state.)

These days, she is rarely seen outside her Los Angeles home. Derek has heard gossip that her younger husband, Frédéric Prinz von Ahalt, is abusing her. I wrote how distressed I felt to learn of her marital troubles and begged her to look after herself.

Not long afterwards a note arrived with a copy of her last memoir, One Lifetime Is Not Enough.

Dear Dale Paul:

You are a darling to write an older actress like me. Frédéric is a difficult man but the report in the Hollywood Reporter *was wildly exaggerated. We are the epitome of conjugal bliss.*

Yours, Zsa Zsa

In the Chow Hall lineup, I was thinking about Zsa Zsa and her health troubles when someone rudely sucked his teeth in my ear. Who else but Aldo is capable of singing a do-re-mi of human spittle?

Hey, man! Zsa Zsa Gabor is fucked. Aldo winked at me with his drooping eye. Somehow, he has found out that I am a fan of the Hungarian actress.

The husband must be glad, yeah? No more poking that dried-up old pussy. He jabbed me with his elbow.

I, too, have sometimes wondered about Zsa Zsa's sex life. In their wedding photograph, she wears a pink brocade dress and a matching pink bow has been strategically placed in her munificent blond curls. The groom stands behind Zsa Zsa's chair, his large, muscled hands resting chastely on the chair's back, a hair's breadth from her aged body. Possibly, Frédéric possesses the ardent inventiveness of Casanova, who made love to an aged countess while a fetching young prostitute exposed herself behind the bedroom curtain.

I had no intention of giving Aldo the satisfaction of sharing his concern. I turned my back on him and walked over to the cafeteria tables, where the men sat chattering in excited voices, all the while trading furiously to get rid of c-coin with her name. They haven't seen her in the sly satirical gem Won Ton Ton: The Dog Who Saved Hollywood. *Nor did they watch her remarkable star turn in* The Beverly Hillbillies *film.*

Well, that is my news for now, Tim. Waiting eagerly to hear how you fare on getting me out of here.

3

NUGENT IS WAITING for me in the visitors' lounge. He tells me he has heard from the admin at Butner and they have refused to accept my transfer to their prison. Before I can protest, he gives me an old novel about the murder of a girl in the Adirondacks, although I have no interest in reading such a depressing tome, especially one recommended by him. Now, with a little smile, Nugent directs my gaze to a table where a young man in a blue beret sits reading. How did this happen? Am I seeing a mirage? I try the usual clichéd ploys, pinching myself and rubbing my eyes, and there is not a scintilla of doubt. *Davie. Here in the flesh.* It feels for all the world as if I've come back from the dead, although it is Davie who has undergone resurrection. I lurch to where he sits, my bad, old heart beating in double time.

My god! I cry, welling up.

Hey, you're crying, he said. I don't believe it.

Do you think I'm inhuman, son?

He makes a downward patting motion with his hand. Not so loud. My name is Asher Shapiro. Ash for short, okay? I told the warden I'm your nephew.

I should wring your neck! But I'm too relieved. Do you understand how sad I've been. How sad we have all been.

I get that, but, hey, I had to take charge of my situation. Meredith agreed.

Meredith knows you're alive? I ask, feeling uneasy.

Yes. Meredith and Tim are pretty happy about it. An old friend of Meredith's ran into me in France. It was pretty rad. Anyway, when Meredith heard where I was, she persuaded me to come home, and she told me I had to come here and tell you myself.

Thank god! I exclaim. *And thank god she has kept her mouth shut about the trust.*

Mom says you're teaching the men in here about money? She was impressed.

Esther knows you're alive too?

Yup. He takes off his beret and rubs his scalp, and for the first time I notice the way his blond hair is receding from his forehead. *My young son is starting to go bald.* I take an anxious breath. Davie … The look on his face stops me.

It's Ash, okay? You can call me by my real name when nobody is around.

Okay, Ash, I had some problems with what Nugent wrote in the *New York Times Magazine.* He insinuated I was guilty.

And you don't think you are? He regards me with Esther's unfathomable blue eyes.

Of course not. I am a victim of prosecutorial zeal.

I don't know. We're all guilty of something, aren't we? he says gravely. I mean, is being guilty so bad?

I'm sorry I cannot do a better job of explaining the delicate equation I carry around in my head. I have my own personal scale of justice, and it balances what I did with what other people think I should have done. Are you with me?

No, I don't get it. Didn't you realize what your fraud did to us? How could you be so cruel? His face turns dark and threatening, as if he wants to strike me. Then he composes himself. Let's talk about it another time, okay? Because there's something you should know. Surf Song's been sold, and Janie Tablow, the real estate lady, said I could stay there until the new owner takes possession.

You're at our beach house on Paradise Island?

Janie said I could live in one of the staff cabins if I did some work on the grounds. Maybe it's a dumb idea. But Janie is cool with it, and Caroline's brother is down the beach so I have company. Anyway, I found some textbooks under one of the beds. They're yours, right?

I read those books years ago, when Pater wanted me to be an academic.

I think back. To please my father, I studied Schopenhauer (gloomy but convincing), Hegel (a thinker with an unforgettable idea), Toynbee (rolling waves of magisterial thought), and Marx (well, enough said). But I liked the course in European literature best.

I can see you as a prof, Davie says. The way you talk. The florid expressions … He pauses when he sees the look on my face. He wrote the word *florid* in his note asking me to stop phoning him.

Hey, sorry, he says softly. I wonder if you remember this novel? He holds up the book he's been reading, and I recognize my edition of *The Great Gatsby*. There's a lot of underlining, like somebody thought the story was killer.

Davie and his hipster jargon. I clear my throat self-consciously. I have always admired Gatsby. How did Fitzgerald describe him? There was something gorgeous about Gatsby, some heightened sensitivity to the promises of life.

Yeah, I can see that. You admiring Gatsby, I mean. What about Roquentin in *Nausea* by Sartre? I'm reading that novel too.

I prefer Albert Camus to Jean-Paul Sartre. The lugubrious tone of *Nausea* makes me laugh.

Cool. There's this crazy section I can't get out of my head … you know, where a guy feels like he wants to vomit when he looks at a chestnut tree and says that everything is filling up with gelatinous slither. I mean, gelatinous slither? Weird right?

Sartre saw the life force as irrational. And therefore meaningless.

He gives me a strange look, and I wonder if he is thinking how bizarre it feels for the two of us to be chatting about literature, considering he has virtually returned from the dead. Of course, the conversation offers a way back for us both, a method of normalizing our situation.

Your aunt disliked Sartre. She used to say he resented women because men can't create life.

Yeah, Kis would say something like that. So you're not upset that I'm staying in one of the old cabins at Surf Song?

I mumble some vacuous reply, my thoughts drifting back to my beach house, with its winding paths through the hibiscus bushes. Obviously, the new owner hasn't had the chance to pull down the decrepit staff bungalows. Against my better judgment, I let Caroline persuade me to keep those graceless shacks. I demolished the old clapboard house, though, and built a four-storey version of my Hôtel de Ville on Long Island, right down to the Lutron lighting. Caroline holds the bulldozing of the main house against me. It is one of her grievances, like my refusal to give to her fund for the congenitally blind and deaf Great Danes.

When I get out of here, I hope to get Surf Song back. I nod at the vending machines. Would you mind buying me a cappuccino?

He looks shocked. Oh shit. I forgot you can't have money in here. He walks over to the machine, bouncing up and down on his toes with what appears to be his old pep. Ah, he's proud of himself. He's pulled off a public vanishing act with no help from me. My boy is resourceful. Neither Meredith nor his mother give him enough credit.

When he returns with my coffee, he puts a finger to his lips and scribbles some words on the Styrofoam cup: *Look under the first garbage bin by the warehouse.*

I keep a straight face in case the C.O. standing by the vending machine glances our way.

Check under the floorboards, he hisses. Let's put in some family time online, okay?

The word "yes" comes out in a whisper. Davie is asking for family time with me. My boy, who has been lost to the world, is saying he wants to be close again. My eyes devour his bright, smiling face. If only somebody wasn't trying to kill me. *Oh, Lordy, whoever you are, stop. Grant me the chance to know my son again, and if you deliver this favour, I promise to give you whatever you seek.*

4

I AM AT a loss as to what to do about the cellphone until I remember Derek is helping out at the food warehouse. The next day my trusty bunkmate comes back with Davie's present hidden inside his pants. It took Derek only a few minutes to find the small Styrofoam package tucked under the floor of the industrial garbage bin. Davie-Ash has left a note with the smart phone nestled inside: *Have fun with it, Dad.* His iPhone comes with something called Gchat. Sequestered in a washroom stall, I follow Derek's instructions and summon my boy; seconds later, he appears as a blank silhouette.

Good man! You got it working! I'd really like to connect with you Dad! Email works on the cell too but it can't phone long distance.

Thanks … Ash. How did you get your new name?

Hey, you don't need to call me Ash here. I found a dead boy with no social security number.

You hacked into social security?

Yup. Stay chill, okay? And hey, I flew back to the Bahamas yesterday. Caroline is flying in from London tomorrow to stay with Charles, and I'm going to surprise her. She doesn't know yet that I'm not dead. Too bad you won't be with us. I want to know what you think about *The Stranger.* Charles says the guy in the Camus novel reminds him of you. The way he goes to his execution, looking forward to everyone hating him: *I opened myself to the gentle indifference of the universe … For everything to be consummated, for me to feel less alone, I had only to wish that there be a large crowd of spectators the day of my execution and that they greet me with cries of hate …*

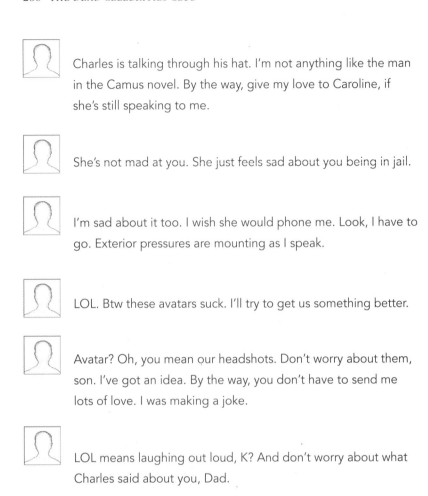

Charles is talking through his hat. I'm not anything like the man in the Camus novel. By the way, give my love to Caroline, if she's still speaking to me.

She's not mad at you. She just feels sad about you being in jail.

I'm sad about it too. I wish she would phone me. Look, I have to go. Exterior pressures are mounting as I speak.

LOL. Btw these avatars suck. I'll try to get us something better.

Avatar? Oh, you mean our headshots. Don't worry about them, son. I've got an idea. By the way, you don't have to send me lots of love. I was making a joke.

LOL means laughing out loud, K? And don't worry about what Charles said about you, Dad.

5

OF COURSE I worry about Charles telling my boy malicious tales. I last saw the Limey grifter eight months before I was formally charged. It was the day I left behind the bucolic charm of Paradise Island and flew north to meet the government stooges investigating my hedge fund companies. I'd already gone over Dieter's travel list, ticking off the items I'd need for the trip: credit cards, bottled water, Tums for my indigestion and Rythmol for my bad, old heart.

I stood in my bedroom, pondering Caroline as she slept beneath sheets of Egyptian cotton.

Below our window, reflections from the boughs of the traveller's palms swayed invitingly across the pool. At this hour, the tepid water would feel comforting, like a forgotten bath. But I had urgent business with Charles. Careful not to wake Caroline, I grabbed my bathrobe and a pair of flip-flops and tiptoed down the staircase.

Wrapping my bathrobe around me, I hurried to the beach and stood looking back at my villa, which nestled (if a home of mine can really nestle) on a sand dune behind a bright pink coral wall. Caroline had chosen the ghastly colour because it matched the blossoms on the hibiscus bushes.

For a moment, I lost myself in the noise of early morning: the screech of a sea bird, the hollow thunder of the waves striking the sand. In the distance my old friends the Shelbys were slowly making their way along the shore, dressed in shapeless plaid bathing suits. I waved, and they lifted their chins haughtily before turning and walking off in the other direction. Who did they think I was? A malicious sea creature rising from the ocean surf? The thought of their hatred felt galvanizing. I began to jog along the beach, my chest heaving, my head down, as if the soft ocean breeze was a bracing gust.

Huffing noisily, I climbed up and over a rocky promontory; I was visiting the last house on the beach before the lighthouse, and there was no other way to get there unless I took a boat from Nassau Harbour. Once more on terra firma, I put on the pair of flip-flops I'd been carrying and walked toward a ranch-style bungalow half-hidden in some Caribbean pines.

Caroline had persuaded me to lend Charles two million dollars for the beach house, and he often whined about why he couldn't pay me back.

I entered his security code on the keypad and padded across a wide patch of brown grass that crinkled like dried-out human hair. An elderly Haitian man, in a sunhat and dark clothes, stood sweeping the stone pathway near the house. Charles hired refugees because they will work for low wages. The Haitian called out, asking me to wait. I did what he said, and his eyes held mine while he mumbled into his cellphone.

As I waited to be cleared, I heard a threatening growl behind me. Charles's Doberman had been tied to a sea grapes bush, the angle of its ears warning me not to approach. I whispered the dog's name, and Ulysses wagged the stump of his tail.

The Haitian put away his cell and beckoned, and I followed him to the house, passing the ludicrously expensive tomato-red dune buggy that Charles had paid for with my American dollars.

My host was on the screened-in back porch, eating breakfast. The reprehensible weasel. The nefarious ingrate. He jumped to his feet, smiling at my bathrobe and uncombed hair. I feel like your mistress, old boy, what with you sneaking up on me in your knickers.

It was always a shock when Charles opened his mouth. I let him air kiss my cheeks in the fatuous European style, then I hurled myself with a crash onto a rattan chair.

Elizabeth, bring us some cappuccinos? Charles waved at a Haitian woman chopping pineapple. Turning my way, he cocked his head gravely, or was he being supercilious? I could never tell if Charles was serious. Did you see the story about you? he asked. When I shook my head, he read out loud from the *Nassau Guardian*:

> International hedge funds manager Dale Paul says he disapproves of the corrupt nature of America's plea-bargaining system. That it convicts 95 percent of its defendants, Dale Paul says, mostly on severe mandatory sentences, is evidence that something is seriously wrong with American justice.

Aren't you afraid you'll anger your accusers? He narrowed his eyes the way he does when he thinks he has something on you.

I'm innocent. I grabbed a croissant from a straw basket on the table.

He nodded, frowning.

As the last of its buttery dough melted on my tongue, I mulled over his habit of borrowing my pass to the Ocean Club, where he passed himself off as Albert Finney. Instead of paying the bill in full, he covered the amount in the first column and ignored the column that said tax and total.

Has Caroline talked to you yet, Dale Paul?

I slit my eyes. Was he going to tell me something unpleasant about Caroline and myself? I was a man on the way down, and there were many tiresome things I was obliged to hear. I'm here to talk about my loan, I replied, grabbing two blueberry muffins from his basket.

Won't the prosecutors seize the money if I give it to you, old boy?

Nobody will find out, I said biting into the first muffin. I need my money back. It's not for me — it's for those who depend on me. I finished the muffin and picked up the second.

Yes, of course. But stop eating for a bloody minute and listen, will you? He grasped my arm. There's a reason I can't pay you back.

And that reason is?

Dale Paul, if you'd just calm down and hear me out …

For Christ's sake! I cried. I don't want to listen to your trumped-up excuses. Just pay me the money back. But you can't do that, can you?

No, but that's because …

I don't want to hear another word, you addled lager lout! You scrofulous poseur!

Shaking free of his hand, I said goodbye, opened the screen door, and walked briskly down the steps. On the veranda, Charles shouted some incomprehensible nonsense. I kept walking. The Haitian gardener stopped his sweeping to watch me go.

As I staggered across his lawn, my heart — my bad, old heart — started knocking *bumpety-bump*. I felt light-headed, and there was a boiling sensation in my gut. I stopped near the bush where Ulysses was tied. I couldn't help it. I began to retch, spewing my breakfast over the scorched grass. Ulysses dropped his head and started lapping up the sulphur-coloured goo. His slurping sounds disgusted me. Wiping my mouth with the back of my hand, I hurried past the creature.

6

CAROLINE WAS WAITING for me in our breakfast nook, the one room I'd allowed her to decorate, ignoring, as was my wont, the debts she was incurring. She had put up hand-pressed wallpaper and replaced Esther's ironstone plates with a set of Willow pattern china.

Caroline smothered me in a perfumed hug. How did it go, darling?

I blanched at the sight of the croissant basket that Dieter was holding and said I was too distracted to talk about Charles.

No wonder, you poor darling! Mother gave me a commiserating look. You and Caroline have a long trip ahead.

Mrs. Paul, I'm staying here to look after my brother. Caroline's voice quavered. His cancer has come back, you see.

I didn't know that, Caroline!

He said he was going to tell you this morning.

A shocked hush fell over the breakfast nook. Davie stopped eating his soft-boiled egg and stared sympathetically at Caroline. Meredith, who looked perplexed, stayed silent while Mother made a tiny unhappy noise and then began tearing at her toast and rearranging the bread into neat rows of small, doughy balls. An early symptom of her mad cow disease, one of the signs we overlooked.

For god's sake, Mother, I said. You used to tell Kis and me not to play with our food.

Like a child, she stopped what she was doing and hung her head.

7

IN DOWNTOWN NASSAU, I spotted G.T. Galbadon taking out cash from an instant teller. He was one of the investigators from the Securities Exchange Commission who were pocketing my hard-earned coin. If there were a more sinister creature, you'd be hard-pressed to find him. Galbadon, with his drooping moustache and narrow shoulders, resembled old Cootes, my pervy geography teacher at Munson Hall.

That cretin is stealing what's left of my funds, I hissed.

Be nice, Caroline whispered. Maybe you should ask him to dinner.

Don't make me barf, I retorted and climbed out of our car.

Good sir, are you enjoying your ill-gotten gains? When I started toward him, he lumbered off down an alley, moving abnormally quickly for a man of his bulk. Behind my back, I heard Caroline yelling. I turned on my heel, feeling annoyed, and a photographer ran out from behind a parked suv and shoved a camera in my face. There was a harrowing click as I shoulder-barged the lummox out of my way.

You manhandled that man, Caroline said when I climbed back into our car.

Meredith cleared her throat. Dale Paul hardly touched him.

Caroline threw me a withering glance. I knew what she was thinking: Good old Kister, always taking your side.

8

WE WERE RUNNING late by the time we pulled into a gas station on President Kennedy Drive. Yet Meredith chose that moment to visit the powder room. Caroline and I waited in silence while my cousin threaded her way through the taxis lined up at the gas pumps, the cabbies turning to gape at the tall, older woman with the long grey braids. As soon as Meredith disappeared, I said: I don't want to get into a discussion in front of Kis, but why aren't you coming with me?

Try to think of somebody beside yourself, Caroline replied nastily. Charles looked after me when our parents weren't around. Now it's my turn to look after him.

Caroline, do I have to order you to come?

Please watch your tone, Dale Paul! Her large blue eyes sparked with an emotion I couldn't identify. I am not — and I repeat — I am not your servant. She uttered the last sentence in a lowered voice because Meredith's head had suddenly appeared in the car window. As we sat there glowering at each other, my cousin climbed inside and Caroline started up the car, pushing her foot to the floor as if she couldn't wait to be rid of me.

9

BACK AT ESSEX, I doodle some Gchat avatars, photograph the images in our washroom, and email them to Davie. His resembles a long-haired elf, while mine is the visage of the old coot I see each morning in the mirror. Perhaps you'll recognize my craggy, time-blasted features and, ahem, the coat hanger eyebrows and pouchy eyes. There is nothing for it. As John Giaccone would say, It is what it is.

From: ashapiro@gmail.com
To: Dale Paul
Subject: Some questions

Hi Dad:
Meredith said I should tell you about my experience at the Buddhist retreat in France. That's where I went after I disappeared and Thich Nhat Hanh, the monk who runs it, helped me get over my anger at you. He said the task is to hold your anger with love and not to chase away anger in yourself or someone else. Instead,

we need to invite in another energy that will care for the anger.

He said I did the right thing revisiting the place in my childhood where I was happiest. You had time for me at Surf Song, and for a while, you and Mom were happy there, too. I know Mom's drinking was becoming a problem, and it's still a problem. Though she tells me she's drinking less now.

And, hey, I'd forgotten you could draw! It brings back the times you and I used to sketch soldiers from the photographs in your Civil War books. Remember when you kept a set of watercolours in your desk? You did great sketches of Abraham Lincoln. Can I be honest? You scared me. You even knew cool stuff about the German philosopher Hegel and his idea of the individual surrendering to the state. But, hey, I know Hegel was against authoritarianism and "surrendering" isn't a fair reading of his noble theories.

Half the time I never knew what to say to you. So much went over my head. Mom said you used to be a bookworm when she met you, and that she was one too. I mean, how great is that!!! It's sad that you two fell out of touch, but these things happen, right?

Anyway, Dad, I hope you can understand how your reputation has made it hard for people to see who I am. They treat me like I am guilty too! Maybe you didn't understand that? But moving forward, I really would like you to answer some questions I have about what you did. Thanks, man.

Hi Dad: K, a bunch of questions coming up. Ready?

Fire away, Davie.

Why didn't you give adequate funds to Mom in your divorce settlement? Are you for real, Dad? Mom said you wanted to get back at her through me. Honestly, how could you be so mean to the person you had a kid with? All you thought about was yourself.

That's not fair, son.

Answer the question, Dad. Here's another one. Why did you give yourself a ten-million-dollar bonus when your company got in trouble?

A corporate bonus is a symbol of financial success, and in my case, it gave our troubled company time to get back in the black.

Yeah, but it's still dishonest, isn't it? And why did you invest in Coca-Cola when that company has unethical practices? Coca-Cola bottles water in Rajasthan, India, for basically free and then sells that same water BACK to the locals at 1,000 times the price! You understand that Rajasthan is a very dry part of India, right? And the locals already have very poor access to water?

Look, you just don't understand how business works. My share-holders favour the personal accumulation of wealth over acts of charity, so you might find yourself making a similar decision if you ran Quaestus Capital.

Not a chance! I'm not like you. And why did you refuse to give Caroline money to help Great Danes with eye problems?

Her organization depended on personal donations and it didn't have a wealthy patron. For a while, her brother helped them out, but you never gave her a dime.

I don't want to be unfair to the dogs, Davie, but they shouldn't have been born.

I can't believe your bullshit. That's emotionally stunted. K, last but not least, I finally read Tim Nugent's article about you getting the prisoners to bet on the death of aging celebrities. Really? Seems weird. And tasteless.

I'm sorry you feel that way. The workshop is teaching the men important skills. Look, let's talk about this in person, okay?

Young people have it in for the old. It's part of the human chain of generational frustration. If you're young, you're against what has gone before, and if you're no longer young, you need to reinvent yourself to keep up with the times, although the Lord Help and Keep You if you make the young take on the role of your adversary. Trying to defend yourself only mires you deeper in their anger.

Point being, Davie is guilty of the sin he accuses me of: selfishness. Has he apologized for putting all of us through his faux death? No. The only person he has been thinking about is himself. It was cruel of him to make us suffer. And to accuse me of being stingy with child support! Pater would have been furious if I had challenged him the way my boy is challenging me.

But I have something more serious on the brain. Is Meredith going to tell him about the trust? Not even Kis can keep a secret like that for long.

10

HOW RIGHT I was! Two days later, Davie sends me another email:

> From: ashapiro@gmail.com
> To: Dale Paul
> Subject: My grandmother's trust fund
>
> Hey Dad:
> Yesterday I phoned the family lawyer to see if I could borrow funds
> and he told me there is no money left in my grandmother's trust.
> Meredith confirmed it. How could you do this to our family, Dad?
> That money belonged to all of us. I was so wrong about you. You
> haven't changed. You are still the same hard-nosed bastard looking
> for ways to take advantage of the people who love you. Don't you
> know how much damage you cause? Don't bother answering.

I delete Davie's email and set off for the Chow Hall, pausing every now and then on the rickety stairs outside our dorm to see if my stalker will creep up behind me and finish me off. The way I feel tonight, it would be a mercy.

Nothing happens. The cold mountain wind lifts my hair off my forehead, but there are no springy footsteps behind me on the old wooden staircase, no dark silhouette billows up and threatens to swallow me whole.

11

May 24, 2013
Dear Tim:

Two days ago, as I filed out of Chow Hall, Martino called me over and said I needed to be in the warden's office at noon the next day because some big shot wanted to see me. (FYI: Martino is the guard who smuggles my letters to you.)

So around eleven-thirty the next morning, I joined the men lining up behind the fence. Just as they once did for me, television crews fought one another for parking spots, their cameras trained on a white limousine that came gliding toward us.

Earl climbed out. He gave all of us standing behind the fence two hearty thumbs up before he turned to Nathan Rickard and they strolled off together. From this distance, it was impossible to notice anything odd about the way he walks unless you already know how things are with him.

I could guess why he came. Earl belongs to a committee of wealthy businessmen who are advising the Administration Division of the BOP on how to cut prison costs, and I often see him on the prison television talking about the need to privatize our jails.

A few hours later, a C.O. escorted me to the warden's office, where Earl and the warden were looking at pictures taped to the wall above the warden's desk. They were photographs of security drones, large and small, along with drawings of handheld shields used by swat teams and prison guards.

The pair stood studying a diagram of a full-body shield that fits over a man like a life size plastic doll. Its metal mouthpiece gave the thing a Darth Vader aspect. I shuddered at the thought of a human wearing something so claustrophobic.

Warden, are you thinking of Star Wars costumes for our C.O.s? I asked. The two men whirled around in surprise.

Heck no, Dale Paul, they throw in this futuristic stuff to get our attention, the warden said. Closing the door gently, he went out. As soon as the warden left, Earl sat down in a chair by the open window and loosened his baggy shirt; the style of his loose garment reminded me of the maternity blouses Esther used to wear when she was carrying Davie. Did I say loosened? He undid his shirt all the way down to his belt, as if its ample cloth didn't give him room to breathe. Point being, Earl has always felt free to let his guard down with me. However, this degree of inhibition was something new. Then I understood: his throat had grown a dewlap the size of a football. How did he keep his shirt done up over something like that? Lord knows what else was hiding under his capacious clothes. He saw my *raised eyebrows and smiled.*

Your condition … I hesitated.

Yeah, it's a hell of a lot worse. But nobody seems to notice, okay? Or maybe they just don't give a shit. He turned his head in the direction of the open window and closed his eyes. He seemed to forget I was there, and for a moment he sat warming himself in the sunlight flooding the warden's office. Then he sat up abruptly, as if he had been caught napping. He pointed at the warden's photographs of the drones, and I realized he was letting me know that he was still the same old Earl.

See those drones, he asked. They're designed to avoid objects. And they return home when the batteries get low. These fuckers will come in handy in a war, okay? His shirt was still open, so I could see his dewlap pulsing a light shade of pink. While I stood there, staring, the colour of his throat deepened to a wine red. Possibly, the prospect of doing battle with the drones was triggering aggressive feelings in him.

I guess you know why I haven't called, Dale Paul.

You tell me.

Look, you're a good guy, but the world doesn't know you're a good guy, okay?

I experienced an involuntary twitch. When Earl says okay, it is like a poker tell that signals he is about to deliver a load of tripe. It's all right, Earl. I'm not angry with you.

He seemed to relax. Old friends, right? You can't beat 'em. Look, Nate says you run a workshop on financial skills. It's a waste of tax-payers' money, okay?

It helps the men get jobs after they leave.

You mean so they can screw some sucker when they get out?

So they won't come back, Earl.

Something flickered in his heavy-lidded eyes. Surprise? Interest? An acknowledgement of what I had just said?

Well, I don't know about that. Your workshop might get cut, okay? He rubbed his hairless head, which gleamed under the ceiling light as rich and soft as new pigskin.

It rankled to think of him destroying something I had created. I pulled out my notebook and began to doodle. Hands this time, doing magical tricks.

Are you listening, Dale Paul?

I listen better if my hand is busy, I replied. It was the same thing I'd told Meredith, and he nodded doubtfully.

Okay, yeah, I see. You must have some skin in that dead pool you set up, right? His broad smile exposed his high pink gums. Remember what the teacher wrote on our report cards? All Dale Paul and Earl Lindquist want to know is — what's in it for us? He chortled.

Earl, my workshop is a helpful pedagogical exercise, and I'd like to keep it going. I helped you once. Remember?

My memory is shit, but yeah, I remember a few things. And you know what? I never saw anything at Munson Hall to get excited about. It was all dumb crap. Cold weather. People talking in British accents …

Nobody spoke in British accents, good sir.

Yeah, whatever. Okay, let me tell you something. You used to be a class act. Nobody could break your chops. You had sharp clothes and your daddy's limousine. And now look at you, okay? How come you were stupid enough to get caught? But look, I gotta see the next guy. Tell me how to fix this dump. In five minutes. No, tell you what. Write me a letter. I'll make sure the warden sends it to me.

Do you recall what Thompson did that afternoon in the forest … how he and the other boys humiliated you? I paused, letting him absorb the word humiliated.

That day in the forest … you mean the shit hole called Norgate?

Yes, Norgate. Do you remember what happened there?

The scaly flesh of his dewlap turned a chalky shade. Perhaps his thoughts were drifting back to that deathly lonely place where an icy river winds through an unending clot of skinny maple trees.

Look, I'll help you keep your workshop, okay? he said finally. If there's a way, I'll do it. I'd even get you a pardon.

A pardon?

He swivelled his head slowly from side to side. Sure, a pardon. You're innocent, right? You shouldn't be in a dump like this. And don't tell me any more garbage about the old days. Okay, let's see your funny money. You got some on you?

I handed over a c-coin with Zsa Zsa Gabor's name.

Isn't she the crazy bimbo with thirteen husbands? He made a snickering noise; then he turned away to perform some function with his mouth. I couldn't see what he was doing, although hand on heart it looked as if his tongue was licking his right eye, washing it clean with a froth of saliva.

Nine husbands.

Okay, nine. But look, no matter what happens to your workshop, no hard feelings, okay, Dale Paul? You and I did some crazy shit together. You scratched my back. I scratched yours. He did up his shirt and heaved himself to his feet. What I'd been allowed to see was once again well hidden. He was all saurian intent now.

And with that, Tim, our old schoolmate walked out, calling over his shoulder to me: See you around, pal.

Best regards,
Dale Paul

12

May 27, 2013

Dear Tim:
Something distressing has happened. I saw the lights again when the Michael Jackson dancers did one of their routines. They were doing it for Earl and Nathan Rickard, who were reclining on lawn chairs by the tennis courts while I stood behind the fence with the other scofflaws — a sad reminder of my altered circumstances.

John was there too, with his runners. When he spotted me, he waved me over. Banging the arms of his wheelchair, he turned toward his women. Hey, ladies! Meet the great Dale Paul. Maybe you read about him in the New York Times? And now he's enjoying the prestige. I don't blame him. World-Renowned Hedge Fund Manager Runs Financial Workshop Inside the bop. When he gets out, that story is going to pay off big-time. I'm not trying to get a medal, but he is.

I could feel myself turn red. Tim, I haven't blushed since public school and likely not even then. Why does John keep picking on me, you might ask? Because our ten celebrities are still alive! It's absurd. Nobody can control their health.

Pretending John's barb was all in good fun, I directed a gentlemanly bow toward the women and then we all turned to watch the dancers doing their high-stepping military drills on the empty tennis courts. As I watched, from out of nowhere, tiny golden sparkles began to flash in front of the men's bodies; the lights were small at first, and then grew larger, forming patterns that evoked the bright streaming lines in time-lapse photographs of night traffic. I am not sure how long the lights danced and flickered, but when I came back to myself the rehearsal was over and John was tugging impatiently on my arm.

I believe he was telling me the value of Bitcoin has skyrocketed. Despite some ups and downs over the past months, one coin is now worth one hundred and thirty dollars. If it keeps going up like this our Bitcoin jackpot could be worth millions.

Best regards,
Dale Paul

June 2, 2013

Dear Tim:

Thank you for asking for my version of what happened at Norgate. You haven't forgotten, have you, Pilot?

I'm talking about the May weekend that you and Earl and I took part in the school games at the country estate that some fatuous old boy had donated to Munson Hall. Pater and Googie were too busy to attend, but Meredith and Mr. Eric came along with the other parents to watch us race rafts made from logs left behind by nineteenth-century lumbermen. Nobody cared that the half-submerged barges might come apart at any moment.

After the boat races, I set off to find Earl, who was nowhere to be seen; as you will recall, he often stole away to escape the taunts of our school-mates. He didn't understand the school code: Don't brag like a bully. Take what you want, but act like a gentleman.

Near a high granite outcropping, I stumbled on a group of boys tormenting something. When I crept closer, I saw Earl spread-eagled on his stomach, his trousers in a nearby heap. Several of the boys were holding Earl down while Thompson tried to shove something up Earl's rectum. Some of the boys were yelling at Earl, who was yelling, too, and Thompson was swearing at him to shut his mouth.

Without thinking what I was doing, I began screaming for our geography master, Mr. Cootes: Lord help us, old Cooties! Save Earl from these bullyboys, these thuggish poltroons, these clay-brained knaves! I beg you! When Thompson turned my way, I screamed even louder: Help us, Cootes, in the name of Justice and Mercy!

I have no idea why I invoked his name. The scenario was something our pervy teacher would have enjoyed.

When they saw I wasn't going to stop, the group melted into the trees. After several fumbling attempts, Earl removed the Pepsi bottle and staggered to his feet.

Without meeting my eyes, he threw the bottle as hard as he could at the tall granite cliff, and we heard the satisfying sound of shattering glass.

13

Meredith Paul

ON A LATE August day, Meredith sits reading on a patio chair the movers have left behind. She is finishing a chapter about Norgate in Dale Paul's memoir, and she's grateful Tim has left out the rest of what happened that terrible afternoon.

She had been necking with him in the woods near a rock outcropping on the Norgate property. They were both in their underwear, and she had screamed just as he was unhooking her bra. After the bit of glass flew into her eye, changing her forever, she had collapsed forward, blood running down her cheek. Out of nowhere, Dale Paul and Earl appeared. Dale Paul ordered Earl to fetch the school doctor, and for once Earl did as he was told while Dale Paul and Tim helped Meredith put her clothes back on. A few moments later, the school doctor showed up with the headmaster. They expected accidents in the rough and tumble of the Norgate games; they just didn't expect the victim to be a girl with a pop bottle shard in her eye.

Afterwards, Tim had tried to visit her in the hospital, but she didn't want to see him. She didn't blame him. She lacked the energy to reassure him because he seemed to hold himself responsible for the accident.

With a sigh, she puts down the memoir chapter and picks up something she found in Dale Paul's study. It's the glass paperweight she bought her cousin as a joke. It had reminded her of the snow globe in the film Citizen Kane. Inside, tiny glittery flakes of ivory are falling on miniature New York skyscrapers. She gave it to Dale Paul for Christmas, the year they had moved into their Long Island home Tomorrow, new owners take the house over. It's an old, familiar story. You go and somebody else takes your place.

From nearby comes the sound of a man's voice. She has been too absorbed in her thoughts to notice Tim.

It's a shame you have to let this place go, he is saying. Are you sad about losing it?

Not really. It's a lot to keep up.

And Mrs. Paul?

Well, it's strange. When she was alive she underestimated me, and now that she's gone, I miss her. It's not as if she was my mother.

Are you sure about that?

You think she was?

Maybe, he says. She was around when you were growing up, right? Good or bad, she's your maternal figure. Can I ask you something?

Isn't that what you do?

He laughs. Are you upset with what I've written about Dale Paul?

We've talked about this before, and the answer is no. As for Dale Paul, he's never cared what people think. He isn't a people pleaser like me.

Maybe not caring what people think is the same thing as not caring about people, Tim says.

She feels her chest open suddenly. A brightness.

Now it's my turn to ask you a question. She hesitates. Are you sure about the marriage?

Never been more sure! Don't forget. I've wanted to straighten things out between us for a long time.

Tim. She smiles fondly. It's okay.

14

Dale Paul

TRISH BALES, THE BOP psychologist, is waiting for me on a bench outside the pool building. I suppress a twitch of irritation, although she is a serious-minded woman. She must have something important to say or she wouldn't waste my time.

I sit down on a bench near her chair, and she lights up. While I wait, trying not to fidget, she smiles.

I know, I know. She shakes her head apologetically. It's illegal to smoke on the grounds, but I'm stressed about the budget cuts. I want my study at Essex to continue, and you must feel the same way about your workshop. Will you help me get testimonials from the men? Maybe you could write one yourself.

Trish, someone like Earl Lindquist doesn't care about rehabilitating the men. He told me himself these programs are worthless.

Oh, that's right. You know him, don't you? And he wouldn't listen. Well, that's no surprise. She takes a heavy pull on her cigarette. By the way, there's a rumour making the rounds that you are going to be the next celebrity to die.

I grab her package of Kools. When she looks up in surprise, I tap my chest with my finger. Had to stop. My ticker. Listen, Trish, what rumour are you talking about?

My source in the admin claims you are on the list. He says he saw your name in the warden's box. You know, the black metal box that Mr. Rickard uses to keep his letters in. It's on the shelf behind his desk.

Words fail me.

15

FROM THE WARDEN's window, the hills of the Adirondacks float on the horizon like green clouds. There's no sign of the leaves turning yet, although it's already mid-September.

I have set up a phone call with Earl, and given half a chance, I intend to turn the situation to my advantage. The warden's letter box is right where Trish said it would be — on the shelf behind his desk.

The phone rings, and I press the speaker button anxiously. The warden is hunched over his desk, pretending not to listen.

That you, Dale Paul? Earl bellows.

It's me, yes. You have news? I bring out my notepad and start to doodle.

I said I'd help you keep your workshop, right? But the guys on the committee think it has to go. It's fucked, okay? The American taxpayer can't afford to throw money away on losers. Hey, you still on the line? You're not angry, are you, Dale Paul? It's too bad about your workshop, but maybe you can write a book or something. So, look, I gotta go. Give my regards to Nate. He's a good guy too. And write down this number. It's about a deal. The biggest deal I ever made. I want you to come in on it with me.

I thank him for the phone number and we say goodbye.

When I put down the phone, the warden isn't there. Gone to the washroom if I'm lucky. Cautiously, I pick up the letter box and shake it; it's not locked, so I open the lid and peer at the tidy stack of envelopes tied with an orange elastic band. Each one bears a name. I rifle through them until I come to an envelope labelled *Mystery Celebrity*. Someone has done a sloppy job of gluing the envelope back together, so I open it easily. Inside on a piece of prison notepaper I see the words "Dale Paul."

Alas, I know what Pater would say. He would say when you lie down with dogs you get up with fleas. And yet, what if you think you're a dog too?

16

BAILEY IS ON his cot reading the Virgin Mary's *Book of Quotations*. On a dorm radio, Whitney Houston finishes her lush diminuendo.

Something untoward has taken place, Bailey.

He sits up, his eyes bewildered behind his oversized spectacles. Somethin' untoward? Can you break it down for me?

I'm the mystery celebrity. Does that make any sense to you?

B, I heard that rumour too. A lot of guys betting on you.

You mean, betting on the mystery celebrity?

Yeah. They sayin' that on Inmate dot com. Bailey groans and shakes his head. You know I don like Mr. Jack. Feels like you don see him clear. You think he be colourful, like he jes stepped out of a movie or somethin'. But he jes playin' you.

I rock back on my heels. Why didn't you say something?

I don know. I ain't … I don't have proof. Just vibes, okay? And you act all happy when Mr. Jack around … He shrugs.

All right. I accept that. Do you know who attacked me in the sauna?

Bailey stands on his bunk and peers cautiously over the cubicle divider. When he sits back down, he picks up the Virgin Mary's *Book of Quotations* and holds it to his chest. She knows I saw Aldo comin' … comin' out of the sauna, and she askin' me to tell you. I've been meanin' … meanin' to. I just a bit scairt, nah mean?

I rush out of our cubicle, my bad, old heart beating double time against my ribs.

17

I TALK A guard into letting me call Nugent on the prison phone. I am uncharacteristically short and sweet.

Nugent, you have to help me escape from this place.

What are you talking about, Dale Paul?

Mr. Jack wants to kill me.

That doesn't sound very likely.

I'll explain it all later. I'm serious. Help me get out of here. I'll cut you in on the dead celebrities pool. You need money, don't you, Pilot?

I can't get involved in that scheme of yours. And don't call me Pilot.

All right, good sir. But surely you don't want to see your old friend murdered in cold blood?

Spare me the drama. I'll have to think about it.

Nugent, I need you to do it now. Or there will be no book. Do you understand?

Let me get back to you on this, he says and hangs up.

18

Tim Nugent

TIM ISN'T FRIGHTENED by Dale Paul's threat to cancel the book. If Dale Paul manages to escape, a memoir with a jailbreak will mean bigger sales, and Dale Paul won't turn down an opportunity to make money.

His worry is that Dale Paul is telling the truth. His old friend has a habit of getting under people's skin, and there's no reason to think the convicts are any different. Why do we help other people? Tim wonders. He remembers the answer the masters gave them at Munson Hall — by helping others we help ourselves. Maybe those garrulous old men had been right. Maybe the urge to help is tied to a primitive anxiety about your tribe's survival. And yet a case could be made that someone like his friend who has done so little to help others deserves no help at all.

Finally, after a day of soul-searching, Tim comes up with a plan. Dale Paul will swim to the other side of the small lake near the prison and Tim will pick him up in a car and drive him to Tim's grandparents' abandoned farmhouse, near the Ontario border. But where will Tim pick him up? He needs to research it, think it through.

Without telling Meredith, Tim heads north in a rental truck, taking the I-87 to Strawberry Lake, where he buys a canoe from an outfitter's shop off the main street. He uses a fake name and pays with cash.

He chooses a small dark green canoe with a round hull, shaped like a rowboat. He explains that he isn't experienced with canoes, and the outfitter assures Tim this style of canoe has been designed for flat-water lakes like the ones in the Adirondacks. It rides high in the water and is easy to steer. The broad beavertail paddle will be easy to use too. The outfitter throws in a thick plastic cushion as a bonus.

Tim arranges for the outfitter to drop the canoe by the mouth of the Oswego River, a fast-running creek that spills into the far shore of the lake behind the prison. The outfitter looks at him quizzically when Tim explains that a friend is coming up to the mountains for a holiday and the friend wants the canoe placed there for his convenience.

You know it's near the prison? the outfitter asks.

Tim says he is only following his friend's instructions.

19

Dale Paul

THE SEPTEMBER MORNING is unseasonably warm. I am standing near the tennis courts watching Derek's dancers perform drills for their show at Thanksgiving, and Martino is letting me watch.

I have filled Derek in on Nugent's plan: the canoe and the hand-drawn map, with its terrifying details. I will swim to the other side, where Tim has left the canoe in some bushes by the mouth of the Oswego River. The river will take me to the first swamp, where Nugent will be waiting by a duck blind to drive me north to Canada. This way, I can avoid the higher peaks that stretch for miles beyond the far side of the lake.

I take out the map and go over it again. Possibly, Nugent is overestimating my paddling skills. He is a child of the north. He grew up there, endured its winters; all I know of the wilderness is the hideous two weeks I wasted as a teenager at summer camp in Algonquin Park. When I complained, Pater brought me home faster than you can say water polo.

20

THE SCREECHING SOUNDS of "Thriller" by Michael Jackson assault my ears. On the tennis court, the dancers are forming their lines while I concentrate on Nugent's map of the Five Swamps Wilderness Preserve. It's two thousand and twenty acres, bound to the south by Strawberry Lake and a portion of the Oswego River, the fast-flowing river that Meredith, Caroline, and I drove across on our way to the prison. In the east, the swampy region is bound by the town line, and a road leading to a lake called St. Regis. Nugent has listed the dangers: deadheads in the swamp, ticks, leeches, and possibly quicksand.

And now, suddenly, a brouhaha. The dancers are screaming at one another, and the C.O.s rush in, waving their clubs like maniacal soccer fans with phosphorescent batons. I check the time on the clock by the tennis court: 9:55 a.m. The fracas Derek has arranged is right on cue.

Using a clump of cedars as a screen, I take off my prison sneakers, thread the laces in a knot, and hang the sneakers around my neck. Next, I put the map and my Rythmol pills inside a cellophane wrapper. Someone has stolen my cellphone or I would have brought it too. When I am certain no one is watching, I slip into the lake dressed in my prison browns.

The water stings my skin like ice-cold acid. Derek tested the temperature of the lake this morning: it was sixty-nine degrees Fahrenheit. Icy, but swimmable. Did he lie about the temperature? Don't be demented. He has no reason to make things difficult for me.

I start with the breaststroke face down in the water, swimming quickly to keep myself warm. I've been advised to follow the thickly treed shoreline to the other side, although swimming straight across the lake is the faster route. When I am far enough away, my head will look like the head of an animal — perhaps a bear or a beaver. I pray the C.O.s are too busy to notice.

21

I'M ALMOST THERE. Luckily, the lake is longer than it is wide, and I can see the narrow beach on the other shore fairly well. It's lined with cedars and birches. The canoe will be somewhere nearby.

I relax and let myself float for a few minutes, scanning the trees. Lord knows what I am looking for. Wild animals? I drift into shore, and gingerly haul myself out of the lake, hoping the guards in the maximum-security prison can't see me from their towers. Possibly, Nugent forgot that detail.

But, thank god, the guard towers appear to be hidden by the curve in the shoreline. I walk south a few yards, feeling pleased with myself for making it this far. I take the map from its cellophane wrapper. The paper is a little damp, so some instructions have blurred, but I seem to be in the right place. I stop and listen. Fine. All right. I hear the faint sound of running water. I hurry down the beach toward the noise. Ah. There's the mouth of the river, and there's the canoe, just as Nugent said it would be, a shiny green shape half-hidden in some underbrush. As I push my way through, I trip over the branches of an indigenous shrub that Sofia Rigby used to grow in her back garden. Its branches are rooted in the sand, the plant's trap for catching unwary creatures.

In the canoe, I find a large zip-lock bag with equipment for my day trip. Inside: a change of clothes, wool socks, a rain jacket, an emergency blanket, matches and a lighter, and a roll of toilet paper. There are also ham sandwiches, hard-boiled eggs, and bottled water. I drink some and leave the sandwiches for later. According to Nugent's instructions, it is one and a half miles from the lake to the first swamp, which is one of the places where the river widens. The swamp water is filled with leeches and sunken logs, and I will need to be careful.

I bury my prison browns in the sandy soil near the viburnum bush and put on the pair of extra-large jeans and the lumberjack shirt with dark blue checks. The clothes don't fit properly, but never mind. Feeling foolish, I climb unsteadily into the stern. The canoe rocks back and forth when I kneel to paddle. To my surprise, I remember the words of my old dunderheaded counsellor: *At the end of your stroke, drag the blade tip through the water for a few inches to keep the canoe on course.* Fortunately, the river is calmer than I expected so the canoe surges forward easily.

22

PADDLING IS TAXING. The relentless tug of the current against the canoe pushing it downstream instead of up; the hysterical blackflies that dive-bomb my head; the still suffocating heat of the forest — all of it adds up to loathsome work. And now I have come to a waterfall that Nugent has left off his map. Of course, he wouldn't know it was there. He just wrote down what the man at the outfitter's store told him. Alas, the falls are high, a considerable climb for a novice such as myself, and fairly steep, the river tumbling down a series of glistening rock ledges, descending stepping stones, spilling water into the frothy pool before me.

I consult the map again, and for the first time I notice two small, puzzling vertical lines beside the word *portage*. Nugent has noted the falls, after all. Good old Pilot. But I have no idea how to portage.

It seems I am to carry it up the cliff, although it's evident nobody has portaged here for a while. The bushes are overgrown, but there remain vestiges of steps carved into the rocky bluff. Is that what the vertical lines mean? I settle the canoe on my shoulders and test the first step with my foot. Point being, I have a fear of heights. Halfway up, and Lord knows how I get that far, I lose my balance, and the unwieldy canoe slides off my shoulders.

There is a boom of wood hitting wood, followed by whispery schussing sounds. I force myself to turn around and look. The canoe has come to rest at the end of what appears to be a wooden waterslide. I didn't notice it before because the slide was hidden by cedar bushes. It must have been constructed to lift a small boat past the falls because ancient rope pulleys run up and down the sides of the half-rotten contraption. This, then, is Nugent's portage. Relieved, I make my way down the rock stairs and over to the boat lift to see if I can make its pulleys work.

23

I HAVE BEEN paddling for what feels like hours, passing through more clouds of blackflies. My new clothes are soaked through with water and sweat and my paddling stroke is becoming erratic. Goddamn Nugent for putting me through this! He must have known how difficult it would be!

After several minutes, I round a bend in the river and, lo, a sea of bulrushes appears before me. To my amazement, the canoe floats forward easily. The water here is sluggish; there's no current to fight. Air like furnace-hot steam hits my face, and when I glance down at the dark brown water, I notice the aforementioned leeches swimming like bloated lumps of flesh.

Ugh. What do I do now? Paddle along the path cut through the rushes? On the shore, I spot something resembling a duck blind; it's a small wooden wall near a place large enough to land a boat. It must be where Nugent and I agreed to meet, but I see no sign of him.

Feeling anxious, I paddle to shore and pull the canoe up onto the muddy ground. Immediately, a swarm of mosquitoes bears down on me.

Their absurd humming is disorienting. As I slap them away, a motor-bike's roar shatters the quiet and an ill-kempt yobbo drives out of the trees. He hops off his bike and takes an axe from some luggage tied to the back. He walks my way, staring ahead with a look of concentration. Before I can react, he disappears behind a wall of bulrushes and I hear the hope-less crashing sound of wood collapsing inward. What on earth is he doing? More loud and crashing sounds follow. Is my canoe next? Maybe John sent him to destroy me. And now he is biding his time, wearing me down, like a cat toying with a mouse.

I head for the canoe, fighting down panic. I'll go deep into the swamp where he can't reach me. Too late. Somebody is splashing through the bulrushes.

I spin around and a man yells: Hey you. Wait up!

I stand crouched in anticipation of his blow. He looks at me curiously.

Sorry, mister, he says. Didn't mean to scare you. I guess you heard the report too.

What report?

About the escaped convict, the man replies. They say he's armed and dangerous.

It takes a second to realize he is talking about me. No, I manage to croak. I haven't been listening to the radio.

I get it. He nods. Need to get away from it all. I know the feeling. Well, the guy escaped this morning. All the roads are blocked with patrol cars. I have a pass because I'm helping the ranger destroy the duck blinds. They're illegal in this part of the park, see?

Is that so?

Yeah, but that don't stop hunters from trying to build them. He looks concerned suddenly. Hey mister, he says, pointing. You've cut yourself.

I recoil at the sight of the deep gash on my wrist. I have no memory of how that happened.

Better put some alcohol on it, eh? He winks and claps my shoulder. If I had some, I'd give it to you. But the cut ain't too bad. Wash it out tonight with soap and you'll be in good nick again. Well, gotta get back to work. Just be careful, okay?

Yes, I reply. I will. And thank you, good sir.

He grins. Sure. Anytime.

24

I PUSH THE canoe back into the water and paddle toward the other side of the swamp, far away from the duck blind where the man has started chopping again. *Armed and dangerous.* The phrase buzzes unpleasantly in my head. I have never set out to harm anyone. Nor do I intend what I do to be taken personally. The pain I have caused others is just something unfortunate that happened along the way.

Trying to ignore the frenzied noise of the man's axe, I sit in the canoe and eat my sandwiches. If he is right and there are police blockades, Nugent won't be able to get through. What should I do now?

Nugent's map doesn't cover the territory beyond the first swamp so I have no idea where following the river will lead me, other than back to its source. What's more, I lack the requisite camping skills to wander the woods, and if I take the road out, I will run into the road block.

Across the swamp, the noise the man is making sounds wild and sorrowful.

Then at last, the chopping stops and I hear his motorbike fade away as he disappears into the forest.

A heavy sadness settles over me. Taking a wide aim, I toss Nugent's zip-lock bag into the swamp. I leave the canoe by the duck blind and head off into the woods.

25

Tim Nugent

TIM CHECKS HIS watch. It's 2:30 p.m. He's driving a rental again, and he's lost his way. He wrote down the instructions from the outfitter, but the man must have left off several forks in the road or Tim has made some wrong turns. He decides to drive back to the main highway and start again.

It's 4:00 p.m. by the time he finds the right logging road, but he can't get through because three police cars are blocking his way. One of the cops tells him they are hunting an escaped convict so nobody is allowed in the park. He feels uneasy, apprehensive. What will Dale Paul do when he discovers that Tim isn't waiting at the duck blind? Will he give himself up? He won't have much choice, but that has never stopped his old friend before. Has he sent his school chum on a suicidal mission?

He tries to put himself inside Dale Paul's mind and draws a blank. It's odd how you can spend hours with a person, listening to their thoughts and feelings, and yet in the end all you get is an aspect of personality with a few attitudes and habits tossed in — a shorthand sketch of the layered human being who lies behind the barrage of words.

When he's out of sight of the police cars, he climbs out of his rental and shouts Dale Paul's name over and over. Nothing happens. There's not a sound except for a blue jay calling somewhere in the forest.

It's a hot, still afternoon, but the air is alive with mosquitoes and blackflies. He looks closely at the pines and birch trees by the road. All forests on the East Coast of North America are the same, he thinks, a mammoth compost heap, ushering in new life. Rotting logs in the underbrush; deadheads in the swamps; lichen-covered rock outcroppings;

feeble mosquitoes flying out of the cedars when you jostle the branches; the soft forest floor squishing like muck under your feet.

There's no use waiting. The man at the outfitter's told him the woods are impenetrable unless you're a seasoned hiker. He'll have to think of something else.

26

Dale Paul

I AM BACK where I started — at the mouth of the Oswego River. I have no watch, so I have no way of knowing the time, although it is late in the day because the sun is starting to set behind the hills near the prison. A chainsaw roars in the distance. The reassuring sound of human activity.

For hours, I have followed the river, staggering through the underbrush, holding my wounded hand, wading in the water when I come to impassable parts of the forest. Several times I have broken down in tears. If Davie appeared before me and said I should drown myself, I would do as he asked.

Oh my dear boy, if only I could make you love me again.

I find the viburnum bush and dig up my browns. I put them on, and in the same spot I bury the clothes Nugent purchased for me at the outfitter's. Then I walk down to the beach and wait. It doesn't take long. Several helicopters hover above the far shore of the lake while a C.O. sits in the stern of a prison outboard scanning the forest with a pair of binoculars. Trembling with relief, I shout and wave.

The C.O. quickly turns the boat around and heads over.

27

Tim Nugent

TIM CALLS THE prison and speaks to the warden, who informs him that Dale Paul has escaped and the prison is on lockdown. The warden says he doesn't expect Dale Paul to get far in the Five Swamps. He's already sent out a squad of guards and called in the New York State Police. They will find Dale Paul, the warden says.

The warden's news doesn't make Tim feel any better. But he thanks the warden and hangs up. There is nothing to do now except wait. When he knows what he wants to say, he will call Meredith and tell her about Dale Paul.

28

Dale Paul

THE HEAT OF the day still hangs in the trees. The warden is waiting for me at a picnic table near the tennis courts while some C.O.s barbecue hamburgers nearby. The warden has on a casual short-sleeved shirt and reflector sunglasses. The effect of the mirrored spectacles on his black, perfectly spherical head makes him look like a gangster.

Bowles, the new C.O., takes me to him. I can't stop shivering. I haven't been allowed to change out of my damp and sandy prison clothes, and the cut on my left hand is stinging unpleasantly. There are more cuts on my face and neck.

The warden lifts up his mirrored sunglasses and eyes me angrily. So you made a break for it?

I jumped in the lake, good sir. To cool off.

No more bullshit, Dale Paul. I'm pissed with you.

Warden, I decided to come back and serve out my time.

He looks at me suspiciously. That doesn't sound like you.

I am sincere, I assure you.

You, sincere? He snorts and shoos Bowles away. Okay, Dale Paul. Did somebody help you escape?

He gives me the fish eye when I shake my head. You realize I have been trying to help you? Or maybe you didn't notice?

I appreciate you introducing me to Bergler.

Ha! But you haven't read him yet, have you? Goddamnit, Dale Paul, you should read that shrink! You might learn a thing or two. You like the fear that comes when you push things too far. Know what I'm saying?

I don't put much stock in psychological theories.

Okay. I get that. He scowls. But read him anyway. And like I said, I'm pissed with you, so you're going to the SHU for three days. After they fix you up in the infirmary.

I can't help myself. I smile.

You crazy, man? What are you smiling about?

Encouraged by his softened tone, I say: Warden, I'll be safe there.

Safe from what? he asks.

Somebody at Essex is trying to kill me.

He does a double take. Who is trying to kill you?

Mr. Jack and some others.

Aren't you two pals?

I thought so, but no, not now. I looked inside the box with your letters …

You looked in my private papers! His voice rises.

I know, but I needed to know the name of the mystery celebrity, and I discovered that I am the mystery celebrity. Do you understand what I'm saying? If I die, someone will make a lot of money.

How are they going to do that? The jackpot is Starbucks coffee. Nobody is going to get rich on a few coffee beans. You're in shock, Dale Paul. Get ahold of yourself. You don't have a fucking clue what solitary confinement is like. But, heck, just because you want to go there, I'm going to change my plan and dock your swimming privileges. For three months! Do you hear me?

I believe so.

Say, Yes, sir, he growls, turning to accept a plate of barbequed food from a C.O.

Yes, sir, I reply, struggling to keep my face composed. He rolls up his shirtsleeves and starts to eat, gulping down his burger in the same slovenly way I saw him do on my first day in prison, the meat churning around in his half-open mouth.

29

WHEN THE INFIRMARY is finished with me, I return to my dorm. From all around I hear the laboured noise of sleeping men, a din reverberating with whistling snorts and other revolting respiratory exhalations. Despite the ministering of the nurse, I remain chilled to the bone. I have also come down with a painful earache, which, in turn, has brought on a case of tinnitus. The constant ringing in my ears makes me feel I'm going mad. Nevertheless, I manage to fall asleep.

In the middle of the night, a PA announcement wakes me. When I sit up, I notice the sheets on my bunkmates' cots have been stuffed with pillows to create the illusion that human bodies are lying under the covers. A note is taped to Bailey's pillow: *Meet me at the pool or Bailey gets another shower.*

I'm not interested in taking a new idiotic risk, not with everything that has gone wrong in the last twenty-four hours, but the thought of Aldo hurting Bailey alarms me. Aldo, with his repugnant vulgarity, his lowlife clownishness, stands for all that is crude and crackbrained; all that is distasteful and indelicate; all that is coarse and cruel.

Weaving unsteadily, I put on my prison sweats. My joints throb from the strain of the day's exertion, but anger is propelling me forward, as if I am on the final lap of the day's horrendous journey. I pad out of the dorm and silently pull off the screen on the window above the outside staircase. Someone must have used the window before me because its latches are unlocked. I climb through, lower myself to the landing, and proceed down the derelict steps, trying not to make a sound. For several minutes, I wait nervously in the shadows, listening for the C.O. who is posted in the yard. In front of the dorm the searchlights move slowly across the lawn.

When the searchlights swing in the opposite direction, I head for the Olympic complex, lurching from one shadowy area on the lawn to the next. The door of the pool building has been left unlocked. Cautiously, I open it and peek in. Somebody is moving around inside, although the lights in the building have been turned off. In the gloom, I spy Bailey lying on the floor, trussed up like one of Irene's roasting chickens; his hands have been bound behind his back with thick strips of grey duct tape. Another strip of tape is plastered across his mouth. Aldo is bent over my bunkmate, taping Bailey's feet. Aldo notices where Bailey is looking and spins around.

Aldo, you skunk-faced jackal! I shout. Get away from Bailey!

Aldo rushes me, clutching a swim weight. When I open my eyes again, I'm on the floor. The wound on the back of my skull is throbbing painfully. Was Aldo cunning enough to strike me on the spot where he hit me before? Bailey's words drift back: *Aldo so stupid he smart.* And now, worse luck, a familiar clammy sensation is spreading up my back. I can't faint. Or have I fainted already? I am too weary to know, but possibly I have missed a beat. Bailey lies only a few yards away, his knees tucked up under him, his eyes terrified behind the lenses of his spectacles.

Get up, Aldo says. Get up or you'll be sorry, Brer Fox.

Aldo has bound my hands but left my feet free. I try to stand, and when I do, I fall back down. He kicks me in the ribs. Well, Brer Fox, got any big words now?

He is standing over me, his arm extended as if he is ready to punch me. Instead, he grips my arms and helps me to my feet.

Walk, he growls.

I take a step. He shoves me hard again, and I stagger forward. When I reach John's swim chair, he presses down on my shoulders, forcing me to sit on its seat so he can bind me to it with duct tape. When he's done, my arms and legs are stuck to the odious chair. Sniggering with glee, the ruffian twists my head in the direction of the observation window overlooking the pool. In the dim light, the silhouettes of three men are visible behind the glass. I know without being told that Martino and John are watching. But who is the third man? I can't see his face, although the shape of the man's head is familiar. Then someone switches on the light, illuminating the observation room. I feel sick at heart: the third man is Derek. While Aldo tries to kill me, my friend and ally is standing there egging him on.

You got an audience, Brer Fox, Aldo chortles. Ready for a little joyride?

Aldo is serious; he intends to drown me. Panicked, I start thrashing about, but he's taped my legs and arms too tightly.

He presses the button on the remote control panel and the chair swings out over the pool, its seat rocking unsteadily. The three men at the observation window pound the glass. I think they're cheering.

Without warning, my son's face appears in the air of the pool building. A listless sadness washes through me. Will I ever see my boy again?

There's a screech and the chair swings sideways and stops. Through a fog of dizziness, I see a light as big as the sun; it is coming my way, moving slowly and purposefully. It is not like any light I've seen before.

I saw. I tell you, *I saw*.

EPILOGUE

Dale Paul

IT SEEMS JOHN Giaccone was right: Aldo is a bumbler. The swim chair was designed to not go below the surface of the water. But who knows what would have happened if Derek hadn't changed his mind and gone to fetch a C.O.

Since my heart attack, I've been reassigned to lighter duties. That's why I'm repotting dahlia bulbs on the warden's patio; the warden's old collie dog, Jessie, sleeps nearby.

Martino, Aldo, and John Giaccone have been sent to maximum security. Derek was sent there with them, although he won't stay long because at the last minute he changed his mind and stopped Aldo from drowning me. I have accused Aldo and Martino and John of attempted murder, and, due to the magnitude of my accusation, it is being treated as an outside charge. That means the police will investigate and a prosecutor will take it over.

I ran into Derek while he waited for his escort to maximum security. Glancing around nervously, he pressed something smooth and metallic into my palm. It was Martino's gold ring with the Bitcoin insignia. You get the jackpot if you drop the charges against John, he whispered.

Before he could say anything more, four C.O.s rushed toward him, their beefy torsos straining the shoulders of their blue jackets; their broad, hairy wrists glinting with chunky watches; their thick-heeled boots hammering the ground.

Derek held out his wrists so the guards could cuff him.

Why did you save me? I couldn't help asking.

I figured you can be more help to me on the outside, mate! He saluted me with his shackled hands before the C.O.s led him off to the prison van.

That was three weeks ago. Derek would be pleased to hear I am meditating again. Meditating helps with my convalescence, and occasionally, if I am well rested, I see glittering lights in the air. Perhaps I am seeing what the apostles of Christ called the sign of the Holy Ghost, and I admit that swatches of Sunday school texts pop into my head during these moments, but I don't see an image of the Virgin Mary or hear the voice of God. Moreover, I have no idea how I went from being Dale Paul, the hedge fund whale, to the man who is now able to see that I ruined the lives of thousands and made it hard for my own son to love me. For the most part, it's enough that I'm privy to the sight of those homely spikes of light, although others are more deserving than I am of religious visions.

In fact, I often talk *around* my experience that night in the pool. No one would believe me if I described the physical sensation of something opening inside my chest, as if my bad, old heart were one of the pine cupboards from Quebec that Esther used to buy, a quaint woodworker's cabinet, in other words, with all its small doors and drawers of tools flung open to the air.

There is one subject I can discuss freely: I derive large jolts of pleasure from apprehension and fear, and I will do what I can to create circumstances that ensure I experience those emotions. Like the schoolboy who enjoys waiting for a tongue thrashing over a bad report card, I am addicted to the dread you feel when something frightening is about to unfold.

As for Nugent and my memoir, I have cancelled my book. I am more interested in the changes I am experiencing than in rooting around in my past. Nugent seemed pleased to accept a kill fee from my publisher and says he will use the funds to pay for his honeymoon with Meredith.

And now it's time to tell you about Caroline. Some days ago, a work gang was attacking the roots of a bittersweet vine climbing up the warden's porch. A C.O. was supervising. I stopped my gardening work and ambled over.

The C.O. was one of the guards who used to watch me clean the wash-room. When I told him the men were destroying *Celastrus scandens*, the harmless vine known as American bittersweet, he yelled at them to stop. As he said thank you, his pager rang. He put it to his ear and nodded: You have a visitor.

I followed him down to the visitors' section by the lake. It was a cloudy afternoon, and an eerie sadness hung over the woods, as if the thousands of dead TB patients who came here looking for a cure had left behind their melancholy hopes.

Near the cyclone fence, a pretty blond woman sat waiting on a picnic bench. While the C.O. frisked me, I watched her pull out a sheaf of statio-nery. Perhaps it was a fundraising letter for her Great Danes. She stopped and scribbled a note, the corners of her lovely, downturned mouth twitch-ing from the effort of concentration. There isn't much I dislike about Caroline, I confess.

She jumped up as I lumbered toward her, ever the lowborn knave, and, stretching up on tiptoe, she air-kissed my cheeks. I tried to hug her, and she gently pushed me away.

I've brought some treats, she said, exuding an air of false cheerfulness, and from a wicker picnic basket she fished out a baguette oozing with rosy-red slabs of beef and frills of lettuce slathered with mayonnaise. You poor man! she exclaimed. You must be longing for good food.

I went off red meat after my heart attack. Strictly vegan now, Caroline.

Of course! How silly of me! But you've lost weight. If you keep on like this, you'll be as skinny as a rake.

If you had to eat the prison food, you'd lose weight too.

I see you've kept your sense of the absurd! She reached over and stroked my cheek. The touch of her fingers evoked a shudder. I grabbed her hand and kissed it.

Tell me, how is your appeal going? she asked, gently removing her hand.

Malcolm de Vries doesn't hold out much hope. Not that he's done much for me while I've been here.

I'm so dreadfully sorry! But maybe something will happen. You always had luck on your side, didn't you? I am sure it's still with you — somewhere.

Maybe so, but at the moment, I am just glad to see you.

She gave me a puzzled look.

Have you heard from Davie? I asked.

Have you? she countered.

He hasn't been in touch. But why did you come? Our relationship has been over for a while, hasn't it?

I'm afraid I have been quite cowardly, Dale Paul. You see, I didn't want to tell you during the trial, although perhaps it was wrong of me to keep you hoping. But there is just no future for us now that you are — where you are. I have a demanding job back in London, a job I adore, by the way, and a sick brother, or maybe you've forgotten about Charles. He is often disoriented and difficult. Do you know he still asks if you could give him some dosh? I have explained over and over that you don't have a penny.

He'll never believe you. With all due respect, it's not in his DNA. But if I had money, I would give it to you.

She looked at me strangely again. You surprise me, Dale Paul. You really do.

I am in love with you. You know that, don't you?

I suppose I do know that, yes. She brought out a handkerchief and blew her nose. When she glanced at me again, her eyes looked sad.

Oh dear, it's ten after four. I need to get back to the city. And about us, she adds. There's really no point, is there?

Not unless you're right and my luck returns.

I hope it does. She paused. You know, you seem different.

People tell me that. Well, I appreciate your coming such a long way to see me. Say hello to Charles.

She broke into a lovely smile and walked away. I watched her go, my blood thundering.

A GUARD IS escorting a prisoner to the parking lot. The prisoner is very tall and dressed in a double-breasted suit that no longer fits properly around the shoulders. There's a cat inside the wicker case he holds in his arms.

A group of men are watching the prisoner from behind a wire fence. He waves farewell, and they shout their goodbyes. Sometimes he tells himself the change he feels is just the shadow side of his personality trying to right the balance. Some think such things happen when we stray too far from ourselves. Some say that's why saints dream of robberies and thieves dream of angels.

He has received a presidential pardon for risking his life to rescue his bunkmate. The warden wrote the president on his behalf, and the day his pardon was announced, the *New York Times* printed a full page of angry letters from the military families whose pensions he'd gambled and lost. And then he quickly ceased to be a story of much interest. Newer scandals were unfolding.

His cousin is late. He was surprised and pleased when she offered to pick him up, although she has gone out of her way to be kind since his heart attack. He glances at his watch. What's holding her up?

There's the rumble of an engine. An ancient pickup truck is pulling into the lot. Well, it's not Meredith. His cousin wouldn't be caught dead in an old jalopy.

Through the windshield, he glimpses a youthful face. The passenger door opens. For a moment, he just stands there. His son looks older, more sure of himself. He has put on weight, and the tangle of blond hair has been tied back in a ponytail.

The cat hisses inside its wicker case.

Don't get too close. He's scared of strangers.

I forgot you liked cats.

So did I.

It's only later, at a bar off the highway, after his son has gone to the washroom, that he takes out the Bitcoin ring. He rolls it around on his palm, then puts it on his finger.

Yesterday somebody sent a smuggled note reminding him that the account is his if he drops the attempted murder charges against his old cronies. Will he do what they're asking? He can feel the clammy perspiration at the back of his neck, the signal that he's beginning to feel stress, but there's no point worrying about it now. His son is walking back to their table. He puts the ring away and starts peppering his boy with questions. It turns out his son works in the IT department at a Long Island college. For a while, they chat about teaching, and then his son clears his throat: Hey, I didn't mean to go through with it. The idea of killing myself started as a joke. I intended to go back and pick up my bike, but when I returned to the bridge it was gone ... I guess I got carried away ...

Easy to do.

No, really, it was wrong.

I'm sorry too, son.

You seem different, Dad. Has prison changed you?

The great Bergler would say — if he even believed what a shrink would say — that he is riding the tail end of another cycle until his masochism propels him to start all over again. But he doesn't answer to Bergler. He answers to his son, and what he tells his boy is the answer he'll give you.

He has no idea if the change he's experiencing is long-lasting because he, too, is often awash with doubts and self-suspicions. Sometimes the doubts dwindle into nothing, but other times he's overwhelmed by fears that these changes will morph into the opposite of what he hopes for himself, and, despite his best intentions, he will return to being who he was. So, in the end, hand on heart, he cannot give you an honest answer.

ACKNOWLEDGEMENTS

This book has had many helpers. I'm particularly indebted to Ricki Gold and Rehabilitation through the Arts so I am thanking Ricki Gould and Rehabilitation through the Arts; Ed Bales and Charlie Schrem for their information about US federal prisons and for Charlie's first hand knowledge of bitcoin. I would also like to thank my agent Samantha Haywood; my husband Patrick Crean; my insightful editor Marc Côté; Mariel Marshall for her drawings and Tom Dean whose thoughts about doodles have been expressed through the novel's protagonist.

I am also grateful to the following for their help: Liz Ruork and Brian St. Amant for their business expertise; James Bannon for his help with betting formulas; James Ponzo for his knowledge of Afro-American street dialect; Margaret Atwood; Sheila Heti; Judy Rebick and Barbara Gowdy for early and invaluable reads of the novel; editors Heather Sangster and Janice Zawerbny; Sylvia Fraser for her knowledge of ghost writing; Jane Urquhart; Matt Kassir; Ron Graham; Kara Brown; Shelley Hassard; Douglas Gould; John Fraser; Katherine Ashenburg; Marni Jackson; my brother John Swan and the late John Nix who piqued my interest in celebrity dead pools.

We acknowledge the sacred land on which Cormorant Books operates. It has been a site of human activity for 15,000 years. This land is the territory of the Huron-Wendat and Petun First Nations, the Seneca, and most recently, the Mississaugas of the Credit River. The territory was the subject of the Dish With One Spoon Wampum Belt Covenant, an agreement between the Iroquois Confederacy and Confederacy of the Ojibway and allied nations to peaceably share and steward the resources around the Great Lakes. Today, the meeting place of Toronto is still home to many Indigenous people from across Turtle Island. We are grateful to have the opportunity to work in the community, on this territory.

We are also mindful of broken covenants and the need to strive to make right with all our relations.